LIVING WITH

YOUR SECRETS

AN ALICIA ANDERSON STORY, BOOK 4

BEVERLEY NEILSON

Books by Beverley Neilson

The Alicia Anderson Series

The Dark Side of Pain
Family Always Comes First
Morally Irresponsible
Living With Your Secrets

Living with Your Secrets

For information contact:
Beverley.neilson.author@gmail.com

Cover photo by: EyeEm/Freepik

ISBN:

Ebook (Kindle): 978-1-7390120-3-8
Ebook (Kobo) 978-1-7390120-4-5
Paperback: 978-1-7390120-2-1
Audio: 978-1-7390120-5-2

First Edition: April 2026, v2

Readers - If you encounter typos or inconsistencies in the story, please send me a note at:

Beverley.neilson.author@gmail.com.

Even with many layers of editing, mistakes can sometimes slip through. Thank you in advance for your help in eradicating such nasty nuisances.

If you enjoyed ''Living With Your Secrets,' I would appreciate it if you would help others enjoy this book, too.

Recommend it. Please help other readers find this book by recommending it to friends, readers' groups, and discussion boards.

Review it. Please tell other readers why you like this book by reviewing it on Amazon or Goodreads.

And if you're wondering what's coming next? Follow me on Facebook or Instagram – Beverley Neilson Author.

For:

Wendy Andrews

(I miss you, my friend)

and

William Bradley

(Congratulations to us on
43 years of blissful happiness)

Chapter 1

The short, heavy-set man stands on the edge of the shoreline looking out over the clear blue water, enjoying the view, the weather, and the evening as he rubs his belly through the expensive fabric of his golf shirt. *Sure glad whatever that pain was is gone,* he thinks, smiling as he gazes out at the sinking sun over the bay.

He bends over suddenly, clutching his stomach with both hands as the pain reappears and cuts through his visceral organs as if a sword has been shoved through his body. *What the hell is going on? I felt sick to my stomach but that went away and now it feels like something is ripping my insides out. Something is wrong.*

The man moans as tentacles of the spasm rip through his body, forcing him to his knees. *Something I ate? But why the fuck would it hit me like this? I've never felt anything like this before,* he considers as he rubs his stomach, hoping that it will help alleviate even some of the agony that seems to be running rampant in his innards.

It can't be what I had for dinner. I just bought the stuff at the butcher this afternoon and BBQ'd it. The steak was cooked – still a little pink – but cooked. A rare steak wouldn't cause this. Maybe it was the butter that I put on the baked potato. No, it couldn't have been the butter. It was in the fridge. A fairly new container – only a couple of scoops out of it for toast. Must have been the shrimp. But they were fresh today too. And dinner wouldn't have hit me so fast, would it? Oh my God, this is fucking killing me. It's not going away. It's not just a twinge either. This is a goddamn nightmare.

"Shit," he groans. *Oh my God! It's not just pain. I feel like I'm going to throw up, and my entire insides are going to come with it.*

Maybe it's not my stomach. A heart attack? No, my chest and arm are OK. That's not it. Maybe it's my ulcer. Maybe its burst.

The man continues to kneel on the ground, one hand in the beautiful, manicured lawn for balance, the other rubbing his fairly substantial belly. Suddenly, he begins to shake as if a cold arctic draft has come out of the north, chilling him to the bone.

It's hot out but I'm fucking freezing all of a sudden. Maybe it's just another symptom of whatever this is. I've got to get to the house. Get inside, sit down, relax. It's got to be my ulcer.

The man struggles to stay on his knees as his entire body vibrates from the agony invading his whole being, and his faded denim blue eyes begin to water. He holds his enlarged belly in his hands, tears appearing at the edges of his eyes as he struggles against the unbearable pain, the nausea, the weakness, the cold sweats. After what seems like hours, the ache subsides slightly, enough that he can channel his entire concentration into pushing himself up from his knees to his feet.

He pats down his golf shirt, which bunched up around his midsection, before brushing the grass off the knees of his pants, as he tries to emulate some manner of normalcy. He looks around at the lake, looking for boaters who may have been passing by, that may have spotted him in an extremely weak moment. *No one. No one saw that*, he thinks standing still for a couple of seconds before the torment ricochets through his system anew.

Shit. It's got to be my stomach ulcer. I'll take some of that medicine the doctor gave me. Take an extra shot for good measure. That'll fix me up, he thinks as he turns away from the water and takes a step towards the large palatial two-storey home sitting just beyond the water's edge.

"What the fuck is going on," he mutters out loud as a rumbling moves through his body into his lower intestines, feeling like something is going to explode. He clenches his butt cheeks together and moves his hand to cover his ass, pulling his knees together tightly. *Fuck, now it feels like whatever it is wants to explode out of me. Jesus Christ. It's running through my system like a freight train.*

He stands for a moment, hoping that he'll be able to make it to the house before something horrific happens. He starts to move slowly taking baby steps, his butt cheeks squeezed together, his legs almost crossed trying to hold whatever it is from blasting out. *Pepto Bismol. That'll help.* The TV commercial for the product runs through his mind, three people dressed in shades of pink, dancing and singing about the relief of their nausea, upset stomach and diarrhea symptoms with a single swig of the liquid.

He takes a couple of steps before his breath catches in his lungs, as if they have simply frozen up. He struggles to pull in a gulp of fresh air, gasping and wheezing as his head starts to spin, causing him to stagger backwards. Unable to stay on his feet, he once again falls to his knees, his hands moving to his throat as if his life is being choked out of him. He is unable to stay upright on his knees, and he collapses, his heavy body tumbling to the ground. He rolls onto his side and pulls his legs up to his chest trying to deal with the torture.

My cell phone, where's my cell phone? He slowly moves his hand to his pants pocket and feels the edge of the device. *Here it is. Now if I can just get it out, turn it on. Dial 911. Everything will be OK. Get an ambulance here and take me to the friggin hospital. They'll know what this is.*

He fights to retrieve the device, but he has lost most of his strength and all of his dexterity and cannot free his phone from its confines. *I'll just lay here a sec. Get my breath back. Try again.*

As he lies on his side on the soft grass, he tries to pull oxygen into his parched lungs. *Fuck,* his mind screams. *Calm down, calm down* he thinks, commanding himself to hold it together, to not give into whatever is happening to his body.

Just before losing consciousness, as his lips and skin start to turn a brilliant blue, as his last mouthful of air escapes and he is unable to replenish his wanting lungs, he closes his eyes to the deadly prank that his body is playing on him before he rolls off the soft grass into the water.

Chapter 2

Maeve

The sun shines brightly as the two women sit side-by-side on the hard stools of the swim-up bar in the Olympic-size pool at the Royal Hotel in Playa del Carmen, Mexico. Sunglasses sit on each of their noses, complimented by their classy sun hats as they each take a pull on their fancy cocktail.

"It was a great idea coming here, Maeve," the tall, thin woman says to her friend. "Just what I needed."

"Definitely what we needed," Maeve corrects. "To get away from the humdrum of everyday life, to be pampered a bit, to sit around in the pool," she says looking around at the people splashing and swimming in the warm water. "And of course, you had to be here to help me celebrate my 40th," she smiles, clinking her glass with her friend.

"It's amazing, don't you think, that we've been friends for so long. Who would have thought that two kids who met in grade six would still be friends 30 years later?" Kandis laughs, tilting her glass back and taking a swallow of the frosty alcoholic beverage before setting it on the bar.

"We're lucky. We've been through a lot together – school, work, boyfriends, marriage, kids, family chaos, medical stuff, but all in all we've waded through it together," Maeve replies, setting her glass down and waving to the young well-tanned man behind the bar, who nods in acknowledgement.

"Damn right. We are fortunate to be healthy, wealthy and wise and friends through it all," Kandis adds laughing.

"And we had a lot of fun along the way," Maeve adds. "Remember the time the principal called our parents back in middle school?"

Kandis chokes, almost spitting out her drink as she starts to grin. "Yeah. I remember. We decided we weren't going to eat lunch in the gym like we were supposed to. We ate our sandwiches in the washroom, so we could walk over to the plaza and hang out with the high school kids."

"And then the janitor came in and gave us a hard time. Made us go down to the office like we were doing something wrong."

"Well, we were doing something wrong. We should have gone to the gym, like everyone else."

"No, we should have just left the school grounds, gone to the plaza like we wanted to. Eaten while we walked," Maeve says.

"And then they called our mothers," Kandis howls with laughter. "I got grounded when I got home. My mom told me you were a bad influence, and I should find a new friend."

"Yeah. I remember. And my mom told me not to be so stupid to get caught in the future," Maeve laughs at the difference in their home life, both then and now.

"Here's to listening to my mom," Kandis laughs, raising her glass to toast her friend. "Not."

"Yup, still here after 30 years," Maeve adds as they clink glasses again and take a sip of the alcoholic concoction.

The two are silent for a moment until Kandis adds another story from their history together. "I remember when you told me you were having a surprise bridal shower for Laura. You asked me to go in on a present for her, and I gave you some money. Then you asked me to make brownies from my mom's recipe, and they were so bad that I broke the knife trying to cut them."

Maeve smiles at the memory.

"So, I stopped at the store to buy pastries on the way over. And when I knocked on your door, you opened it, and everyone yelled surprise. The freaking shower was for me."

Maeve laughs. "Remember what you said?"

Kandis smiles. "I do. I called you a few choice words and threw in a couple of obscenities. My mom was so upset; told me I was a terrible friend."

Maeve laughs again as Kandis nods at the memory.

The pair are quiet for a moment, their thoughts far away before Kandis offers another old memory. "And the girls' weekends at the cottage? The only rules for the weekend - no men, no kids, no pets!"

"Lots of food. Always a competition for who could make the best meal. Remember the year we had a synchronized swimming contest in the lake and I almost drowned?"

"How about the year we learned how to walk the runway? All the fashion shows we used to have to model our new clothes that we bought on the drive up north."

"How about the time there was that major water leak when we were up there, and you and Lori had to MacGyver it? And when we went in to get the right parts, the guy at the hardware store was amazed at your ingenuity."

Kandis smiles, remembering the craziness, the friendship, the adventures that they enjoyed together before Maeve asks, "How about the garden party we went to at Felice's?"

"Mmm. Yeah, we all dressed up like we were royalty going to afternoon tea - fascinators, boa scarves, wild glasses, scads of fake jewellery, white gloves," Kandis pauses before adding, "I think that was the beginning of our annual afternoon tea excursions."

"How about some of the fantastic concerts we went to?" Maeve continues.

Kandis thinks for a moment before she starts rhyming off artists that they had seen together. "Bob Seger, Burton Cummings, the Guess Who, the Eagles, Rod Stewart, Don Henley, Neil Young, Gordon Lightfoot, Bryan Adams," she says beginning to slow down before Maeve picks up the list.

"April Wine, Chilliwack, Loverboy, Van Halen, Foreigner."

There's silence for a moment before Kandis adds, "All the old classic bands. Who would have thought looking at us that we're closet rockers?"

"A holdover from growing up with hippie parents," Maeve smiles. "So glad you love the same kind of music as me."

"How many times do you think we've seen Burton?" Kandis asks, only using the musician's first name as if they had been friends for years.

Maeve laughs. "We should have counted – over a 100 at least. And he's still my favourite!"

"There's still a lot of bands that I want to see. How about Nickelback? Are you in when they tour again?"

"I am." There's silence for a moment until Maeve asks, "How about our trip to New York City?"

"Remember the guy at the Empire State Building? Asking if we were sure we wanted to go up because it was foggy out and we couldn't ask for a refund on the admittance fee," Kandis chuckles.

"But we went up anyway. And the guy was right. We couldn't see anything. Nothing," Maeve laughs. "But it was fun. And we couldn't go all the way to New York and not go up the Empire State Building!"

"And the weekend shopping sprees to Buffalo? Back when the exchange rate made it a deal."

Maeve chuckles, "That's where we discovered the three degrees of honesty with the border guards."

"Yeah, I would tell them exactly what I spent, and Lori would tell them about half of what she spent. And then there was you," Kandis smiles. "Telling the guy, in your sweetest voice ever that you bought almost nothing! When you spent five times what I did!"

The women smile before falling quiet, their numerous adventures streaming through their thoughts.

"Ladies," the bartender interrupts their silence, putting drinks down on the bar in front of each of them, a delicious wide smile on his face, his brown eyes twinkling. "You're still drinking your way through the alphabet, correct?" he asks.

"We are. These look interesting," Maeve replies, shoving the memories from her mind while pushing her empty cocktail glass towards the bartender.

8

"For the fourth letter, I've prepared two Deep Blue Sea Martinis. We are staying with a vodka base. This one has a very fruity, island flavour with a taste of pineapple and the sweet addition of Blue Curacao." He stops and watches as each of the women lift their glass tentatively to their lips and take a small sip. Smiles radiate on both of their faces, as they swallow the potent substance and set the glasses back on the bar top.

"Good. Very good, Juan."

"Do you want me to work on your next drink?" he asks the pair.

"Yes, please. 'E' is the next one on the hit parade," Kandis answers, as she puts the glass to her lips for another sip.

The bartender smiles, and half bows to the women before moving down the bar towards other guests, shaking his head subtly at the women's mission to drink through the alphabet.

"Bet he would be great in bed," Maeve chuckles, as she raises the glass to her lips, watching the backside of the young man as he walks away.

Chapter 3

Maeve

After a fantastic dinner at the steak restaurant in the hotel, Maeve sits on their balcony, leaning against the railing to watch below as Kandis exits the building from the main level and sits on one of the lounge chairs at the pool. Maeve sits back in the chair once satisfied that her friend is OK, and leans her head back looking at the night sky and its plethora of bright stars.

Always looking towards the heavens that girl. And she can name all of the constellations, point them out and tell you stories about the Gods that named them. Says the view of the sky is different in the south so she wanted to take the opportunity to just lie out and gaze at their splendour.

Maeve leans back on the lounge chair and brings the glass of wine to her lips. *Bloody Caesars are definitely a Canadian drink. Juan looked at me like I was crazy when I asked for one.* Maeve chuckles as she remembers their afternoon at the swim-up bar and the delectable drinks they enjoyed. *Where the hell did we get in the alphabet? K? L? Whatever. We'll have to go back tomorrow and finish. It's our mission for the week!*

She looks down to make sure her friend is still there, not being bothered by anyone, simply enjoying the night air.

We've been through a lot. I've been lucky she's always been there for me. Always. She knows more about me than anyone else in the world, and understands who I really am. She supported me when I met Lewis, when I decided to live with him, when we had the kids and started the business. She's always been there to listen to me rant when things went wrong, and celebrate when things went right.

Maeve smiles as she remembers meeting her husband. *I was working in the office of that construction company, something temporary, something just to bring in a pay cheque until I decided what I wanted to do. And then I met*

Lewis. He was working there; his father was a supervisor, and he hired him to swing a pickaxe, dig trenches, pour concrete, anything that needed to be done.

Everyone from the company used to get together on Friday after work at the bar around the corner. I never went, until one Friday the girls finally talked me into going with them. I gave in and said I'd go for one, but then I saw him sitting there. His shoulder length blond hair, his sparkling blue eyes, his striking smile.

He came and sat beside me and introduced himself. And we talked, talked for hours as our colleagues slowly left and we were alone. He told me about his dream of opening his own company and I talked about my dream of finding a purpose in life, maybe going back to school. That night was our beginning.

We had nothing, no money, no furniture but somehow we scrimped and saved for first and last month's rent and got enough together for a one-bedroom basement apartment. What a fucking dump! But we stayed the course and worked hard. Lewis learned everything about construction, while I worked at a bunch of unchallenging office jobs to bring in a few bucks.

I remember when he first became a supervisor with his own crew. My God did we celebrate, and I believe that's when Izzy was conceived. She grins to herself, looking over the balcony railing to make sure her friend is still safe.

We moved up to a three-bedroom, and I thought we had gone to heaven. I put Izzy in daycare and went to work at another construction company, more hours, more money, and to learn about the inner workings of the business, while Lewis worked his way up to Project Manager, then Operations Manager, continually getting closer to his goal.

Finally, we decided to go for it, and we mortgaged ourselves to the hilt, took out loans, anything to get a couple of bucks. We were a team working the business together, him looking after the day-to-day operations, me looking after his paperwork in the evening – quotes, billing, invoices, payroll, and anything that needed to be done, It was hard and there were a few hiccups along the way, like that time I had to ask Dad to lend us some money to make payroll. Thank God he came through for us.

And then we had Rand. I stepped back a bit; the company was viable enough that they didn't need me. We were comfortable, we had finally made it, so we bought the house on the water, and I got to renovate and decorate it to my heart's content, creating a haven for Lewis, Izzy, Rand and me. A sanctuary for the family. A real home.

A frown comes to her face as she reflects on their present situation. *Not sure when we lost each other. We were so busy working, so busy building our lives that we didn't even notice that we had drifted apart. Lost our passion. Lost each other. We smiled for the outside world, but inside the relationship was dry, withered up like a dead weed.*

And then the fucking bastard screwed around on me. Asshole. I was pissed off when I found out, but then I just let it go. I was too tired to fight. I guess I didn't care at that point. I had the life that I wanted, I had all the money that I needed, and I knew I was secure. Lewis would always look after me, but then he met that bitch, who was going to ruin everything.

Chapter 4

Kandis

Kandis sits on the lounge chair beside the pool. She snuggles back, gets comfortable and looks up to the dark night sky. *Absolutely gorgeous. A midnight-black sky is the best canvas for the sparkling diamond-like stars,* she thinks. *My eyes will adjust in the next couple of minutes, and I'll be able to see the Southern Cross and Scorpius and hopefully Sagittarius, and perhaps even Cassiopeia. Oh look, there's Mercury and Venus. And Jupiter. Wow!*

She gazes at the night sky, enjoying the quiet, dark, spectacular vista on display. She sits quietly drinking in the panorama, a smile on her lips at its size, its expanse, its beauty.

Her mind begins to wander as her eyes dance from star to star.

Why can't life be this simple? I thought Kyle was different, exciting, so grown up, so sure of himself. We were good together, loved each other, enjoyed life but when we had Abbie, things changed. He couldn't quite get his shit together, couldn't quite accept that he had to work every day, every week to support his new daughter. He couldn't get up in the morning to be on time. He didn't want someone telling him what to do. He thought he was worth more than anyone was willing to pay him.

Then the alcohol and drugs took over and it was downhill after that. Said he was going to start a band, make some hits, go on the road, get a recording contract and look where that ended up. A bunch of drunk assholes hanging around in the garage, not a decent voice or a talented musician among them.

The first time he forced himself on me should have been my wake-up call. The first time he hit me, I should have dumped his ass. I should have taken Abbie and left, but I was unsure, didn't want to look bad, didn't want people talking about us. He told me he would never let me go. That he would follow me. That he would beat me into submission, and I believed him.

He has moments though when the kind, considerate Kyle shows up. Like a miracle of sorts. He treats me like I'm a goddess. Loves me like no one else can. He works around the house, cleans, paints, cuts the grass, and does all the things a husband is supposed to do. And he loves me. And he is so good at loving me. But then something always happens. Something small, something unexpected and the cycle starts all over.

I need to move on. Forget the good Kyle. Forget what could have been, forget that I still love him and concentrate on looking after me and Abbie.

The worst part is that I've subjected our daughter to all of this. His love. His hate. She has watched him for years spiral from one extreme to the other. She's watched him drink and do whatever else he does in that fucking garage. And now she has a drug problem too. Like father, like daughter, I guess. I need to help her get straight. I need to do whatever it takes to save her from the craziness of Kyle and his influence.

It's amazing that I have a senior management job, that I can manage a whole frigging department and be responsible for about a million-dollar budget but I can't stand up for myself against the piece of shit I married. Full of self-doubt. No confidence when it comes to Kyle and our life together. Still loving the piece of shit. Always hoping that he'll reform, that he'll realize what we could really have together. And where the hell has that got me?

Was it my upbringing? Maybe if my mom had stood up to my dad. The beatings were many. Drunken fights, punches thrown, tables tossed. But I can't blame her for this. This is all me. All my weaknesses. Why am I like this? Why do I depend on someone that beats the shit out of me and makes my life a horror story?

Get your shit together, Kandis. Stand up. Brush yourself off and get on with life.

Chapter 5

Present Day

"911. What's your emergency?" the operator asks succinctly.

"The police need to get out here fast. There's a body in the water," the caller cries frantically into the phone.

The emergency dispatcher, who has been working in the crisis call centre for 25 years and is trained to attend all emergency calls, stands up from her desk, waving her arms to signal her supervisor that she has a hot call – a call that could mean life and death, something that needs police officers and medical experts to attend to quickly.

The supervisor sees the signal from her seasoned operator, Donna, and drops her paperwork. She hurries over to the agent's desk, picks up a headset and plugs in to hear the call as the operator tries to calm the close-to-hysterical caller.

"Can you try and calm down a bit? Take a big breath. Let it out slowly," the operator pauses, listening to the caller breathe in and out loudly. "Now again," she says patiently, listening until the caller's heavy breathing quiets a bit. "Tell me what's happened."

"There's a body. A dead body," the caller replies, quieter, calmer.

"Are you sure the person is dead?"

"Yes. He's floating in the middle of the lake," the caller clarifies, her soft voice beginning to ratchet up again.

"Tell me your name."

"My name is Robyn."

"And are you alone, Robyn?"

"No, I'm with my husband. My husband, Ray," she adds, her voice rising, the turmoil of the situation becoming a reality again.

"Can you give me your cell number, Robyn? Just in case we get disconnected, or something happens while we're talking."

"705-555-1790."

"Thanks, Robyn. Now tell me what happened. Tell me where you are."

"We're out in our boat. At the mouth of Kempenfelt Bay. We're anchored out here. We were having a picnic on the boat and were about to go in for a swim when we saw this thing, this bloated mass of green something. We watched it, thinking it was a pile of green algae and weeds, that it would simply float away but it stayed around. It was moving very slowly even with the current, you know. Then my husband saw a hand."

"A hand?" the dispatcher asks.

"Yeah, he said he saw a hand in the middle of the weeds, but I didn't believe him, so I looked closer. It took me a couple of minutes but then I saw it too. And then an arm and a shoulder appeared, tangled in the weeds. Then we saw something catching the light and realized that he had a watch on, and it was reflecting the sun. Then it all came together. It was a body, not just weeds. Somebody must have gotten caught in the weeds when they were out swimming. I don't know. You need to get someone out here now," the voice escalates, fear and trepidation filling the words as the caller begins to sob. "Please. You've got to get someone out here," she begs between gulps of air.

Chapter 6

Wyatt

Richard Wyatt stands, holding the windshield of the Stanley marine boat with his left hand, his right hand trying to steady the binoculars as he looks towards the mouth of the bay, scanning for the white boat with the red bimini that has called in the distress call. *Where the hell are they? Dispatch said they were in the bay. The co-ordinates are in the bay. Maybe they didn't put their anchor in and got carried into the lake with the current,* he asks himself as his eyes move back and forth, eliminating the score of other boats out enjoying the sun and warmth on this summer day.

Finally, he catches a glimpse of a boat off of the Big Bay Point government dock. "There," he says to his partner, pointing about five kilometres up the bay.

"I don't see it yet," Darcy Hudson, the helmsman of the boat and Wyatt's partner replies, as he squints towards the end of the bay.

"Give it a sec," Wyatt replies, his eyes affixed on the boat, waiting for it to visually materialize for Darcy as they speed towards it.

After a couple of tense moments of anticipation, their racing boat gets closer to its goal, and Darcy finally confirms, "I see it. Four minutes out," he estimates.

Wyatt pulls his cell phone from his pocket and asks, "You still there?"

"Yes, we're here," the emergency dispatch supervisor confirms.

"We see 'Knot on Call'," Wyatt advises. "ETA is four minutes."

"We'll tell the boaters. Wait a sec." There's a short pause before the supervisor comes back and confirms, "They see your flashing lights. You're coming straight for them."

"Is the body still there?" Wyatt asks, knowing that in the craziness of the call, of waiting for the police to get there, the

18

body may have drifted away, especially with all of the boat wake in the area, the wind and water current moving from the bay into Lake Simcoe.

He waits for a moment before dispatch confirms that the body is still near the boat.

"I'm going to hang up now," Wyatt tells the operator. "I've got a visual of the two people on the boat."

"No problem. Let us know if there's anything else we can do for you."

"Yeah, before you go, who are the detectives on this one?"

"Alicia Anderson and Helen Hodgins. They are on their way to the government dock right now. We've also called the medics, though it doesn't sound like you'll need them. I've also put in a call to the coroner."

"Thanks. Appreciate you getting the cavalry lined up," Wyatt comments before disconnecting the phone line as Darcy slows the boat for their approach to 'Knot on Call'. Wyatt waves to the occupants of the red and white boat as they move closer.

"Where? Where is he?" Wyatt calls out as both boaters point to the starboard side of their boat. "Darcy, let's tie off on their port side. Once we're secure, I'll get my wet suit on."

Chapter 7

Alicia

The antique market is crowded with shoppers on this beautiful warm Saturday afternoon, as the couple roam up and down the numerous rows of tables, all overloaded with interesting objects from years gone by. Some tables feature old kitchen items including fancy cups and saucers, depression glass, and different colours of mountain pottery, while others are crammed with dented pots and roasting pans like ones that granny would have used for the annual Christmas turkey dinner. There are a variety of booths displaying ancient furnishings – old wicker rocking chairs, Singer sewing cabinets, some with the machine, some without, while another table features pictures, paintings and postcards, while another contains knickknacks such as old cameras, lighting fixtures, cast iron door stops and a few old, well-read books.

The woman pauses, watching as her companion stops at a table full of old treasures and picks up a bulky gold-coloured handset from a not-yet antique phone and holds it to his ear. He nods his head as if listening to someone on the other end, the corners of his mouth upturned in a silly grin, his dark brown eyes sparkling.

"It's for you," he says, handing the receiver to her, just as her cell phone rings.

"Can you ask them to hold for a minute?" Alicia asks, digging into her purse and producing a still-ringing cell phone. She looks quickly at the call display before putting her index finger up in a motion to ask her companion to wait, as she hits the button and answers precisely with "Detective Anderson." Alicia moves away from the people crowding the aisles of the large market and slips between two booths, towards the vendor storage area, devoid of people, filled with piles of boxes of wares that have not yet made it to their tables. Her eyes squint as she listens to the voice of the police dispatcher on the phone above the noise of the open-air bazaar. Her boyfriend Jeff's smile dissolves as he shakes his head 'no' to the vendor who is hoping to sell the old phone. Jeff places the receiver back on the phone's cradle and follows Alicia, his joke quickly forgotten.

Alicia nods her head a couple of times as she listens intently to the call. The Barrie marine unit has been dispatched to a situation in Kempenfelt Bay where there's a dead body in the water. Additional details are sketchy. Jeff watches as her relaxed posture shifts, her shoulders move up as her body tenses, and her stance becomes stiff. He knows immediately that their leisurely day is going to be cut short for her job.

After several moments, Alicia tells the dispatcher, "Call Helen. Tell her to meet me at the precinct. Tell the marine unit to come to the Big Bay government docks once they've contained the situation."

She listens for another moment. "I'm on my way. ETA is 30 minutes, 45 tops. Let me know what Helen's timing is once you get her."

The pair move in unison towards the parking area, Jeff stepping in front of Alicia, leading her through the rows of vendors, pushing around the crowd of people as she finishes the call. She pockets the phone quickly, matches his stride, and reaches out to link her fingers through his jeans' belt loop, as they make a concerted effort to get free of the multitude of shoppers.

The crowds dwindle as they reach the parking area and Jeff clicks the button to unlock the doors on his black BMW Z4 convertible. He goes directly to the passenger side of the car and opens the door, waiting for Alicia to get in. She stops, gives him a quick kiss before lowering herself into the vehicle.

"What was that for?" Jeff asks, standing beside the car.

"Just for being you," she replies. Jeff closes the door and moves around to the driver's side, and folds his tall, athletic body into the driver's seat.

"For being me?" he asks, turning to her as he starts the car.

"Yeah, we had all these plans for the weekend and now they're spoiled. And just now, you helped me get out of that frigging crowd in one piece," she smiles as she gestures towards the market. "You always make it easy for me, you never complain, you just seem to accept the inevitable," she finishes, looking at him.

Jeff's dark brown bedroom eyes smoulder as the corners of his mouth upturns into a sexy smile. "Well, I'm not really OK with it," he confesses, taking her hand in his and holding it. "But your job is important. And if one Saturday gets fucked up because of it, well I'll just have to put on my big boy pants and accept it."

"Thank you for understanding, Jeff," Alicia murmurs moving in for another kiss, holding it for a few seconds before pulling back and looking into his eyes. "Not sure what I did to deserve you, but I'll take it," she laughs.

Jeff lets go of her hand before putting the gear shift into 'drive' while still looking at her, a smirk on his face. "You can't use that line. That's mine!" He pauses as he manoeuvres out of the parking space and pulls into traffic. He asks, "Where to?" already knowing that she will want to go home and get her car before meeting her partner.

"Home, please." Alicia says as she sits back against the seat, wondering what has happened on the water on this glorious summer day and what catastrophe she's going to see when she meets the marine unit at the docks.

Chapter 8

Wyatt

An hour later, Darcy steers the Stanley patrol boat easily into the government dock allowing Wyatt to jump from the boat and secure the lines.

"Where the hell is everyone?" Wyatt mumbles looking towards the dirt lane leading to the main road, just as a large black Chevy SUV pulls in, parking directly in front of a 'no parking' sign. Two women get out of the vehicle – one a short, petite woman with long chestnut-brown hair pulled back in a ponytail, wearing jeans and a light blue t-shirt; the second a tall blonde, her shoulder-length hair bouncing with her quick footsteps, also in jeans topped with a navy jacket. The pair walk swiftly down the dock towards him.

"Wyatt, right?" the dark-haired woman asks as they move towards each other. The marine police officer smiles as he nods his head in agreement.

"I believe we've met at one of the precinct's annual conventions," the dark-haired officer says, as she reaches out to shake the man's hand. "Detective Alicia Anderson and this is my partner, Detective Helen Hodgins," she clarifies, pausing a moment as the two police officers shake hands in greeting. "What do we have?" she asks, looking past Wyatt to the boat tied at the end of the wooden dock.

"A 911 call came in from Ray and Robyn Gardiner. They were out on the water in their boat, 'Knot on Call'. Just picnicking, enjoying the sun when they saw this weed bed floating on top of the water. They didn't think much of it, other than they weren't going to go swimming until it floated by. When they examined it a bit closer, they saw a body amid the green goop," he finishes, as a white van with 'CORONER' on the rear panel, backs into the dead-end laneway and parks. A tall, thin woman jumps from the van, her long red hair tied back, wearing light blue coveralls specifically made for forensic investigators at crime scenes.

The coroner moves towards the group on the dock, as the two detectives smile, thankful that they have the city's expert on death investigations and forensics in their midst – Dr. Jules Diamond.

"Hey Alicia, Helen, Wyatt," the doctor greets as she approaches.

"Dr. Diamond," Wyatt says reaching for her hand. "Good to see you. We've got a bad situation here and need your expertise."

"What have you got?" the coroner asks quickly.

Wyatt repeats the short synopsis that he has already given the detectives as the team move down the dock towards the police boat. They stand for a moment on the pier, finishing their conversation before Wyatt jumps onto the boat's deck and holds his hand out to Jules to help her onto the vessel. The coroner pulls a pair of booties and sterile gloves from her black doctor's bag and puts them on before offering her elbow for his assistance into the bobbing vessel.

"Thank you," she replies. "I've never been a boat person like you guys," she smiles at Wyatt before moving towards the tarp on the rear deck of the boat. "Can we get someone to move these people back?" she asks looking up at the crowd that has somehow appeared at the once quiet part of the lake. People are now clustered on the dock, and some even forward enough to wade into the water beside the boat to have a look.

"Sure," Helen replies, moving her arms demonstratively as she cajoles the crowd away from the boat, off the dock, out of the water and back to shore.

"Now let's see what we have," Jules says, bending down as Wyatt pulls the tarp off the top half of the body.

Alicia cringes inwardly as she takes in the mass of weeds, the green foam of bacteria which is entangled in the mess and the single open eye – fixed, dilated, a light blue almost white colour, which seems to be looking directly at her from the bottom of the boat. The body is distended, bloated beyond recognition, the skin a translucent green, open sores and

24

several small pieces of skin missing on the victim's cheeks, ears and chin.

Alicia and Helen move to cover their noses as gases begin to seep from the corpse.

Chapter 9

The Chief

"So, tell me what we have," Chief Margaret O'Malley says to her two detectives as they enter her office and move towards the visitors' chairs. "Did you have a chance to talk to Jules? Did she share anything when the body was pulled? Or after her initial examination? When's the autopsy scheduled?" she continues, her active mind moving quickly as her clear ocean blue eyes move between Alicia and Helen, as she waits for answers.

"I did get a couple minutes of her time this morning," Helen starts. "The autopsy is being scheduled for later this week. Alicia and I will be there." The detective stops and looks at her notes. "Not sure if the two marine police officers will be there but the invitation has been extended." Another pause before she gets into the specifics from the coroner. "Jules advised that the victim is approximately 50 years old, probably weighed about 250 pounds, about 5 foot, 4 inches, thinning blond hair, balding on top. No noticeable scars, no tattoos, no medical implants, and he has all his teeth. He did have a couple of contusions – one on his head, another on his shoulder. Jules believes both happened premortem. She didn't think either was the cause of death, but we'll have to wait for her to confirm. There was no ID on the body. He was wearing a pair of designer jeans and a light-yellow high-end golf shirt. No socks, no shoes, but they could have come off in the water."

"Dental impressions?" the Chief asks.

"Not yet, but it's on the list of things to do before the autopsy."

"DNA?"

"Yes, she has a sample. We'll run it through the DNA database, see if we can get a hit," Alicia advises.

"Fingerprints?" the Chief pushes.

"No. The body was in the water too long. Decomposition had already started and with the help of marine life, there is not enough to even try and reconstruct."

"Did she have a look at the lungs? Was there water in them?"

"She did not," Helen confirms. "Told me that's usually determined during the autopsy."

"Got it. If there's no water in his lungs, then he wasn't breathing when he went in. If that's the case, it might have simply been a heart attack. Or it could be murder. Someone killed him and pushed him into the water hoping that he would sink to the bottom and never come up," the Chief says thoughtfully. "They didn't take into consideration that bodies initially sink but they always come up rather quickly."

The room is silent, each contemplating what could have happened to this man. Was it a simple accident or was something sinister going on?

"Well, we know he wasn't out swimming. The guy was fully clothed. But maybe he did have a heart attack and fell off a boat or a dock or something," Alicia puts forward.

"I hear there was a Rolex recovered. Is it registered?" the Chief asks.

"I made an initial call to Rolex, had a hell of a time finding the right person to talk to, but finally found Hans Schmid, a lawyer who guards customer information closely. He won't give me anything without a warrant which is being signed this morning. I will get it to him today," Alicia advises.

"Good. Good. What about the clothes?" the Chief ask.

"They've been sent to forensics, but they haven't had a chance to look at them yet. We're hoping the jeans have a brand name stitched inside the waistband. Hopefully something exclusive. Something traceable. Maybe they are only sold at one or two stores. Maybe he was rich, had them made to measure or had his initials stitched into them," Alicia suggests.

"Any idea how long our victim was in the water?"

Helen, who has a page of notes in front of her, looks down before responding, "Jules guesses at three days based on the lack of fingerprints, the colour and abuse of the victim's skin. The body is still basically intact, but she confirmed that marine life had started to take advantage of the situation. The skin was blistered from the sun and had started to turn green. Said she should be able to give a better time of death once she has a look at his internal organs."

"Isn't three days a long time for a body to float around the bay, especially with the good weather we've had lately and the number of people on the water? Why wasn't he found earlier?" the Chief asks "Were there any signs that the body was submerged for an extended period?"

"Nothing that Jules mentioned, but I will ask her specifically at the autopsy," Helen replies making notes.

"Ask her about rope burns. Marks on the wrists or ankles or around the body from a chain. Chafing or cuts on his skin from something rubbing on it, something that would have been used to weigh him down."

Helen nods her head as she continues to write.

"Alicia, any missing persons that fit our vic's description?"

"I did a quick scan, and I don't think so, but I'll take another look with the additional details we now have. Three days is a long time for someone to be missing and not be reported. No friends? No family? No job? I guess he might live alone or possibly he's on vacation alone and no one's missed him yet. I'll extend the search to province-wide to see if I can find anything," she offers.

"Did Jules have a preliminary ruling?"

"I pressured her, Chief, but she wouldn't commit to anything before the autopsy is done," Helen answers.

"Always playing it safe," the Chief huffs. "The autopsy will give us the answer to how this guy died, whether it was a natural death or a possible murder. Either way, we need to find out who he is," the Chief tells her detectives.

"I had a conversation with Richard Wyatt, the marine officer who pulled the vic out of the water. Apparently, they have software that might be able to plot the vic's watery journey and tell us where he went in," Helen says.

"That would be helpful. Give you guys a place to start canvassing. Keep me in the loop on your progress," the Chief directs, effectively dismissing her detectives, her eyes moving to her computer screen.

Chapter 10

Alicia

Alicia logs onto her computer looking for an update from Rolex. *Frigging nothing. What is taking so long?* she wonders before leaning back in her chair, searching her thoughts for another possible lead to the identity of the victim that they pulled from the always-cold waters of Kempenfelt Bay. Her lips curl into a grin as she picks up the phone and enters a three-digit internal code. The phone is answered before the first ring is finished.

"Hello Alicia," the cheerful voice answers.

"Connor," Alicia acknowledges. "How are you today?"

"Life is good. No complaints here," his voice light and musical. "What can I help you with?"

"Wondering if you've had a chance to look at the clothes from the victim that was pulled out of the bay?"

"Grant has done a preliminary. No saliva, semen, skin cells or fingerprints on the clothes, which is not surprising seeing he was in the water for a couple of days. The victim was wearing black Ralph Lauren Classic Fit Denim Jeans, size 38 waist. They're sold in several places in Barrie including Moore's, Tip Tops and the Ralph Lauren store at the Outlet Mall. You can also get them online. The jeans have been shortened; I'd say by a professional tailor." Connor pauses for a second to catch his breath before continuing. "The victim was also wearing a yellow Michael Kors cotton-blend button-up golf shirt. Again, found in a variety of places or available online. No socks. No shoes."

"So, nothing that's going to tell us who the hell this is?" Alicia grumbles into the phone.

"I don't think so. Sorry," Connor offers.

"K. Let me know if anything comes up that will help us identify this guy." Alicia hangs up the handset and sits back in her chair, catching Helen's attention.

Helen turns towards her and asks, "Everything OK?"

"Not really. Nothing from Rolex. Nothing definitive from forensics. I think we need to get Blake over to the coroner's office this morning so he can make a sketch of this guy. We need to write a media release and get his picture out there. Someone must know him. Or at least know of him," Alicia answers, her frustration evident.

"Makes sense. You call Blake and see when he can get over there. Also, let the Chief know what we're up to. She should do the media release, add to the importance of finding out who this is ASAP. I'll write the message for her," Helen suggests, minimizing her Google search and opening Microsoft word.

***

The lobby of the police precinct is crowded with reporters holding cameras and microphones. Alicia and Helen are positioned slightly behind the Chief, as she stands at the podium and reads from the release. An enlarged sketch of the victim is posted on an easel to the Chief's left as she runs through the very little information they have about the victim and asks for the public's help.

There are several questions from the media, which she answers quickly before the news conference ends. She moves from the podium and walks down the hallway to her office.

The two detectives stand for another moment giving the press additional time to take pictures of the sketch or pick up a copy of the press release that are sitting on the lone table in the entrance hall before they move into the bowels of the police station to their desks in the Detectives' Den.

Chapter 11

Alicia

Helen manoeuvres the police vehicle to the police marine unit's office located in Friday Harbour Resort in the town of Innisfil, just south of Barrie. She drives to the east side of the complex and finds a parking spot behind a large two-storey building – both levels are totally glass with stores and offices open to public view, with Harbour Master boldly displayed on several signs, just as the marine officer, Richard Wyatt, opens the office's door.

Wyatt waves as the detectives get out of their vehicle. "Thanks for coming. Appreciate it," he greets.

"This is quite the office," Alicia replies.

"It certainly is. It's just a couple of years old. Right on the water. Right in the middle of all the action," Wyatt agrees, looking around at the docks, the boats, the pedestrians. "Come on in and Darcy can show you what we've put together," he continues, holding his hand out to guide the detectives to the side door of the building and up the stairs. "This way," Wyatt directs, moving along the hallway towards a large room at the front of the building. "When we moved into these premises, we had the opportunity to upgrade our computer systems."

"And we took advantage of it," Darcy chimes in, as the team enter the boardroom. "Bought the best software available, physical oceanography stuff that we weren't even sure we would ever really need. This is the first time we've been able to use it for a valid reason," he smiles as he sits down.

"The program, Physical Oceanography, allows us to put in physical attributes for the situation – the geography of Kempenfelt Bay, the structure, its depth, the shoals, the holes on the bottom, all of which impact how the water ebbs and flows. It also lets us include the surface water temperature for the week before the body was discovered, the wind direction and speed, tides or in this case known currents, probable boat activity and other possible influences," he explains.

"Other possible influences?" Helen asks.

"Yeah, like the density of the water, and the fish population."

"Fish population?" Helen echoes.

"Yeah, if there are lots of fish, which we can predict from the lakebed structure, then the water is typically healthier, less polluted. Anything in it will move easier as it gets less resistance," Darcy clarifies.

"Interesting. I never would have thought so many things would have an impact on movement within the water," Helen says.

"And then we had to input all the information we knew about the vic – height, weight, clothes. We assumed that he was dead when he went into the water. We haven't heard from the coroner yet whether this is true or not but thought it was a viable assumption. If we're wrong, and he was alive when he went into the water, we can update the parameters, which might move his course."

"OK enough grandstanding, Darcy," Wyatt laughs. "Show the detectives what we're thinking."

"Let me just connect to the white screen," Darcy says as he pushes a few keys on the keyboard and his computer screen displays at the front of the room. "There you go. Now we can all see it instead of hovering around my small laptop," Darcy comments before getting down to business. "We played around with it a little bit after we put in all the parameters. We initially proposed that he went in the water at the west end of the bay, in the city marina along Lakeshore Road. If that was the case, this is what we believe his destination would be in three days," Darcy says, sitting back after hitting a key on the keyboard, watching the large screen.

The group watches the outline of the bay as a red dot starts in the middle of the marina area. It begins to sway back and forth, before slowly moving towards the mouth of the bay, but only making it to Minet's Point, a small spit of land on the south side of the bay, ten kilometres short of where the body was found.

"If our data is correct, then he didn't fall in at the marina; he didn't get far enough into Kempenfelt Bay in the three days he was supposedly in the water. So, we moved him, thinking he might have gone in at the transient boating area near Heritage Park."

The team watches the original red dot disappear, replaced by a yellow dot just off the shoreline northwest of the initial guesstimate. All eyes are on it as it progresses slowly, swinging back and forth as it moves in a southern direction across the bay.

"This entry moves him up the bay, almost to Tynedale Park if our parameters are correct, but still not close enough to where he was finally found. So, we moved his entry point to Johnson's Beach Park."

All eyes are glued to the screen as an orange dot appears, and they watch it shift and move slowly across the bay.

"Still shy of the area where the victim was found, so we tried putting him in the water along Ridge Road. Maybe he came off one of the docks or a boat that was anchored there."

The four pairs of eyes watch as a blue dot appears, and floats across the screen but not far enough. A green dot appears farther down the coastline and drifts closer to the extraction point. A purple dot is added to the map, and the team watches as it slowly glides just past the point where the body was retrieved.

"With the information that we have, we think that the victim went into the water somewhere in this area," Darcy says, pointing to the screen, indicating a swath along the north side of the bay.

"We were able to superimpose a street map on the land. With the current, the temperature, the boat traffic, the size of the guy and if he was actually in the water for three days, we think he went in between Sideroad 5, just outside the city boundary and Line 3 South in Shanty Bay," Wyatt explains.

There is silence in the room as their eyes watch Darcy rerun the trip of the blue, green and purple dots and where they end up.

"Lots of nice homes on big lots in that area," Alicia offers.

"Yeah. Black Forest Lane, Pemberton Lane, Bay Street, Trafalgar. Gorgeous places."

"That's impressive guys," Alicia says. "Gives us a place to start canvassing."

Chapter 12

Kandis

The women stand in line at the Cancun International Airport waiting to board the Boeing 737 which will jet them home. Maeve Preston is short, heavy set, with cropped auburn-red hair, sticking up like she's put her finger in a light socket. She is wearing elegant jet-black capris and a matching jacket, with a flowing bold leopard print t-shirt and sandals. Kandis Sheridan is tall, pencil-thin, her brooding grey eyes with green flecks flash as she looks about. Her shoulder-length mousy brown hair is pulled back in a hair clip. She is wearing a pair of well-worn skinny blue jeans and a flashy tie-dyed t-shirt that her friend talked her into buying while they were on vacation.

"That was a fantastic trip," Kandis says, smiling at her friend. "Thanks for including me in your birthday celebration."

"It was a fantastic vacation. I think we should plan something else," Maeve suggests, watching her friend closely before adding, "You mentioned wanting to see some new bands. How about a road trip to Nashville? Go for a couple of days, take in a show, maybe go to the Grand Old Opry?" she suggests, always ready to organize and go on a trip.

Kandis is silent for a moment. *I would love to. Love to go everywhere that you want to Maeve. But I know there's going to be a knock-down-drag-out fight when I get home. Kyle will be an asshole and obliterate all the good of this week. And then there's money. If the bastard only had a job and contributed, I could do more. And if he was a normal husband, we could even go together. Nah, that's never going to happen,* Kandis thinks.

Maeve waits, knowing her friend is imagining the reception she will receive from her deadbeat husband when she gets home, as Kandis' smile slowly slips off her face.

"I would love to," Kandis finally offers. "But I've got to make sure everything is OK with Abbie first."

"Understandable. Did you talk to her today? How's she doing?" Maeve asks, as they move a couple of steps forward.

"She's struggling, but she's definitely trying. She says she misses me. Says she'll be glad when I'm back. For some reason, I've become the buffer between her and Kyle," Kandis shrugs before continuing. "And if that's what it takes to keep her drug-free, then that's what I'll do." She pauses for a moment. "Drug Free Kids Canada has been a great help, supporting her as she navigates back to the life of a teenager without the crutch of drugs. But I still worry about her. Especially when I'm not there."

"I understand that Abbie is your priority. And it's fantastic that there are some programs to help both of you. And what about your other half? Is he involved with Abbie's rehabilitation?"

"He's got his own issues with alcohol. But he said he would try. And he did go to AA," Kandis says, her voice petering out.

"And how did that go?"

"Well, he went to one session but when he came home, he said he could do it on his own. Said he doesn't need them. Said he doesn't want anyone to see him in that setting."

"So, he's not going to go? Has he quit drinking?" Maeve asks her friend.

Kandis looks at her friend, tears clouding her eyes. "Yeah, for about two hours before the meeting that he went to," she replies.

"Piece of shit," Maeve says under her breath, loud enough for Kandis to hear.

Kandis grimaces at the words, nodding her head in agreement. "Yeah," is all she says as they move a couple of steps closer to boarding the plane.

"No worries, my friend. Hopefully, Abbie has it licked this time, and she can get back to being a carefree teenager,"

Maeve offers before adding, "Kyle, on the other hand, is not going to change, and you know it."

Chapter 13

Alicia

Alicia slams the desk phone down; stress and disgust etched on her face as Helen approaches.

"What's going on?" Helen asks, sitting down beside her partner.

"Frigging guy. I sent the warrant electronically. And they got it. But now, he's telling me his legal team has to look at it, talk to their police force. Says they have some bloody process to make sure it's an approved legal warrant before he can give me the owner's information. Do people just call Rolex with watch serial numbers to try and get the owner's info? What the hell is happening in this crazy world?" she spits out.

"And how long will that take?"

Alicia laughs. "That's where this guy is a real tool. Says it could be as quick as a day. Or more likely a week or two. And then he declared that he might not even have the data when he already confirmed that he did. I reminded him of our conversation the other day when he said he had the information, and he just hemmed and hawed trying to make up shit, like he was lying then or lying now. I don't know."

"That's quite the timeline and list of possible limitations," Helen replies before adding, "Do you want to ask the Chief to lean on Rolex?"

Alicia thinks for a moment before retorting. "Yeah, I think that's a good idea. This Hans Schmid asshole confirmed they got the warrant, and he was the guy I was talking to the other day. We need someone to cut through the bullshit and speed up the process and get the friggin name of the watch owner," she finishes, picking up her phone and dialing the Chief's assistant, Charlotte, who can always get things done quickly and efficiently.

After a short conversation, Alicia hangs up the phone. "Says she'll get back to me as soon as she hears something.

Says she'll call first, throw the Chief's title around and if she needs more muscle, she'll get the Chief to call directly," Alicia tells her partner.

"Well, we'll just have to sit on that for a bit then. How about we knock on a few doors? Maybe we'll get a hit," Helen suggests.

"I was so hoping we wouldn't have to do that. I was hoping there would be a hit on the DNA database, or someone would file a missing person's report, or someone would recognize the sketch on the news," Alicia advises.

***

Hours later, the two exhausted detectives make their way back into the precinct, throwing their briefcases and cell phones on their desks.

Helen releases a big sigh. "What a day! How about we go for a drink? We can brainstorm the scenario again. See if there's anything we're missing. See if there's another way to find out who this guy is."

"I would love to, but I need to go home. I got a text from Luke earlier asking what time I would be there. Apparently, he has something to tell me," Alicia replies guardedly.

"That sounds kinda ominous."

"Yeah, I'm not sure what's up with him but hoping for good news," Alicia replies, crossing her fingers.

Chapter 14

Alicia

Alicia pulls her car into the driveway of her small bungalow, noticing her son Luke's beat-up black Toyota Corolla, a car which he bought second, probably third hand, but has worked diligently on to get it in working condition. *What does he want to talk about?* she wonders as she exits the car and walks towards the side door. *I hope to hell it's got nothing to do with Annie's brother. I don't know how she came from that fucking family. She must have got the whole family's brains, all their morals. Don't think of her criminal brother. He's not part of her life anymore.*

She opens the side door of the house and walks up the three steps into the kitchen of her rental home, listens, and hears whispers and chuckling coming from the living room. "Luke?" she asks loudly, as she throws her purse and briefcase on the counter and continues to move into the dining room.

She quickly takes in the helium balloons placed strategically around the dining area and into the living room in bunches of blue and pink. Alicia smiles, knowing that he has chosen blue as her favourite colour and pink as Annie's. *But what if it's blue for a boy and pink for a girl*, she wonders as her eyes move to the two standing at the opposite end of the dining room table, grins on their faces, happiness radiating from the pair, her son, tall, well built from constantly working out at the gym, his sandy-brown hair shorter than in the past, his bright blue eyes watching her every move. Annie Tunes, his girlfriend, stands beside him, almost as tall, her long strawberry-blond hair pulled back with a large silver hair clip, her brilliant green eyes watching.

"What's going on?" Alicia asks, several possibilities running quickly through her head. *She's pregnant. They're getting married. He's moving out. Whatever it is, they think it's great news. Smile Alicia. Whatever it is, don't rain on*

41

their parade. She stands and smiles at the couple before her eyes move to the dining room table, where a cake sits in front of the pair. "Cake?" she asks cautiously.

"Look at what it says," Annie tells her, gesturing to the cake with her hand, nodding her head.

Alicia walks around the table to get a better view and reads the inscription, 'We made it!'

She looks up at the pair, still unsure what they are celebrating, and smiles before asking, "Made it?"

Luke and Annie both pick up separate pieces of paper from the table. Luke unfolds his and hands it to his mother. Her eyes review the letterhead and the first paragraph quickly before looking at her son, a huge grin on her face.

Annie hands her a second piece of paper and she looks at it quickly, reaching out to hug the girl, before hugging her son.

"I am so proud of you," she says directly to her son, before turning back to Annie and repeating her thoughts, "I am so proud of you."

Luke reaches out and pulls the two most important people in his life into a hug. "We made it, Mom. We've been accepted into the Police College in Alymer." He pauses before adding, "Together. We're going down together."

That's only four hours away. Maybe five. Not too far. Drivable, Alicia thinks as she holds on to her son and his girlfriend. *And he won't be gone too long. Only a couple of months hopefully.*

Chapter 15

Kandis

Kandis lies beneath her husband, gasping for air as he drives into her, the mountainous amount of alcohol which he consumed earlier inhibiting his ability to hold an erection and have an orgasm. He's sweating as he continues his attack, unaware of the pain that he is inflicting on his wife of 16 years, uncaring of his brutality, only conscious of the need to dominate her and satisfy himself.

"Fuck," he mutters as his hips grind against her unmoving body. He stops for a moment, hovering over her limp, unresponsive form and looks into her face, disgust clouding his expression. "What the hell, bitch? Move with me. Make me come, you cow," he grunts, pushing even harder and faster as his wife lies still in a dead-like state, closing herself off from him, the indignities and the violence that is being inflicted upon her.

What seems like hours but is probably only several more minutes of grunting and grinding into his wife, Kyle reaches a climax and falls on top of her, panting, waiting for his heart to slow. He pulls out of her and pushes himself up on his hands and knees. "What the fuck was that?" he asks in disgust as he gets up and sits on the edge of the bed. He turns to look at his wife. "What the fuck, Kandis. If you're not interested, there are plenty of others that are," he declares, as he gets up from the bed pulling his jeans on commando style. "Plenty more," he continues as he bends over her inert body and slaps her brutally several times. "That'll teach you," he mumbles, as he moves towards the bedroom door, opening it and staggering down the hall.

She listens as he stomps through the house, listens as he opens the side door and moments later, the garage door as it slams behind him. *Asshole. He should fucking stay out there. A place where he can drink until he falls down. Take whatever fucking drugs he wants. Just leave me alone! I need*

43

to get my shit together. I need to get rid of him. I need to be free of him.

She touches her right eye lightly, feeling the swelling which has already started. She grabs a Kleenex from the bedside table, flinching as she dabs her bottom lip, before pulling the tissue away with traces of blood on it. She leans back on the bed, closing her eyes as tears escape.

***

The loud buzz of the alarm startles Kandis, making her jump from a deep, dreamless sleep. She hits the button on her phone to stop the insistent buzzing before she looks over to Kyle's side of the bed. *Thank God he didn't come back. Probably sleeping in his fucking garage,* she thinks, gingerly moving her legs to the side of the bed, her pelvis and genitals sore from her husband's brutal assault. She slowly stands up, feeling like she's been hit by a bus, tiptoeing towards the bedroom door.

Kandis quietly walks down the hallway towards the kitchen, opening the door to Abbie's bedroom and closes it quickly when she sees the girl's midnight-black hair peeking out from under the blanket as she sleeps.

She steps back, leaning against the wall in the hallway. *I can't keep doing this. One day he's going to do something even worse to me, put me in the hospital or even kill me. And then what will happen to Abbie? He won't look after her. He doesn't look after her now. Says she's not a child anymore.*

How the hell did it get this bad? Why didn't I stop it? Fucking asshole doesn't work anymore, doesn't help with this family, doesn't even try. I've been supporting him for years.

Drinks like a fucking fish. If he quit or at least cut back, we could get back to a decent life, but who the hell am I kidding? He needs to get help and get into a program. Yeah,

yeah, he's tried that before, and it didn't work, so not sure why I think he'd try it again.

But when he's sober, when he remembers what we had, he rallies. Treats me right, treats me like royalty, but those times are so few and far between that it's not even worth holding out hope for anymore.

Maybe Eric can help. Kyle might listen to his brother. Eric can play the sympathy card. Tell him his mom would have wanted him to get sober. Eric probably doesn't even know how bad it is. I should call him. Ask him to intervene. Ask him to help his brother. To help me.

Kandis staggers into the kitchen, looks to make sure that the water reservoir is full on the coffee maker and turns it on, before stumbling down the hallway and into her ensuite bathroom. She stands in front of the bathroom mirror, a plethora of makeup spread out on the vanity, as she leans her head back and puts Visine eye drops into her right eye. She blinks a couple of times before looking at her reflection.

Not sure that these fucking eye drops are going to help today. How many goddamn times can I tell people that I tripped or ran into a door, or I'm allergic to something? They aren't stupid and they've probably already guessed what's going on here, she thinks as she picks up her green concealer and lathers it on her eye, on her brow, and on her cheek.

After a moment, she stands back to look at her work, smoothing it out gently with a blending sponge before putting on another layer of concealer, one that matches her skin colour.

After artistically adding the second layer, she stops and looks at her face. *Fucking dickhead. This has to stop. One way or the other, this has to stop.*

Chapter 16

Helen

"Good morning," Alicia says warmly to her partner as she places her briefcase on the desktop, making Helen jump. "You OK?" Alicia asks, looking closely at her friend.

"You just startled me is all," Helen laughs. "I've been waiting for you for 30 minutes now. You're usually in here before me."

"What's going on? Did we get some hits on the hotline? Or get some information from Rolex?" Alicia asks, as she sits down beside her partner.

"There were a bunch of calls from the hotline but nothing that sounded viable, but I found something else. There's a new missing person's report that was placed with the OPP detachment just north of here yesterday that you need to take a look at," Helen replies, as the screen on her computer changes, displaying the document that she has been talking about. Helen pushes her laptop towards Alicia, saving her the time of signing on and finding the notice.

Alicia squints at the screen reading the missing person's report before a grin spreads across her face. "This could be him," she says, looking up at Helen.

"Could be," Helen agrees. "Look at this – the guy's address is right in the region that Wyatt and Darcy suggested. His place is right on the water. He's the right age, right weight, from a part of town that would be wearing Ralph Lauren and Michael Kors. Hasn't been seen for over a week. Why has it taken so long for him to be reported?"

"The missing person's report says his wife has been out of town," Alicia answers.

Alicia reads the report for a second time before looking up at her partner. "Can you print this?" she asks, preferring to hold a piece of paper in her hand as opposed to looking at a screen.

"Already done." Helen stands up and walks to the department's printer. She returns to their desks and hands the document to Alicia.

"Have you called the OPP? Can we go see this woman, this Maeve Preston?"

"Yup, they said we were good to go. She lives right on the border between the OPP and Barrie jurisdictions. As long as we keep them in the loop, they are good."

"The wife, eh? If I remember correctly, 40% of homicides are committed by family members."

"Yeah, but only half of that number is typically the wife," Helen adds.

"That's if we have the right guy, the right family. Have you called her? Set up an appointment?"

"Not yet, partner. I was just waiting for you," Helen replies, picking up the phone.

***

A couple of hours later, the detectives pull into the palatial grounds of 555 Trafalgar Road, Shanty Bay, the home of Lewis and Maeve Preston. The driveway winds through clean crisp lawns, similar to the greens on an exclusive golf course, to a luxurious two-storey brick home. The dining room and family room are at the front of the house on the main level, their windows large and unencumbered by any coverings, giving the detectives a view of the well-appointed and expensive furnishings within. An ornate double front door sits between the two rooms. The door is open, and a woman stands waiting for the pair. The woman's brilliant hazel-coloured eyes are intent as she watches the detectives walk towards the house, her brows knit in worry. She is well dressed in a long flowing bright yellow sundress, her make-up and hair perfect, highlighting a deep summer tan.

"Detective Hodgins?" she asks, stepping out onto the front porch.

"Yes," Helen replies, striding towards the woman, her hand extended. "I'm Detective Helen Hodgins. This is my partner, Detective Alicia Anderson," she finishes, as Alicia holds out her hand in greeting. The older woman shakes first Helen's and then Alicia's hand.

"Have you found him? Have you found Lewis? Is he OK?" she asks quickly, her hand moving towards her mouth, covering it in anticipation of bad news.

"Can we come in and talk?" Helen asks, nodding towards the house.

"Of course. Forgive me," Maeve replies, stepping back and motioning for the detectives to enter the front foyer, following them in before she closes the front door. "Come in. We can sit in here," she gestures to the room on the right of the large open foyer.

The detectives enter the family room, one of the rooms that they had glimpsed from outside the house. The room is large and features two over-stuffed chocolate-brown leather couches facing each other, set apart by an oval glass table with a vase of fresh flowers sitting at its centre. Two matching club chairs huddle at one end of the coffee table, facing the floor-to-ceiling stone fireplace.

The room is cluttered with pictures on every horizontal surface – pictures of children through the years, some with only one child, some with a pair but mostly a cluster of what looks like the whole family – Mom and Dad, a son and a daughter. Alicia's eyes zero in on a fairly recent photo of Maeve arm in arm with a heavy-set man, both with smiles on their faces as they squint into the bright sunlight. Alicia catches Helen's eye and moves her head slightly towards the picture, knowing that it is the face of the man that was pulled out of the water, the man that they've been trying to identify.

"Would you like a coffee?" Maeve asks as the detectives sit in the individual chairs facing the large stone fireplace and she sits down at the end of the couch closest to the detectives. Before they have a chance to answer, she yells, "Janie, can you get us coffee?"

"It's OK. We're good, I think," Helen says as a young, dark-haired woman appears in the doorway.

"Three coffees," Maeve demands, nodding at the young woman, dismissing her immediately, turning back to the detectives, as the youthful domestic scampers from the room. "Thank you for coming. I just filed the report last night. Have you found Lewis?" Mrs. Preston asks again.

"Have you been away, Mrs. Preston?" Alicia asks.

"Yes, I was away for a week with a girlfriend. We went to the Riviera Maya in Mexico," she smiles. "Why are you asking? Did something happen while I was away?"

"Do you usually talk to your husband when you're on vacation? Maybe call home to check in?"

"Not normally, no. He would call if there were any concerns like if one of the kids was sick or something else was going on, but Lewis is pretty busy. He owns Preston Construction, and I never know where he is, or what he's doing. Unless it's urgent, we don't usually call. And after 20 years of marriage, a week of silence is kinda nice." She stops for a moment before blurting out, "Oh my God. What happened to Lewis while I was away?"

"Where did you stay in Riviera Maya?"

"We were at The Royal. Right on the beach in Playa del Carmen."

"We?"

"Yes, I went with my best friend Kandis."

"That is a gorgeous ring," Alicia says, nodding to a large heart-shaped diamond on Maeve's left ring finger.

Mrs. Preston looks down and smiles. "It is beautiful, isn't it? Three carats. I saw it in one of the small shops on the pedestrian street in Playa del Carmen. I loved it and just had to have it. I bought it for myself as an anniversary present from Lewis."

The conversation pauses for a moment as Mrs. Preston looks down at her latest purchase, extending her hand, and wiggling her fingers to admire the sparkling jewel. "Enough of this," she says, putting her hands back into her lap. "Tell me what you know about Lewis," she demands sternly, though she continues her saga without waiting for a reply. "I thought he was away on a business trip, but when I called the office, his fill-in assistant said no. Then I thought he might have gone to our cottage, though his car was in the garage. I called his cell phone, but it just went to voicemail, which isn't surprising if he was up there. The service is very spotty. I called his friends and got nothing. They hadn't seen him. Then I got scared and called a couple of his VPs. Asked if they knew where he was, if he was on a business trip, and they said no, they hadn't heard from him for a couple of days either. Checked with the Royal Victoria Hospital here in Barrie, but they didn't have anyone by his name or his description. Even checked Facebook and Instagram," she fumes before continuing. "That's when I called you guys," she pauses, catching her breath before adding, "What the hell happened? Is he at Soldier's Memorial Hospital in Orillia? I knew I should have called there."

Just as Maeve finishes her rush of words, the young maid appears at the doorway, staggering into the room, balancing a large tray loaded with coffee, cups, cookies, cream and sugar. She puts it down on the edge of the oval coffee table, picks up the large flower arrangement from the centre and moves it to an end table, before repositioning the tray. "Would you like me to pour?" she asks, looking at the lady of the house.

"No, we're good," Mrs. Preston says, dismissing her quickly and efficiently, waiting until the girl has left the room before asking again, "Where is Lewis? What's happened?"

"Is this your husband's watch?" Helen asks, pushing a picture in front of Mrs. Preston who looks at it for a moment, her anger dissipating instantly.

Her eyes slowly move from the photograph to the detective's face. "Oh my God. Was there a robbery? What else did they get? Where's Lewis?" she asks.

"No, we don't believe it was stolen," Helen replies.

There's silence in the large space as the detectives watch the woman intently, looking for any clues to her possible knowledge of the situation. They wait for several moments before Mrs. Preston stands up and moves to the fireplace, her back to them momentarily before turning to face the pair. "You're killing me here. What's going on? Where is Lewis?" she demands, her intense fiery personality reappearing.

"There was a body recovered from Kempenfelt Bay a couple of days ago," Helen starts, as the homeowner's shoulders slump and she begins to shake, and leans against the fireplace to steady herself.

"Recovered from Kempenfelt Bay?" Mrs. Preston repeats questioningly, as she moves back to the couch and sits down, her face slack, her shoulders bending in, making her look smaller.

"Yes," Helen clarifies.

There is silence in the room before Mrs. Preston finally states adamantly, "It can't be Lewis. He was a good swimmer. Always in the water, well mostly the pool, but he knew how to swim."

The room is silent for a moment before Helen explains. "We believe it may be Lewis. From the description you gave the reporting officer last evening, from the watch, which was found on the deceased's body, from your pictures," she nods to the mantel before continuing, "and where the body was found."

Helen and Alicia watch as the silent woman slumps back into the plush leather couch. Another minute passes before she sits upright, moving her back straight, her shoulders at attention. "But you're not sure?" she asks, seeming to grasp at straws.

"Well, no, not conclusively," Helen admits.

"So, how do we prove it? One way or the other?" Maeve asks.

"The body would need to be identified, either visually or by DNA," Helen answers.

Maeve is quiet for a moment, her eyes beginning to squint as if looking into the future. She hangs her head, her shoulders slumping once again as the detectives watch. After a few moments, she raises her head and looks directly at Helen. "I will identify him," she says succinctly.

"Are you sure?" Helen asks.

"Yes, I can do it. Better me than one of the kids. And that will be faster than DNA testing," she answers as she looks at one of the larger pictures of her family sitting on the mantel over the fireplace. "And when it's not Lewis, you can get on with looking for my husband."

Chapter 17

Maeve

"Are you sure you want to do this alone? Maybe one of your children should be with you? Or a friend? Or another relative?" Alicia asks, as she watches Maeve Preston pace the length of the small viewing room at the coroner's office. Helen has gone in to advise the medical examiners' department that the next of kin is ready to complete the morbid task of putting a name to the as-yet-unidentified body.

Mrs. Preston turns as she reaches the distant wall and looks at Alicia as if she has never seen her before. She pauses a moment before answering. "No, I can do this. I don't want to bring one of the kids here in case it isn't him," she says quietly nodding. *And don't fucking ask me again. Don't think for a minute that Milly Ellis raised a weak feeble woman. No, I had to be strong for her, for me, to put up with the bullshit my father heaped on us. And I learned to hold my head up and always look out for number one. Always. Doing it by myself is the right thing to do. Don't scar the kids for life, they've already been impacted enough by Lewis' bullshit lifestyle.*

"And if it is him?"

"Then I'll deal with it. I'll have to call the kids and tell them what's happened. I don't want to involve them in this until we're sure. It wouldn't be fair. No, I can do this," she says forcefully as if trying to convince herself, turning to pace the length of the room again.

"I respect your decision but it's going to be difficult and someone to lean on is always a good thing."

The woman stops mid-stride, her bowed head straightening, her eyes glaring at the detective. "I understand your concern, but the decision has already been made."

The two stand for a moment, looking at each other. "If it truly is Lewis, I don't want their last memory of their father

53

to be a body laid out on a steel table with a sheet over him. And you said he was in the water for three days? No, that would not be fair to them."

"I understand," Alicia acknowledges impressed by the woman's determination, as the only door to the stark space is opened and Helen walks in.

"The team is sorry for the delay, Mrs. Preston, but if you're ready now," Helen says, moving to one side of the woman as Alicia moves to the other, ready to hold her in case she's not as strong as she believes. The three move in unison to the large picture window located at the centre point on the far wall. It is shrouded with blinds closed on the other side of the wall, and nothing is visible.

Mrs. Preston's shoulders, which have been hunched over, seem to rise to take on the challenge, adding a couple of inches to her height. *I can do this. I can do this. How bad can it be? So, he's been in the water for a couple of days.* She squares her face, turns to Helen, and grimaces weakly. "I'm ready," she says.

Helen nods her head in agreement, reaches out and knocks on the window. The blinds are pulled up quickly. A small stark room is visible through the window with a young man standing at the head of a raised table, a light blue sheet covering what they all know is a body.

"Ready?" Helen asks once again, thinking that the reality of the situation may now be sinking in.

She waits for a moment before Mrs. Preston nods her head and whispers, "Yes."

Helen nods to the man inside the room and he efficiently grabs the corners of the sheet and pulls it down, away from the corpse's face, setting it on his chest. He watches through the window as the woman stares at the body, her once-placid face crumbling at the sight.

The three women stand for a moment looking at the cadaver before Helen asks, "Is that your husband? Is that Lewis Preston?"

Mrs. Preston stares into the morgue area not making a sound, mesmerized.

Helen asks again, "Mrs. Preston. Is that your husband?"

There's silence in the room until she is able to nod her head. "Yes, that's Lewis. That's my husband," she clarifies, turning her back to the window, moving slowly to the chairs at the opposite end of the room and sitting down heavily.

Helen looks towards the window and nods to the attendant, who lowers the blinds, cutting off the morbid display.

Chapter 18

Alicia

The detectives stand on the Preston's front porch, the victim's toothbrush and hairbrush in separate evidence bags in Alicia's hands.

"This will help us corroborate your identification," Alicia says to the new widow, who is standing squarely, shoulders back, her face placid as she waits for the detectives to finish their unpleasant task and leave her in peace. She nods her head in answer.

"The coroner's office will be in touch with you for details on where to send your husband," Helen adds and Maeve nods again.

"We are sorry for your loss," Alicia reiterates, before the detectives walk down the three steps and move in unison towards their police SUV parked in the driveway.

The detectives get into the vehicle and put on their seat belts, both watching as the widow walks purposefully through the front door of the expansive house, shoving the door closed brusquely behind her.

"Strange, don't you think?" Alicia asks.

"What do you mean?"

"No tears. You would think after all the years they'd been together there would be a bit more emotion or even some shock."

"A bit puzzling, yes. But everyone handles stress differently. Maybe she's crying now. Too proud to show any emotion in public. Perhaps she has a high tolerance for daunting or intimidating situations. Possibly a learned response from the highly visible life that she's been living."

"Maybe. I mean her face kinda caved in for a minute, but no crying, no tears, no gasps when she saw the body," Alicia says.

"Very undemonstrative. Very conservative. Could be used to the public eye and just put her game face on."

"Possible, but I would say she seemed heartless. Even if you can posture for the camera, put on the poker bitch face so no one knows what you're thinking, the eyes usually don't lie."

"The eyes?" Helen parrots.

"Yeah, the eyes. The eyes didn't change from when she was talking about her vacation to looking at her husband's dead body. There was no sadness there."

"Interesting take," Helen suggests as she starts the SUV. "What I find interesting is that no one she called, the people at Preston Construction, her husband's friends, no one saw the news report on the unidentified body that was pulled from the bay. Not one of them. Don't you think that's strange?"

Alicia pauses for a moment before answering. "With all the ways to consume news in this day and age, I think people aren't as likely to watch their local TV channels. They're more interested in what's going on in the national or international forums, if they're checking the news at all."

Chapter 19

Kandis

The slamming car door echoes through the rural subdivision as Kandis pushes it with all her might.

What the fuck is going on? It's only 6 o'clock and there's already a crowd in the garage, laughing, hollering, trying to play their fucking instruments. Not one of them can carry a bloody tune, she thinks as she trudges to the front door of her house and grabs the doorknob, twisting it. *What the hell? The door is locked.*

Her keys are still in her hand, and she thumbs through the mass to find the one for the front door. *Here it is,* she thinks as she shoves it into the lock, walking into the front hall. *Well at least Abbie is home*, she muses as she pushes her daughter's shoes and backpack away from the entrance door.

"Abbie," she yells as she takes her shoes off and moves into the kitchen. "Abbie," she shouts again, stomping through the kitchen, throwing her purse and briefcase on the kitchen table crowded with dirty dishes, fliers that must have come in with the mail that day, an open guitar magazine, pens, sticky notes, a set of keys, everyday stuff.

Kandis continues down the hallway to her daughter's bedroom and knocks on the door. "Abbie," she calls again. "Are you in there?" she asks, rattling the door handle, then pushing against the door to open it, but there is something big on the other side, something pushed up against the door so she can't get into the room.

"Abbie, what's going on?"

Kandis stands for a moment and listens. A quiet voice comes through the narrow opening of the door. "Mom?"

"Abbie, what's going on? Open the door," Kandis demands, fear starting to creep into her consciousness.

"Mom?" she hears again stronger this time.

"Abbie, what's going on? Let me in," she asks more gently.

Kandis hears movement on the other side of the door. *What the fuck! Did she push the dresser in front of the door? Why the hell would she do that?*

Moments later, the door opens a little wider and Kandis can see her daughter's thin drawn face, her black hair hanging in clumps, her light grey brooding eyes. Her mother-instincts take over quickly and she pushes the door open.

"What's going on?" she asks.

"That friend of Dad's. Alex, I think his name is."

Kandis sharply breathes in before asking, "What did he do, Abbie?"

Abbie tells her mother that he approached her in the kitchen, that he told her how beautiful she was, how he reached out and stroked her hair, how he put his hands around her, tried to pull her close to him, but she pulled away and ran into her bedroom.

"And then?" Kandis asks.

"I waited. I was quiet. I could hear him in the kitchen. He was looking in the fridge, I think. Then he left, went back out to the garage."

"And then?" Kandis asks again.

"I crept into the kitchen to make sure he was gone, and I locked the front and side doors. I ran back into my bedroom and moved my dresser in front of the door, just in case."

Anger grabs Kandis immediately. *Son of a bitch. Who the hell does that piece of shit think he is, coming into my house? Touching my daughter.*

"And where was your dad during all of this?" Kandis asks.

"He was in the garage. I didn't want to go out there. He's with all his friends, so I stayed in my room until you came home," the girl confesses.

Kandis pulls her daughter into her and pats her back. "I'm so sorry this happened to you, Abbie. So sorry," she says, swaying slightly, holding her daughter tightly.

They stay this way for several minutes, Abbie shuffling her feet, looking down, not returning her mother's hug as Kandis gets angrier. Finally, Kandis stands back and looks into her daughter's eyes. "You stay here. I need to talk to your father," she says.

"Mom?"

"Don't worry. I'll look after this," she tries to comfort her daughter for several moments before Abbie steps back, letting her mother go.

Son of a bitch, Kandis thinks as she rushes through the house, out the front door and into the garage. She walks boldly into the crowded space and rips the electrical cords violently from the wall socket.

"What the hell!" her husband Kyle exclaims as the music from his guitar dissipates. His head comes up and he sees his wife standing with the cords in her hand. "Kandis, what the fuck are you doing?" he yells, taking a step towards her.

"I think that's what you should be asking your friend, Alex," she replies, turning to look at the bass player who has stepped back behind the drum set as if trying to hide.

"Alex?" Kyle asks, turning to look as his friend retreats. "What's going on?"

"Yeah Alex, what's going on?" Kandis asks, cords still in her hands.

"Alex, what's she talking about?" Kyle asks, setting his guitar in its stand and stepping towards his friend. There's only silence as Alex steps back again, bumping into a set of speakers.

"Your friend thought it was OK to accost your daughter," Kandis answers for the silent man.

"Are you fucking kidding me," Kyle screams. "Abbie. You touched Abbie," he yells as he jumps around the drums, microphone stands falling in his wake and grabs his friend by the scruff of the neck, their faces within inches.

"I didn't. I swear I didn't," Alex lies.

"You fucking piece of shit. She's mine, asshole," Kyle mumbles as he hits the man, hits him so hard the crack of his jaw resonates throughout the garage.

Chapter 20

Maeve

Maeve staggers through the house remembering the sight of Lewis at the morgue, his inert body lying on the slab, his pure white cheeks with small areas that looked like they'd been puttied to hide holes or chew marks from something that had munched on him. *Thank God my mother made me a strong woman.*

The detectives said they'd done an autopsy on him, and they were waiting for the coroner's ruling. I read somewhere that a person's organs start to decompose and turn to mush depending on how long they're submerged in water. Three days! They won't be able to tell what happened to him, so they'll have to rule it a natural death. Probably rule it as a heart attack.

I better call the kids and tell them about their dad. I hate funerals. I need a drink.

What was that drink that Kandis and I loved in Mexico? That Juan was quite the bartender – his dark brown eyes looking at you like he could see inside your mind, his strong tanned shoulders bursting at the seams of that way-too-small t-shirt, his dimples accenting his smile. Now that's someone I would like to wake up beside. She smiles at her racy thoughts, forgetting for a moment that she has just identified the dead body of her husband and is about to start calling her children to tell them that their father is dead.

Mojito. That was one of the drinks that Juan made for us. Fantastic with all that rum, a bit of lime and mint. I don't think we have any lime or mint here, Maeve thinks as she moves into Lewis' office and looks in his liquor cabinet. *Nope. I'll have to put that on the list for Janie to pick up. Hmm, how about a Bloody Caesar? We've got all the makings for that. I'll have just one to take the edge off, to help me make these fucking phone calls. And to help erase the sight of Lewis that is etched in my brain.*

Maeve makes herself the drink and moves into the kitchen to add a pickle to the concoction, the final touch, before walking into the family room.

Here we go, she thinks, taking a large gulp of the tangy, crisp drink before picking up her phone.

***

"This Grey Goose is pretty good. The silky texture. The hint of sweetness. Yup. This is good," Maeve murmurs to herself as she drains the glass before making a fourth Bloody Caesar. *I called both of them and neither one asked how I was, how I was coping with the death of their father. Nope. Selfish. Self-centred. Just like their fucking father.*

She moves behind Lewis' large ostentatious office desk and sits in his generous ergonomic chair. *Mmm, this is comfortable. Guess it had to be with all the time that asshole spent locked up in this room.*

She sits back, her phone sitting in front of her on the desk, a drink at her lips, sipping leisurely. *I better call Kandis and let her know what's going on. She'll understand what I'm going through. She'll ask how I'm doing. She'll even come over here and commiserate with me,* Maeve thinks as she pushes the button for her friend's cell phone.

"Hey Maeve," Kandis greets. "Was I right? Was Lewis up at the cottage? Maybe hiding away with his VPs discussing how to take over the rest of the construction world?"

"Hi Kandis," Maeve says, setting her drink down on the wooden desk. "No, he wasn't at the cottage. Wasn't working on taking over the world," she sighs. "I got a call from the police about a body they pulled out of the bay, and I had to go to the coroner's office to identify Lewis today," she starts.

"Identify Lewis? Pulled out of the bay?" Kandis says breathlessly.

"He must have had a heart attack and fell in. I had to go identify him. You know how they do it on TV. It's something

62

like that but it's a surreal experience when it happens. Like a fucking nightmare."

"You should have called me. I could have been there with you. Are you OK? Do you want me to come over? Do you want me to call the kids?"

Maeve hesitates, a vision of her dead husband floating around in her mind.

"Did you hear me Maeve? Do you want me to come over?"

Maeve shakes her head before answering, trying to get rid of the haunting image of her dead husband. She finally answers, "That would be great. We can have a couple of drinks and toast the dead son-of-a-bitch."

Chapter 21

Kandis

Kandis looks at her phone as the line goes dead. She sets it down on the kitchen table and shakes her head as she takes a minute to digest the news of Lewis Preston's death. *Holy shit,* Kandis thinks, leaning back, as the muffled bass beat of the drums in the garage permeates her consciousness.

She stands up, moves down the hallway to her daughter's room and knocks on the door.

She hears an almost inaudible, "Come in," before she opens the door to her daughter sitting on her bed, her back against the headboard, her stocking feet on the bedspread, her knees bent and Kandis' iPad in her lap.

"What are you watching?" Kandis asks innocently.

"Just some stuff on YouTube," Abbie replies without looking up.

"I need to go to Maeve's," Kandis advises, watching her daughter for a reaction, but there is none. "Your dad is in the garage," she stops, watching her daughter's body language, which doesn't reveal any stress. "I've talked to your father and Alex won't be back. He's gone for good." Kandis pauses but there is no response. "You have a choice. Come with me or stay here," she tells her daughter, but it's like she's talking to a brick wall. "Abbie, did you hear me?" she asks, frustration now evident in her voice.

Abbie lifts her eyes from the screen, hearing the stress in her mother's voice. She pauses for a moment before telling her, "I'm good. I'll stay here," before her eyes return to the screen.

"Are you sure?" Kandis pushes.

"I'm sure," her daughter replies.

"I'll be home later," Kandis advises, watching for some type of acknowledgement from Abbie. "Lock the doors after me," Kandis tells her daughter, who simply nods.

Kandis moves towards the front door, grabs her purse and keys and walks outside. *What the hell. Look at all the cars in the driveway! Now I have to go into the fucking garage and get whoever owns that little black thing to move their car, so I can get the hell out of here. Don't any of these guys have to get up in the morning for work? All assholes. Every single one of them.*

***

Hours later, Kandis drives through the empty streets of Barrie towards home. *Maeve had to identify the body! What the hell! He must have fallen off the dock or the boat or something. Must have had a heart attack. But still, so much stress after our nice week away.*

She said the kids were coming up tomorrow but really, what are they going to do? It'll probably take a couple of days for the autopsy and then Maeve will want to plan everything. She's always been the planner, the glue in the family and she'll want to make sure that the funeral is up to her grandiose standards. I guess it's important to do it right. Lewis did have his own company, did a lot for the community, employed a lot of people.

She turns onto her street and instantly sees the crowd of cars in her driveway and parked on the road. *Shit! What the fuck are these guys still doing here? They need to shut it down,* she thinks as she pulls over to the curb and gets out of her car. She walks towards the garage, her mellow, tipsy mood from the excessive alcohol she's consumed while consoling her friend, suddenly gone.

Chapter 22

Alicia

Alicia sits at her computer in the Detectives' Den, reviewing emails as she waits for her partner to arrive. "Hmm," she murmurs to herself noticing a message from Rolex. *About frigging time,* she thinks as she clicks on the note from the watch company. She reads it quickly, a smile gracing the edges of her lips. "Thanks for nothing Rolex," she tells her computer screen as she forwards the email to Helen and Charlotte.

"Talking to yourself?" Helen asks as she rushes in, throwing her briefcase and purse on her desk before pulling out her chair and sitting down.

"We finally got a confirmation from Rolex – the watch belongs to Lewis Preston of Barrie, Ontario."

Helen smiles. "Well, at least it's good to have a secondary confirmation, I guess."

"A week ago would have been better but I guess better late than never," Alicia agrees.

"Well, I guess that's a wrap then unless Jules comes back with something on the autopsy," Helen suggests.

"Agreed. We have the wife's identification of the body. We have an independent confirmation of identification from Rolex. I've sent the toothbrush and hairbrush over to Jules to compare with the DNA from the body to ensure it's Lewis Preston, though it's almost moot at this point. I'll do the paperwork and hold onto it until we get that confirmation," Alicia says.

"Excellent," Helen agrees.

Chapter 23

Jules

Jules hits the send key on her computer and sits back in her armchair sighing loudly to the empty room before looking at her watch. *Amazing where the day goes,* she ponders as she moves back to the keyboard and shuts it down for the evening.

Well, the preliminary results are in, but there's a lot more testing that's required to confirm why the man actually died. I don't typically rule homicide without that proof, but it wasn't a natural death. I've sent all the data from the body to John, our forensics pathologist, and he'll ensure the microscopic, chemical and microbiological exams on the organs, fluids, and tissues are completed to identify the cause of Mr. Preston's death. It might take a while for the toxicology results, but Alicia and Helen will be able to start their investigation with my ruling of homicide.

He had a few prescription drugs in his system – perindopril for high blood pressure, rosuvastatin for high cholesterol and allopurinol to lower uric acid in the blood, usually to reduce kidney stones and gout, and a small amount of valium. The trace of valium is kind of weird. He didn't seem to have a history of anxiety, seizures or muscle spasms. Not something that someone would take as a one-off to calm down. And he didn't have a prescription for it.

He did have a premortem bruise on the back of his head, like he had fallen. It wasn't the cause of death, but it could be something that led up to it.

I'll leave it to the experts - John can figure out the medical specifics and Alicia and Helen will find the killer.

I'll have to go talk to the wife tomorrow. Tell her it's a homicide. Tell her that we're keeping the body to do some tests. She must be a strong woman coming to the morgue by herself to identify him. I'm sure she'll want to understand what happened to her husband.

Jules' laptop finally shuts down, and she unplugs it, tucking it into the top drawer of her desk. *Nope, not taking this home tonight. I've done enough today. I think I'll relax in my whirlpool tub for an hour or so. The warm water will certainly help after this 12-hour day,* she thinks as she throws her purse over her shoulder and walks to her office door, locking it behind her.

Chapter 24

Kandis

Kandis and Abbie walk pensively out of the community centre towards the parking lot, both quiet, both ruminating on the things they have just heard at the support group for teenagers and substance abuse.

Kandis unlocks the car doors and they get in, pull on their seat belts before she asks, "What did you think?

Abbie simply shrugs her shoulders and looks out the front window of the car.

There's silence for a moment, before Kandis pushes. "Talk to me. What did you think?"

Abbie turns her head towards her mother, tears in her eyes. "It was sad."

"Sad?" Kandis asks.

The quiet continues for several moments, Kandis watching her daughter as tears slip down her face.

"So much sadness. So much pain," Abbie answers quietly.

"There is," Kandis agrees, reaching out to her daughter and holding her hand. "Life is hard. Harder for some more than others," she offers.

"It is," Abbie agrees.

"Do you think we learned anything here tonight?" Kandis asks, still clutching her daughter's hand.

"Learned anything?"

"Yeah, like if you're having problems at school, or with a friend, or if something upsets you, there are people you can talk to. Maybe someone at Drug Free Canada. Or you could even talk to me. Maybe I could help you through whatever it is."

Abbie looks at her mother as if she's someone she's never seen before. "Not sure they said that tonight," she replies.

"Well, they didn't say it that way. They talked about not letting things fester; they talked about having someone in your corner, someone to help you think things through," she stops.

Abbie smiles weakly. "I did hear that. But didn't hear anything about confessing everything to my mother."

Kandis smiles in turn. "I get it Abbie, but what I want you take away from tonight is that there are people here to help you. You can talk to the support group. You can call the counsellor directly. Or you could simply talk to your old mother."

"Sure Mom," Abbie agrees swinging her head back to look out the front window of the car. "Let's go home and see what the other deviant is up to."

Kandis sits for a moment, watching her daughter shut her out, knowing that she can't push too hard, too fast, worried about her daughter's future, before she turns the key to start the engine.

Chapter 25

Luke

The phone rings once, twice, three times before it is picked up. "Hey Mom," Luke says breathlessly.

"Did I catch you at a bad time?" Alicia asks. "I just wanted to make sure everything's OK. I haven't heard from you for a bit," she explains.

"Sorry, we've been busy what with the new place, the course and George."

"George? Is everything OK with King George," she asks, the vision of the cute little black and tan miniature pincher crossing her mind.

"He's OK, but he got into the flower garden at the front of the complex, did some snorting around and something happened to his eye. We had to take him to the vet because he was scrunching it up all the time. Wouldn't open it. The vet said that he scratched the cornea."

"Shit. That doesn't sound good," his mother replies.

"Definitely not. We're supposed to wash his eye out every six hours and give him two different kinds of antibiotic drops," Luke advises.

"Supposed to?"

"Well, he's not happy with it. As soon as he sees us coming with the little bottle, he runs and hides. It's been a bit of a yelling match but so far, we're winning," Luke laughs.

"Glad to hear it. Poor little thing," his mother says commiserating with the dog.

There's silence for a moment before she asks, "How's the apartment?" referring to the main floor, one bedroom furnished flat that they have rented near the Police Academy.

"Different," he says simply.

"Different? Different good or bad?"

"Different good – we're redecorating a bit, painting the bedroom, the kitchen, trying to freshen it up. Annie has rented one of those steam cleaners, and cleaned all the furniture, so the place is coming together. But it's not home."

"Well, make it livable for a couple of months and then you'll be home, Luke. How's school?"

"Fantastic. We're learning lots, making lots of contacts, getting some leads on jobs when we're done."

"Fantastic," his mother replies. "Don't forget Chief O'Malley told you to look her up once you were finished."

Luke laughs. "I'm surprised she hasn't told you. We had a conversation just after I was accepted and depending on my marks here, she said we could talk again."

"That's fantastic. Maybe I'll get to see more of you," Alicia laughs.

"Maybe," her son agrees. "Listen Mom, I don't mean to cut you off, but we're at dog school and it's my turn to work with George."

Alicia laughs. "All of you at school. You guys are busy."

"Sorry, I've got to go," Luke says breathlessly as Annie stares at him, signalling to wrap up the conversation. "I'll call you. I promise," he pauses before adding, "Oh Mom, thanks for the money. It sure has helped with the apartment. We bought a couple of things that we needed. Oops sorry, I got to go. I'll call you soon," he finishes as the phone line goes dead.

Chapter 26

Kandis

Kandis sits at her kitchen table tapping on the keys of her laptop, her brows creased with concentration as she works on the monthly cost analysis required for tomorrow morning's meeting with her boss. She has ear buds in, listening to the local rock station, something that helps her concentrate and makes her oblivious to the loud noise coming from the garage, until a loud banging sound of someone kicking her front door permeates her consciousness.

"What the fuck," she mumbles to herself as she gets up, stomping into the front hallway, noticing for the first time that the TV is off, and the room is empty. "Where the hell is Abbie?" she asks herself as she looks at her watch, seeing that it's after 10 pm.

Kandis jerks open the front door just as another kick lands on the wooden slab, shaking the door on its hinges. "What?" she yells, before seeing the culprit, her next-door neighbour Denise Grant. "Why are you kicking my door, Denise?" she asks, looking down at the scuff marks left by her neighbour's running shoe. "What's going on?"

"What's going on?" the frumpy neighbour repeats, surprise in her voice. "The noise that your husband thinks is music is way too loud. It's one thing on the weekend, but another during the week when some of us have to get up and go to work in the morning."

Kandis stands for a moment, taking in her neighbour, the whining guitars, the thumping of the drums, before nodding her head in agreement. "I'm sorry, Denise. I was working on something and guess I just didn't hear it," she tries to explain.

"Didn't hear it? That's not possible. Tell him to turn it down now, or I'm calling the police," Denise yells, before turning around and tramping off the Sheridan's front porch.

Kandis stands for a moment, watching as her neighbour cuts across her front lawn and makes her way home. *Fucking guy*, she thinks as she steps off the front porch and makes her way to the garage, knowing that an argument is in the making, and it too is going to be loud.

Chapter 27

Alicia

The detective sits at her desk waiting for her computer to boot up when the doors to the Detectives' Den open and her partner saunters in. Helen smiles and greets their colleagues as she crosses the room to their work area.

"Morning," Alicia greets, as she opens her email.

"Morning," Helen replies, as she unpacks her computer from her briefcase. "Do we have a new case yet?"

Alicia holds her hand up, her eyes glued to her screen.

"What's going on?" Helen asks, as she opens the lid of her computer.

Alicia's hand is still in the air for a moment, before she turns to her partner. "We got the preliminary autopsy results from Jules."

"And?"

"She's ruling Lewis Preston's death a homicide," Alicia replies, her eyes not leaving the computer screen as she speaks. There's silence for a moment as Alicia continues reading the document. "John Richardson has been assigned as the forensics pathologist on the case." Alicia turns to her partner. "Jules says it'll take six to eight weeks to find the cause of death, but she is adamant that it is homicide, just not sure from what yet."

"Wow," Helen replies as she opens her email and clicks on the message Alicia is talking about. The document opens and she reads it quickly before turning back to her partner.

"Looks like the Preston case is back on. I'll send scheduling a note to let them know," Helen says, clicking away on her computer before turning around. "So, what's our plan of attack?" she asks her partner, who is still glued to her computer.

Alicia doesn't answer for several moments, opening a second email from the coroner. She reads it quickly and gives her partner a synopsis. "Jules told Mrs. Preston this morning about the ruling of homicide. Told her they were going to hold the body for 30 days to conduct tests. Her lawyer has already contacted a judge, who is applying pressure to shorten the post-mortem time. Says they'll probably agree to release the body in two weeks."

"Wow, must be nice to have friends in high places," Helen replies.

"She definitely does," Alicia agrees.

"Got it," Helen agrees. "I suggest we go to the funeral, whenever that is. Stay in the background, get some cameras recording the crowd."

"Agreed. You set that up with date to be confirmed and I'll contact Preston's assistant and get his calendar for the week leading up to his death. Maybe that'll give us a clue as to who did this."

The two detectives turn to their computers and their phones to complete the tasks and work individually for about 30 minutes before Helen sits back and declares, "Done."

Alicia hangs up her phone and turns, waiting for the full details of Helen's work. "I've got a team of crime scene guys booked to take pictures and videos before and after the service. We just need to tell them where and when."

Alicia nods her head before revealing, "Lewis' assistant is Dominique Guillaume. She's on maternity leave right now but I got her replacement, Trina Gomes. She's going to get approval from HR to send Preston's calendar to us for the week before his death. Said she'll get it to us by the end of the day, if at all possible."

"Perfect. It should give us some place to start asking questions," Helen agrees. "Why don't we start with the Mrs.? Get a take from her on what she thinks happened."

***

Both detectives wear their sunglasses against the bright glare of the sun as Helen pulls the police SUV up the winding driveway to the Preston home. Helen stops the car and looks at the large structure. "Gorgeous home," she comments, as she pushes the driver's door open.

"Certainly is," Alicia agrees, as they walk towards the front door. "Looks like she has company," Alicia adds, nodding towards the brand-new bright white Lexus RX sitting in front of the house.

"Perhaps she gave in and asked one of the kids to help her," Helen suggests, her hand up to knock on the front door, just as it is opened, as if someone had been watching for their arrival.

"Mrs. Preston," Alicia greets the widow. "We are sorry for your loss," she stops for a moment before adding, "Thank you for agreeing to see us today."

"Thank you for your condolences," the stuffy homeowner replies, standing back to give the pair access to the bright spacious entranceway. "I've invited my lawyer to sit in on our meeting," she adds, gesturing the pair towards the family room, the same room that they had been in previously.

"Really?" Alicia replies, surprise in her voice.

"I just wanted someone with me. Rand and Izzy couldn't be here, and Scott is on retainer with Lewis' company. He's been our lawyer and friend for years," she explains, as they move down the hallway.

"Here we are," Mrs. Preston announces, as they stand in the entranceway of the large family room.

A round, squat middle-aged man, shaped similar to the Laughing Buddha, with whisps of grey at his temples that compliment his intent green eyes, sits in one of the club chairs. He's looking intently at his phone until he hears their arrival. He stands up, taking in the newcomers, before reaching out his hand. "Scott Wolfe," he says.

"Good to meet you," he adds before sitting back down. "I would like to keep this meeting to a minimum if we could. Mrs. Preston is under a lot of pressure and very emotional with the sudden loss of her husband," he adds nodding towards their hostess, who lowers herself in the second chair.

"We understand, Mr. Wolfe," Alicia agrees as the detectives settle onto the couch before turning to the homeowner. "We are hoping that you can help us with your husband's case, Mrs. Preston."

"Tell me about the coroner's ruling," the lawyer asks. "It sounds kind of lackadaisical to me. It's homicide but we don't have a cause of death?"

"The coroner is convinced that Mr. Preston's death was not natural. It did not occur because of some internal issue, such as a stroke, a heart attack, or something else. Some external event caused his death and that is why John Richardson, the forensics pathologist for the county, has been assigned. He will determine exactly what happened and what caused your husband's death," Alicia offers, nodding at Maeve Preston.

The room is silent for several minutes as everyone digests this information before Alicia continues, "Let's get started then, shall we? Tell us a little bit about your husband, Mrs. Preston."

"Such as?"

"Why don't you start with how long you've been married? What did your husband do for a living? Tell us about your children."

Mrs. Preston sighs and looks out the window, frustrated with the detectives. Her eyes move to her lawyer, and he nods his head before she begins.

"Lewis and I have been married for almost 20 years. We will ...," she hesitates before changing the tense of her words. "We would have been celebrating that milestone this fall." She looks out the window at the bright sunlight dancing on the paved driveway, the maple trees swaying in the slight breeze before she continues. "We have two children – Isabella is our oldest and our son, Rand," she pauses before continuing.

"Isabella, Izzy for short, is a wild child, always likes to do things a little bit differently. She has a place in downtown

Toronto, a nice little apartment and is one of those social media influencer people."

There's silence in the room again, Mrs. Preston looking out the window, her mind seeming to be a million miles away.

"And there's Rand," her lawyer leads.

The muscles around Mrs. Preston's eyes tighten, and her crow's feet appear more prominent. "Yes, Rand," she agrees. "A headstrong, independent soul, just like his father. He's finally finished high school in Toronto. Not what I wanted for him, but his dad thought it would be best for his future to go to the city. It took Rand an extra year to finally get his high school diploma. I think he dragged it out so he could play football," she snorts at the thought. "But in the end, it worked out for him. He has a full scholarship at the University of Texas to play football. That team feeds into the Dallas Cowboys," she finishes.

"What about your husband? What did he do for a living?"

"Lewis started in construction years ago, swinging a pickaxe. He did that for a while, then worked his way up, moved between a couple of different companies from labourer to supervisor to project manager to who knows what, but he did almost everything in the industry. He always wanted to open his own company, so we took a chance. Preston Construction started small, first with only Lewis, and then it slowly expanded. We worked hard to make it happen, took us about 15 years to get to this," she says, looking around at the palatial surroundings, smiling at her memories.

"And did you work for the company?"

"I did when he first started out - invoices, quotes, receivables and payroll when there was only a dozen or so employees. When the company got bigger and we could afford office staff, I stepped back to raise the kids and look after the house."

"Does he own the company? Does he have partners?"

"Lewis owns the whole thing. There might be a loan or two, but there are no other shareholders."

"Do you know how much he owes?"

"I don't specifically, but his Financial VP, Jake Beckham, would have the details – the banks, the loans, whatever you need to know."

"Does he look after both Lewis' personal and company money?"

"No, Jake only looks after the company. Lewis looked after our personal finances. Says it's important to take control of your own life, that you need to know what's going on," she replies.

"Are there any situations or problems at work?"

"Not that I'm aware of."

"So, no employee issues, no enemies at other competing construction companies?"

"Nothing that I'm aware of but it's a big company. You should talk to his VP of HR, Fallon Shipley, about employee problems."

"Any other VPs that we should talk to?"

The widow thinks for a moment before offering, "Operations is Elijah Greco. Fairly new to us, probably about six months. He came from one of our competitors. Gavin Ferguson is the VP of IT. Not sure what he would be able to add but he is an important part of Lewis' business. Feel free to talk to him."

"Anyone else?"

Mrs. Preston moves her eyes from the detectives to the window, watching the sun beat down on the cars in the driveway, before uttering, "VP of Marketing is Cory Mercer, but again I don't see how marketing will have anything to do with this."

"I understand that Lewis' assistant is currently on maternity leave. Do you know her? What's her name?"

The widow turns to look into the detective's eyes directly, her eyebrows together, her forehead wrinkled, a glint in her eye. "Dominique Guillaume," she hisses.

There is silence in the room, the detectives waiting for more details, more specifics, but there's only silence until

Helen finally asks, "What's she like? How long has she worked for your husband?"

"I don't really know her but from what Lewis says she is very competent, works hard and keeps him organized. She's been with him about three years, I think."

There's another pause in the room as they wait for additional details from the widow, but nothing is forthcoming. The detectives decide to change tact.

"We would like to take a look at his personal effects – his computer, his cell phone, the financials for your household as well as Preston Construction," Helen states.

The lawyer puts his hand up in a stop motion before Mrs. Preston can answer. "That's not a problem once you get a warrant," he advises.

Again, there is silence in the room for a moment before Alicia asks, "You said you stayed at the Royal in Playa del Carmen. You said you were with a friend. Can we get their contact information, please?"

"Not a problem," the widow says picking up a piece of paper containing Kandis Sheridan's name and phone number off the coffee table and handing it to Alicia. "I'm sure the hotel will be able to confirm that we were there for the week."

"Thank you," Alicia replies, taking a quick look at the piece of paper that she has been given. "Is there anyone that you can think of that would want to hurt your husband? Anyone that would benefit from his death?" the detective asks directly.

A look of shock crowds onto the widow's face at the audacity of the question, at its directness. She shakes her head adamantly. "No. Lewis was a good man. A good father. A good businessman. Were there people that didn't like him? Sure. That's life. That's a reality in the business world, but no, I can't think of anyone that would be that upset, that diabolical that they would want to kill him."

The clock on the mantel clicks as the foursome sit, each lost in their own thoughts, until the lawyer asks, "Anything else?"

Alicia and Helen look at each other and shake their heads before standing up. "We are sorry for your loss, Mrs. Preston. And we want to be transparent. We will be putting together a warrant for both the house and Preston Construction," Alicia advises, to which the lawyer sits at the edge of his chair, his attention peaked.

"On what grounds?" he asks.

"A crime has been committed, Mr. Wolfe. We know that the death was not natural, that it has been ruled a homicide. Mr. Preston was at home before he went into the water, so it is reasonable to believe that there might be some evidence at the house."

The widow looks directly at her lawyer, a look of amazement on her face. "Can they do that, Scott?" she asks.

"If they get a judge to agree that they have reasonable grounds to suspect there is evidence here, they can."

There's silence for a moment before Alicia advises, "We'll be in touch." The pair of detectives move towards the front foyer and exit the home. As the large glass door closes behind them, Alicia quietly suggests to her partner, "Something is going on there."

"I agree. She seems more concerned with us looking at their stuff than finding who killed her husband."

The detectives get into the SUV. Helen starts the vehicle, sitting for a moment as the air conditioner clicks in and starts to cool the stifling interior. "Thoughts?" she asks her partner.

"I don't think it was the happy marriage that she wants us to believe. Or maybe the reality of his death hasn't registered yet. She seemed so standoffish, so distant from the whole situation, the whole family. Perhaps he gave her a reason not to care anymore. She certainly bristled when we asked about his assistant. Maybe there's more there."

Chapter 28

Maeve

"Thanks for coming over, Scott. I appreciate it. And thank you for handling that insipid coroner. Thirty days. What the hell," Maeve says, after the police vehicle has disappeared down the laneway.

The lawyer simply nods at her as she leads him to the front door and onto the porch. She stands for a moment as the lawyer moves down the steps before she retreats into the house, closing the door with a shove. She moves back into the large family room and sits down on the couch looking at the family pictures scattered around the room. A smile bubbles up as she spies the family picture taken last Christmas. *It was hell getting them all together for that picture, what with Izzy being Izzy, high as a fucking kite pretending to work at that media bullshit thing. And Rand – like pulling goddamn teeth getting him to leave the city and that mob of girls that always seem to be hanging around him – just like his father.*

Her eyes shift to the picture of her, and Lewis taken on the same day. *My God we looked happy. We got so good at playing the game that it was almost easy to fool the family, fool the world into thinking that everything was still good between us, when it was all just a façade.*

Chapter 29

Kandis

Kandis is huddled over a computer, her eyes glued to the screen as she types in Google search and then reads the results furtively, looking over her shoulder every couple of minutes to make sure no one is watching her or standing too close enabling them to catch a word or two on the monitor. She wears a long dark wig over her shoulder-length locks, has about four inches of make-up on her face to obscure her facial features, wears a flowy gauzy overshirt over a tight pair of jeans and doesn't look anyone directly in the eye. She is well aware of the cameras within the building, and she stays well away from them. She has strewn papers around on the surrounding desk and stops every once in a while and scratches out a note.

There are three locations for the public library in Barrie, and this is Kandis' first trip into the downtown location, and she thinks it will probably be her last. *This place is freaking busy. From kids running around, even though the kiddie section is upstairs, to teenagers meeting up with friends under the guise of studying. It's good to see so many people taking advantage of the library, our sky-high taxes pay for it, but do they all have to be here today? Well, maybe it's good. Just blend in. Do some research. Figure out how the hell I can get rid of that freaking anchor tied around my neck. Something easy, something that leaves no trace, something that won't cause any suspicion. There's got to be something out there*, she thinks.

Here's an interesting article – The Most Common Method of Murder. Most popular – firearms. Nope, that's way too complicated. Got to get a gun. Got to learn how to shoot it. Make sure you actually kill him, can't just wing him. Can't have him wake up and tell the police who shot him.

Number two is cutting up or piercing. Cutting up? Like taking a big knife to him? You would have to be freaking

84

strong, probably have to sedate him first. But then what would you do with all the body parts when you're done? And what about all the blood? No, that doesn't sound reasonable.

Number three is suffocation. Now that sounds a little more doable, but again Kyle is pretty strong. No, this one is too risky. Too much room for error.

Is number four a contender? Striking. I guess that's blunt-force trauma. Again, it needs lots of strength and luck. What happens if he's only wounded or unconscious?

What's number five? Poisoning. Now that sounds better. Just have to figure out what and how to get it. And how to make sure only Kyle ingests whatever it is.

Hmm, number six is fire. That might be good. I'd have to make sure that he is actually unconscious and won't come to. Perhaps it could be mixed with suffocation? Make sure he's unconscious and set the place on fire. Still kinda iffy though. What happens if he wakes up and can get out?

Number seven is drowning. I might have to think about this one. Take him out fishing, hit him with something, push him overboard. Yeah, that sounds good but what happens if he's not dead? What happens if he wakes up when he hits the cold water? And I would have to be in the boat. I would have to report it to the cops, and they would be on me like white on rice. Nope, that won't work.

The last one on the list is motor vehicle. Maybe I could run him down. It's a small car but it could still be deadly. Maybe there's a problem with the steering. Or possibly the brakes. I couldn't stop and the son of a bitch was standing in the driveway.

Nope, I think I'll go back to number five – poisoning. There's got to be something that I could give him. Something that only he eats at the house. Something that I can mix with his rum and coke. Something that he won't even taste. What kind of poison? Where would I buy it? She smiles at the thought of ordering poison from Amazon, the shopping site which sells almost everything.

Kandis looks at the clock in the corner of the computer screen, amazed that she has spent two hours oblivious to the time slipping by. She looks around the library at the stream of people coming through the double doors, at the short line-up of people holding books in their arms ready to check them out and take them home to enjoy, to the young children climbing up the stairs to the kids' section, smiles and looks of anticipation on their little faces as they race ahead of their parents. She sighs, satisfied with the anonymity of the central library as she clicks on 'Settings' on the computer to begin the task of erasing all of the websites she had accessed.

Chapter 30

Alicia

The detectives sit side-by-side at their workstations, each of them pounding on their keyboards, both occasionally picking up their phones and making calls before reverting back to their computers. These activities go on for most of the day before Helen gets up and leaves the office for almost an hour.

Upon her return, she smiles at her partner, setting a coffee and chocolate donut on Alicia's desk.

"Did you get it?" Alicia asks.

"I did. It took a couple of reiterations for Judge Mitchell to be comfortable, but he finally signed it," she says, taking a bite of her apple fritter.

"Give me another hour with Lewis' calendar and then we can talk about it. I've just got two more calls to make," Alicia advises as she picks up her phone and dials.

Helen nods her head, and signs back onto her computer, checking her email before searching a number of police sites for the addresses of Rand and Izzy Preston.

After 90 minutes, Alicia finally turns to Helen. "Done," she says.

Helen quickly closes her computer and turns to face her partner. "Talk to me. Who did Preston meet with the week before he died?"

Alicia looks at her computer and starts to summarize Preston's business activities for the week before he died. "If this is a typical week, Preston was a busy, hands-on owner. He had three phone meetings with city staff – one with the mayor, one with the commercial operations manager and a third with community relations. The mayor was asking for his support and contribution to a committee that he is putting together on real estate risk management, which Preston declined. The commercial ops manager was soliciting his assistance and expertise for a small business program. They wanted him to be a quasi-mentor to small business owners.

He didn't agree or decline but was going to get back to him. The third discussion was about the taxes and development costs of the new Preston Construction building. Preston thought the taxes were too high and was looking for a reduction, seeing his business was growing and he would be employing more people from the area."

"He also met with the National Operations Manager at Amazon, Eva White. It took me a bit to get her, and she was very vague about the particulars, but did admit it was a heads up that a formal request for an RFB was going to come out for a couple warehouses in Canada."

"RFB?" Helen asks.

"Stands for 'request for bid'," Alicia clarifies, Helen nodding in agreement before Alicia continues. "He also had a couple of conversations with Brent Wentworth, the Commercial Banking Manager at CIBC."

"Hmm," Helen replies.

"He wouldn't give me any specific information on their conversation, other than they were reviewing Preston's accounts, the outstanding loans and possibly extending his credit rating to cover new business that he was contemplating."

"Wouldn't Preston's financial guy look after that? His VP of Finance?" Helen asks.

"I asked Wentworth that and he agreed that normally Jake Beckham would be key in these kinds of conversations but lately Lewis Preston was taking the lead and leaving Beckham out of the conversations."

"Interesting," Helen comments.

"I don't believe any of those people are prime suspects for Preston's death, but we'll keep them on the back burner, just in case," Alicia confesses before continuing. "Preston met with all of his VPs, a weekly team meeting. I think we need to talk to each of them," she pauses, her eyes looking up from her laptop to her partner, who nods in agreement.

"He also had individual meetings with Jake Beckham, the finance guru, Elijah Greco, Operations, Fallon Shipley, HR and Gavin Ferguson, IT," Alicia states.

"Anyone else?"

"Yeah, two curious appointments. One with his lawyer, Scott Wolfe. I wasn't able to talk to him today, he was in court, but I left a message. The second one was with Antony Rizzo, President of Rizzo Construction. Rizzo's admin advises he's out of the office for a couple of days."

"Funny, the lawyer didn't mention a recent meeting with Preston when we met him with the Mrs.," Helen comments.

"I agree. You think he would have said something, even if it was a normally scheduled meeting. Might be nothing, might be something," Alicia says. "I'll reach out to Trina and ask her to set up a round of meetings with all the VPs."

"And I think we should add his regular admin to the list too. She's on maternity leave, right?"

"Good idea," Alicia agrees, satisfied with the initial list of potential suspects. "What about the warrant? I saw you on the phone a couple of times before you went to get Judge Mitchell's signature," Alicia asks, changing the direction of the conversation quickly as she lowers the lid of her laptop to give her partner her full attention.

"Judge Mitchell refused to sign a full search of the home. Said we could take Preston's stuff but not the wife's. Said we hadn't demonstrated probable cause that the wife committed the crime and that we were on a fishing expedition."

"Shit," Alicia says quietly.

"Said we could include everything from Preston's personal and business lives, but when it came to the wife, she was off limits."

"I guess I get it, but he's making it awfully damn difficult, like he's eliminating the wife as a suspect."

"I agree but he was adamant."

"So, what did you get in the warrant?" Alicia asks.

Helen picks the paper warrant off her desk and reads, "Everything related to Preston Construction from his office and from home. We are allowed to take his computer, his phone if we can find it, any iPad he had access to," Helen looks up and smiles at her partner, "Even if it belongs to his wife. We can also take any books, journals, or clothes that we think might be related. We can also take any toxic substances from the house, even though we don't know what killed him yet."

"You're thinking poison, right?"

"Yeah. I kinda led the judge that way," Helen smiles.

"Anything else?"

"We can clone the wife's phone," Helen announces grinning. "He wouldn't allow us to take it but cloning it should be almost as good. He did say that once the cause of death is confirmed, he would be willing to revisit the restrictions."

"Well, I guess that's better than nothing," Alicia replies. "OK, let's go see the Mrs. tomorrow with the search team. Then I think we need to talk to the two kids, then the Preston VPs."

"Perfect," Helen agrees.

Chapter 31

Kandis

"Hey Mom," Abbie greets, as she sits on the front porch step of the Sheridan home, her mother getting out of her car in the otherwise empty driveway.

"What's going on?" she asks, the silence from the garage almost deafening. "Where's your father?"

"Is it your birthday?" Abbie asks. "I thought it was in May."

"It is. The 25th."

"When's your anniversary?"

"September 10th. Why all the questions?" Kandis asks, eyeing her daughter suspiciously.

"I'm going to Sam's for dinner," Abbie says, standing up and brushing her butt off from sitting on the bare cement.

"Did Sam ask you to go? Does her mother know?"

"We talked and her mother suggested it," Abbie says, stretching the truth just a bit, as it was truly she who had suggested she should be out of the house that evening.

"OK. Call me when you want to come home and I'll come and get you," Kandis replies automatically before reconsidering her daughter's previous questions. "Why all the questions about my birthday, my anniversary? What's going on?"

"You'll see," Abbie smiles, walking down the front steps and moving down the driveway. "Have fun," she adds, waving over her shoulder.

"What the fuck," Kandis mutters to herself, stepping up the three steps into the kitchen. "Kyle," she yells, kicking off her shoes and dropping her purse and briefcase, looking around at the mountain of dirty dishes on the counter.

She stands for a moment in the silence before yelling again, "Kyle."

"In here," is the reply. Kandis makes her way through the kitchen to the dining room, where she stops, her eyes looking around in surprise. The old, scarred dining room table, which they purchased years ago at a garage sale for almost nothing, always meaning to refinish it, which never happened, is dressed in a cream-coloured tablecloth with a lace overlay. The table has been set with dinner plates, cutlery, napkins, and wine glasses for two. A large bouquet of red roses interspersed with white daisies sits in the middle of the table, as Kyle stands back, watching his wife's reaction.

Kandis moves into the room, leans over and sniffs the very fragrant flowers, before straightening up. "Now I know why Abbie was asking if it's my birthday or anniversary," she pauses taking in her just showered, presentable husband. "What's going on?" she asks.

"Nothing special," Kyle starts. "I just wanted to show you how much I love you."

There's silence for a moment before he continues. "I'm a shitty husband, most of the time. I don't help around the house," he says as his eyes move around the dining and living rooms, taking in the clean, vacuumed, dusted room which he had worked on earlier. "And you're so patient with me, as I work with the band – writing, practicing, making a hell of a racket most nights, as we try and get our shit together so we can book a couple of gigs."

Kandis continues to stand beside the table, her mind taking in what he's saying, knowing that it's another ploy to get on her good side, that he's trying to win some favour, that he's misconstruing their life together and putting a positive twist on it.

"Say something," Kyle finally says as the silence wears on.

"I shouldn't have to thank you for cleaning your own house," she starts putting up her hand to stop his retaliation, "Seeing you live here too, but I will. Thank you."

Kyle nods in agreement, waiting.

"And the table looks gorgeous but spending money frivolously on roses for no real reason," she shrugs her shoulders before continuing, "Not something that we can really afford right now."

"So, just to be clear, this," he gestures to the table, "All this including the steaks that I was just about to put on the BBQ, and the wine, and the mushrooms, and potatoes – you can't have a good steak without mushrooms and a baked potato, and the dessert, and no I'm not telling you what it is, was all paid for by me."

"By you?"

"Yes, by me."

"How?"

"I did a bit of work on Alex's guitar. It was always going out of tune, so I changed the bridge. That was quite a job. Then I replaced the tuners, you know the screws at the top of the neck, and I had to repair the bolt holes. He was also having problems with his pick-ups, so I had to do that too. Anyway, he paid me, and I thought we could enjoy a nice evening with the proceeds."

"Alex, the guy that scared the hell out of our daughter. Accosted her in the kitchen. That Alex?"

"I talked to him. It was all a misunderstanding. He'd had too much to drink and he apologized for being an ass," Kyle explains.

"Not enough, Kyle. He needs to apologize to Abbie. He needs to not ever come into this house again and you should be throwing him out of the band, if that's what you want to call what you guys do in the garage," Kandis retorts, her face beginning to flush red with anger.

Kyle puts his hands up in surrender. "I will talk to him again. We can talk to him. It's all a misunderstanding, I swear, I'm not minimizing the issue." Kyle pauses for a moment before continuing, "I will take care of it. Can we enjoy a nice dinner tonight – some good food, some good wine, definitely good company?" Kyle smiles, his hazel eyes twinkling as he steps towards his wife, his arms outstretched.

Fuck. This is the Kyle that I married. He's back. He's here. He's in this very room with me right now. But can he keep it together? Can he really make music and make money? Shit. This is what he does to me. Sucks me in, treats me like a queen, loves me like no one else can.

Kandis gives in to his charm, to her memories of their good times and steps into his arms, as their lips melt together passionately.

***

Kandis spoons with Kyle, her back pressed against him, his arm wrapped around her waist, his head on the pillow beside her as he snores softly, contentedly. She smiles to herself, the glow of their passionate lovemaking and tenderness still overshadowing her thoughts. She lays there reviewing the evening in her mind, the scrumptious dinner, the tart, flavourful wine, the soft music playing in the background which they danced to afterwards before he swept her off her feet and carried her to bed.

If it could always be like this, it would be heaven. Or at least a version of this. Maybe this is it and he's seen the light, and he's going to change. Going to sell his music. Going to make some money. Going to treat me like he really loves me. That would be heaven on earth. Can he do it? Can he come back to me like it was before we were married? I hope so Kyle. I hope that you've finally got your shit together.

Chapter 32

Alicia

The police SUV pulls up in front of the large home and stops. Helen and Alicia get out of the car, and as they do, the front door is opened by Maeve Preston, her hands on her hips, a look of exasperation on her face.

"Looks like she was waiting for us," Alicia whispers to Helen as they move towards the front door of the house, watching as Mrs. Preston's eyes catch the movement of the two police vans pulling up the driveway carrying the team that will search the expansive home.

"What the hell is going on?" Mrs. Preston asks, standing resolutely on the front porch, physically towering over the detectives.

Alicia holds out the warrant to the homeowner, advising, "We have an approved search warrant for the premises."

"What? Why? You said there had to be grounds for a search warrant. I was out of the country when Lewis died."

"We understand that you were away, but we need to take a look at both Mr. Preston's business and personal life to see if we can find anything that might give us a clue as to who did this to him."

"There's nothing here that will help you. The coroner is wrong. Lewis had a heart attack or something. It was natural." Maeve stands resolutely as four police officers get out of the vans and move behind the detectives, waiting for directions and authorization to enter the house.

"We have a signed warrant," Alicia says, waving a piece of paper in front of the homeowner's eyes before she snatches it away from the detective. "Call your lawyer and he will tell you that we have every right to come in."

"This is not fair," Mrs. Preston says desperately.

"I'm sorry you feel that way, but it is the law, and we are only trying to find out who killed your husband. You are more than welcome to wait out here," Alicia expounds, her arm waving towards the driveway, "but you cannot stay in the house."

Maeve Preston stands at the front door pouting, her options running through her thoughts.

"You can grab your purse if you would like to go somewhere else for a couple of hours. But we will need to look at the contents before you leave. And we need your phone for a little bit before you go," Alicia advises.

"My phone? You're taking my phone?"

"No, we're not taking it. But we will clone it. It'll only take a few minutes."

"Cloning it?"

"Yes," Alicia answers succinctly. "Please get it for me," she instructs the widow. "Is there anyone else in the house?"

"No, I'm alone. Well, except for Janie," Maeve Preston corrects.

Alicia shakes her head, knowing that in Mrs. Preston's mind, Janie is more like a piece of furniture than a person who deserves respect. "Detective Hodgins, can you help Mrs. Preston get her purse and her phone while I do an initial search of the house to ensure there's no one else here?"

Helen nods in the affirmative as Mrs. Preston raises her voice, "I just told you there was no one else in the house. Don't you frigging believe me?" she squawks loudly.

"It's just protocol, Mrs. Preston. Nothing personal," Helen explains. "Let's go in and get anything you might need in the next couple of hours while we search."

"What are you looking for?"

"If you look at the warrant," Helen moves her eyes to the piece of paper Mrs. Preston is clutching close to her body, "It will give you the specifics of the search."

"Scott will figure this out," the widow says almost under her breath, huffing as she follows Alicia into the front foyer of her home, Helen close behind her. "Janie, where are you?" Maeve yells, marching towards the back of the house.

Chapter 33

Maeve

The search continued on the Preston property for hours. The team of police officers hauled property out of the palatial home, including laptops, iPads, boxes of paperwork found in Lewis' office, daily journals and diaries, a couple of guns and several banker's boxes filled with various personal effects of Mr. Preston.

Maeve left the property before the search got underway at the urging of her lawyer and she is now sitting on the spacious balcony of her suite at the Horseshoe Resort, a luxurious inn about 20 minutes north of the city. Kandis, whom she talked into taking the rest of the day off of work to help her get through the craziness of the police search, is sitting beside her. The pair are sipping Bloody Caesars, looking out at the beautiful, tranquil surroundings.

A perfect place to unwind, get away from the bullshit that's going on at my house. I don't know what the fuck they are looking for, but they won't find it. Nothing. Lewis died. That's the whole story, Maeve thinks, as she takes another sip of her savoury drink. *And they won't find anything on my cell phone. There's nothing to find. And Scott says that's legal. Says they could have taken the phone if the judge had allowed it. Judge Mitchell signed the warrant. Lewis was always supporting his legal aid charities. I guess it finally paid off.*

She looks at her friend as they both sip their drinks. *Fucking bastard hit her again. She puts make-up on, which might fool the idiots she works with but if you look closely, you can see the bruises turning dirty-yellow underneath mounds of foundation. Bastard. She needs to throw him out. At the very least.*

"It's been quite the afternoon, what with the police at my house probably making a hell of a mess. Thanks for coming up and keeping me company while they make asses out of themselves. Why don't we go grab something to eat before you go home? There's a great restaurant downstairs."

"Hmm, I would love to Maeve, but I think I should go. Abbie has probably already started dinner, and I don't like to leave her alone too long, especially if Kyle has his friends over."

"Friends? That's what you're calling them now?" Maeve questions sarcastically.

Kandis stands and steps to the railing of the balcony, looking out at the expansive lawns and the green trees, listening to the silence, except for the occasional bird chirping, before she turns back to her best friend and whispers, "It's like he's bipolar, like Jekyll and Hyde. He changes from a fucking crazy man to a loving, affectionate husband."

"He is a piece of work, Kandis. When he's coherent, he loves you, he shows it, he shows your daughter, though it never lasts very long." Maeve shrugs her shoulders before continuing. "But when he's drinking and whatever the hell else he's doing with his friends, then look out," Maeve says quietly in case they can be overheard, even though they are the only people on the balcony, on any of the balconies at the resort. "You need to make a decision – either put up with his bullshit or get the hell out of that house. Or get rid of him. Your choice."

Kandis continues to stand, her shoulders stiff, stoic, unmoving.

"Listen, Kandis. I've offered to help before," Maeve puts her hand up as a stop sign as her friend opens her mouth to say something. "Let me finish. Let me help you now. You can pay me back later. We can move you into your own house. Just leave the asshole in his fucking garage and watch his world fall apart around him. Or we can start divorce proceedings and get him evicted from the house," she offers, watching her friend closely.

"The problem is Abbie. She's struggling to stay sober. All the craziness of leaving him or throwing him out may push her over the edge again," Kandis argues.

Maeve straightens her back, her friend's anguish chilling her to her soul. "What the fuck, Kandis? He's killing you. And you're worried about Abbie? Abbie has an addiction problem, just like her father, probably because of him. Most days he doesn't give a shit that she's alive. He's never acknowledged her problem. He doesn't spend time with her. He's never taken her anywhere, not even to the mall. And you argue that Abbie would miss her father, that it would negatively impact her. I think you're wrong. Leaving him would help her, not hurt her."

The pair remain as if frozen in time, Maeve sitting in the wicker chair, Kandis leaning against the balcony railing, both silent in their thoughts.

Chapter 34

Kandis

"This is the best mac and cheese I think I've ever had," Kyle says after scooping up the last spoonful from his bowl. "Thanks for helping me make dinner tonight, Abbie," he continues, smiling at his daughter.

Abbie simply shrugs her shoulders and moves her food around in the bowl.

"Everything OK?" her mother asks, watching as her daughter plays with her food, not actually eating more than a couple of spoonfuls.

Again, she shrugs, looking intently at her bowl.

"She's just a bit tired, I bet," Kyle offers. "Said she had a double period of Physical Education this afternoon. Apparently they were playing field hockey."

Kandis looks from her husband to her daughter, surprise on her face. "A double period? Isn't that a bit much for 16 year olds?"

Abbie shrugs again, her eyes down examining the food in her bowl as if she's never seen it before.

"Yeah, said she played forward, just like I used to back in the day," Kyle continues, his eyes glued on his daughter.

"That's nice," Kandis offers dismissing her daughter's distance, her silence, her lack of appetite, unaware that anything might be amiss in her life.

Chapter 35

Alicia

Alicia is staring intently at her computer, oblivious to the detectives around her, unaware of her partner as she sits down heavily at her workstation beside her.

"What's going on?" Helen asks.

"We just got the list of stuff they took from the Preston house. Adriana made a note at the bottom advising that there are security cameras at the house, all over the place in fact, but they were all turned off."

"Turned off?" Helen questions. "Why the hell would they be off?"

"From what I can piece together, they were on until about 2:30 pm on the day that Preston went into the water. That's the day he left the office early, said he had something personal to do, and then he was gone."

"Sounds like he didn't want anyone to see what he was up to," Helen offers.

"Agreed. According to Mrs. Preston, she left for Mexico two days before Preston died. I'm just taking a look at the participants in the Security Camera Program for the city. Even though that part of town is officially outside Barrie's jurisdiction, there appears to be several homeowners that have joined the program."

"It's great that residents are taking their security seriously and becoming part of this initiative," Helen comments.

"Yeah, I'm just creating a list of the cameras in the area with contact information. We'll have to give each of the homeowners a call and see if they'll share their footage with us."

"Cool. Anything else stand out from the search?" Helen asks.

Alicia turns from her computer screen and smiles. "Drew called. He was looking at the apps that the wife has on her phone," she advises, continuing to grin.

"And?"

"Apparently Maeve had a short leash on her husband and her kids," Alicia gushes.

"Really?"

"Ever heard of mSpy?" Alicia asks, watching as her partner shakes her head. "mSpy is a parental control that you can download on any phone or PC. It monitors messages, calls, social media, GPS locations, photos, videos, browsing history, apps, calendars – basically everything on someone else's device without the user knowing."

"Bitch," Helen comments.

"Controlling bitch," Alicia corrects.

"Who was she watching? The kids?

"She was monitoring hubby and the two kids," Alicia announces, her smile from ear to ear.

"That's fantastic. Judge Mitchell wouldn't sign off on a warrant for any information on the kids – their phones, their financials, a search of their homes. Said we were reaching with no probable cause."

"But now the issue is how much of the information on the phone can we use. I've just sent a note to our Crown Attorney, Hope McDonald, for her direction."

"We found the app in an approved search. I think we should be able to use whatever we find," Helen argues.

"But it could be argued that the information on the app wasn't specifically included in the warrant. So, we need to cross our t's and dot our i's and make sure. We don't want anything to be thrown out once we make our case."

"Makes sense," Helen agrees.

"Let me finish getting the list of security cameras. Give me half an hour. We can call them tonight – probably get more people home after business hours," Alicia says.

"Perfect. I'll go grab us a couple of coffees to go and then we can go visit the Preston kids," Helen suggests.

"Great plan. We can ask them about their relationship with their father. About the relationship between their parents. Get a feel for the family dynamics. Ask them if they know who would want to kill their father. Ask them if they killed their father," Alicia answers directly.

***

Helen steers the police SUV to the road barriers at the guardhouse protecting the exclusive enclave of high-end townhouses and condominium apartments on the shore of Lake Ontario at the bottom of Yonge Street, a main thoroughfare in the large city of Toronto. She hits the button to roll down the window and smiles as the young sentry stands up in the guardhouse and moves towards the edge of the doorway.

"Who are you here to see?" he asks, craning his neck to see both the car's occupants, as the detectives hold up their police shields for his inspection. He looks closely at the identification, and nods before asking again, "Who are you here to see?"

"Rand Preston," Helen answers.

"Is he expecting you?"

"He's not. And we would prefer it that way," Helen adds, as the officer starts to move back into the security booth.

He smiles and moves back to the driver's window, bending over to see the detectives' faces. "I understand officers, but that's why these people employ the likes of me. To ensure that strangers or the unwanted aren't wandering around the place."

"Understood, however, Mr. Preston's father has recently died, and we have information for him," Helen tells the security guard.

The building's protector hesitates for a moment before asking, "Do you know his unit number? His security code?"

"We do. His mother was kind enough to give them to us," Helen lies.

The young man waffles again before finally making his decision. "Go ahead. But this better not come back and bite me on the ass," he says, as he retreats into the guardhouse, pushes a button and the road barrier rises.

"It won't," Helen smiles as she drives into the lavish private gardens of the complex. "Want to bet he's got a view of the lake?" she asks, pulling in front of the building and parking in a restricted area.

The detectives walk towards the double-glass entranceway of the condo, taking in the flowers, the hedges, and the sitting areas that have been constructed around the elaborate gardens. The front vestibule has a control panel with a keypad similar to a computer keyboard and microphone. Helen pushes a series of numbers.

"I'm not going to ask you where you got those," Alicia comments, as they stand and wait for a response.

None is forthcoming and Helen enters the numbers again.

The pair wait until they hear a muffled, "Whose there?" through the microphone.

"Is this Rand Preston?" Helen asks.

"Yeah. Who wants to know?" the male voice answers.

"This is Detective Helen Hodgins and my partner, Detective Alicia Anderson. We would like to talk to you about your father."

"My father?"

Helen and Alicia look at each other before Helen answers, "Yes, your father. Lewis Preston."

"Is my mom with you?" the voice asks.

"No. Please open the door and let us in," Alicia prompts. The detectives wait another minute before the loud buzzing sound of the door lock vibrates throughout the small foyer.

The pair step into the modern front lobby with light grey walls and a seating area with four wingback leather chairs facing a stone fireplace. "Nice," Helen comments, as they make their way to the bank of elevators.

An elevator door is open, as if waiting for them, and the detectives load in. Helen pushes the button for the 28th floor. The cab is silent as it speeds to the upper reaches of the building.

There are about a dozen apartment doors on the floor. About halfway down the hallway, a tall, lean teenager, with a spray of freckles across his nose, his auburn-red hair long on top and shaved close on the sides, leans against a doorjamb, watching as the women approach.

"Does my mother know you're here?" he asks as they get closer.

"We are so sorry to hear about your father's passing. We'd like to talk to you about him," Helen says, without answering his question. "I'm Detective Helen Hodgins and this is my partner, Detective Alicia Anderson. May we come in?"

The boy looks the pair up and down, his expression a blend of cockiness and curiosity. After an elongated pause, he finally moves his arm into a welcoming gesture, permitting the detectives into the apartment. "Well, you've come a long way to see me, the least I can do is let you in." He stands back as the detectives walk into the expansive living room, floor-to-ceiling windows directly across the room looking out to the harbour and Centre Island, a small landmass located just off the city's shoreline.

"Nice view, eh," the boy almost taunts, watching the initial look of awe that everyone entering the apartment seems to display.

"Definitely," Alicia agrees, turning away from the wonderous scene to face the boy. "Nice place. Do you own it?" she asks, launching into her questions quickly.

The boy chuckles. "I'm a high school student for God's sake. My dad bought the place so I would have somewhere to live while I finished high school in the city," he explains, closing the hallway door, moving into the room and sitting down at the end of the black leather couch. "And he said it was a great investment. He was always thinking about the all-mighty dollar. But who am I to complain," he adds, looking around at the opulence that he finds himself in. "Please have a seat," he indicates the two matching chairs.

"It's kinda strange. You're underage, living in the city, in a condo alone, with your family 100 kms away," Helen states, as she lowers herself into the luxurious seat.

"I wasn't getting enough exposure in that fucking little town. So, my dad made a few calls and was told that the scouts typically search for up-and-comers in the bigger cities. They don't waste their time in backward little places like Barrie, so he set me up here and voila, they found me!"

"Who found you exactly?"

"Texas! They're giving me a full scholarship. I'm going to play football. I'm going to be a Dallas Cowboy someday."

"That's fantastic. Good for you," Alicia congratulates the boy. "And has your dad bought you a condo there too? The campus is in Austin, isn't it?"

Astonishment is written on Rand's face. "Wow, I'm surprised you know that," he says breathlessly.

Alicia simply smiles, knowing that watching all that football with her son Luke has just paid off.

"To answer your question, yes. As soon as the offer was made by the university, my Dad and I went down to Austin, and he bought a place. A bit smaller than this one," he adds, looking around at the spacious surroundings. "But big enough for me for a couple of years," he finishes.

"Lucky for you that your dad was flush with cash," Helen adds almost viciously.

"I know what it sounds like," the boy says, leaning forward on the couch, minimizing the space between the trio, trying to make himself look empathetic to the situation. "But my dad offered. And he's not hurting. And besides, the condos are just investments. He'll get his money back when he sells them," he finishes, suddenly remembering that his father will not be selling either property.

"Sounds like you and your dad were pretty close. Did he have any enemies that you know of? Anything that he might have told you about?" Alicia asks.

"We didn't really talk a lot about work, more about sports, football especially and of course my marks at school. He was some pissed when I took an extra year to finish grade 12," the teenager offers.

"Your dad owns the condo and pays the monthly fees I assume. What about other things like food, clothes, books, whatever else you might need?" Helen asks.

The boy hesitates before admitting, "My dad gives me a monthly allowance for anything that I need. I don't really have the time to work, what with all the football practices I'm involved with before and after school, Nothing that would pay well enough anyway. My dad agreed that I didn't need to work at a menial job. That I should concentrate on football."

"Did he have the same relationship with your sister? Did he help her out with her education, her rent once she moved out?"

Rand shakes his head. "I don't know. I doubt it, but you would have to talk to Izzy about that."

"Why do you doubt that he would help your sister?"

"You obviously haven't met Izzy yet," Rand answers, a long uncomfortable pause follows before he finally continues. "My sister isn't a scholar. She spent one year at Georgian College in a media arts program. Not even sure she finished the year. Anyway, she decided she didn't need the diploma, left Barrie, came to the city and became an influencer."

"An influencer?"

"Yeah, one of those people that post on Facebook, Instagram, TikTok, about where they go, what they eat, what they do."

"Interesting. And how's she doing at it?"

"I don't know. We're not that close. You'll have to ask her yourself," the young man replies testily.

Deciding to leave that subject alone, Alicia asks "What was your parents' relationship like?"

Rand hesitates for a moment before offering, "You'd have to ask my mom. I do know that my dad worked a lot, wasn't home much, and when he was, not sure I saw them in the same room at the same time, but hey, they'd been married for a lot of years."

"Who do you think murdered your dad?" Alicia asks, changing the topic.

"Murdered?" he almost yells, moving to the edge of the couch. "That's not what my mother said. She told us he died of a heart attack."

"That might have been the original assumption, but the coroner has ruled his death a homicide. Do you do any drugs, Rand? Any drugs in the apartment now?" Helen asks, looking around as if she might find a pound of crack sitting on the coffee table.

"Drugs? Someone drugged him?" he replies, but the detectives don't give him any more information. Rand shakes his head. "No, there's no drugs in the apartment. I don't do drugs. I've been trying to get a football scholarship. Drugs would have sunk me quicker than anything."

"So, if we look around the place, we won't find any marijuana or a bong, or any edibles? Or maybe some of those anabolic steroids to strengthen your body?"

Rand looks from Alicia to Helen, his mind reeling at their questions. "Can you do that? Look around my place? Don't you need a warrant or something?" he asks.

"If you give us permission, we could take a look right now," Helen offers, standing up as if she's about to search the apartment.

"Well, I don't give you permission. It sounds like you're trying to pin something on me. Why the hell would I hurt my dad? He was footing the bill for me to play football. I would be crazy to do something like that. Is that why you're here? You think I did this to my dad?" he asks, standing up and starting to pace across the dark wood floor. "No way. No fucking way," he mumbles almost to himself before turning to look at the pair. "I didn't do anything," he states aggressively, anger starting to bubble from within.

"Is there anyone that can confirm your whereabouts the day your father died?"

The boy stops and stands looking out at the water before turning to the pair. "I was here. With a couple of friends. For the whole weekend," he adds.

"And what are their names and contact information?"

The boy looks at the detectives and asks, "Really? You're going to call them?"

"Yes, we need to confirm your alibi."

"Alibi. Holy shit," he breathes deeply, pulling his phone from his pocket, scrolling through several screens before handing the phone to Alicia.

Chapter 36

Rand

The young man stands looking out at the lake, the same view that the detectives marvelled at moments ago. He clenches and unclenches his fists as he watches the ferry coming back from the island to dock at the Jack Layton Ferry Terminal at the foot of Queen's Quay.

Thank God he bought that condo in Austin before all this shit went down. At least, I'll have someplace to live while I'm down there.

And thank God those cops couldn't just search the place. Wouldn't want them to find my stash of steroids. I guess I'll have to find a new distributor down there so I can subsidize my monthly income, seeing dear old Dad refused to up my allowance. Someone's got to do it, and it may as well be me.

I hope the bastard signed the papers leaving the company to me before he died. It was a strange conversation, but I told him what he wanted to hear. How I would look after his precious company when I've finished my football career. How I'll come back and run it with him. What bullshit, but if it got me the company and all his money, who cares.

Fuck, what day did they say he died? Shit, was that the day I was up there? His fucking admin saw me when I dropped by his office. Just dropped by, the prodigal son doesn't need an appointment. And I was simply asking for an increase in my allowance, and it was like he truly snapped. He was such a bastard, yelling that he'd given me enough, that the tap was going to be turned off if I wasn't careful. What the fuck!

He pissed me off, and he came at me, so I hit him. Not too hard but enough to make him go down. I think he hit his head on his desk, but he got up pretty fast, so it couldn't have been too bad. He fucking drove home after it all. He wouldn't have been able to do that if he was fucked up from the punch, would he? No, they're looking for some kind of drug, maybe

110

some kind of poison. It better not be some kind of steroid or I could be fucked.

I better call Kim and Bree and remind them that they were here that weekend, They were both so high they probably don't remember the date. I'll just make sure that they remember it was that weekend from Friday to Sunday. Help them get their stories straight before the frigging cops call them.

Chapter 37

Alicia

"Another nice place," Helen comments, as the pair walk through the decked-out lobby of Izzy's condo building in the Distillery District of Toronto, an internationally much-admired village near Lake Ontario, acclaimed for its shops, galleries, studios, restaurants, theatres and several newly built giant condos. "Mr. Preston's kids sure like to live in style. What floor?" she asks as she pokes the elevator button, and the dark glass slab door opens.

"The penthouse. Where the hell else would she live?" Alicia answers.

"Surprised there's no security at the door checking who's coming and going," Helen says, as they walk into the elevator.

"Maybe they just stepped out for a smoke," Alicia offers as the expansive doors close, and the car begins to rise rapidly to the top of the building.

It stops smoothly. The doors open to a foyer with black marble floor, and walls boasting white wallpaper with prominent streaks of silver. There are four doors off the spacious atrium. "That one," Alicia points to a bright pink door, with an oversized black glass number one hanging beside it. They move toward it and knock, the sound echoing in the empty hallway.

They stand for a considerable time before Alicia steps closer to the massive pink door, placing her ear against it, listening. "Someone's in there. They've got the stereo on," she declares, standing straight and pounding on the door again.

"Keep your pants on," they hear through the door, a young voice giggling the words. "I'm coming," she adds, just before a young woman dramatically pulls the door open. "You could have just left it at the door," she adds before she sees the two women. The girl is naked, except for a colourful tie-

112

dyed knee-length t-shirt. "Who the fuck are you? Where's my food?" she asks, looking around the hallway.

"Izzy Preston?" Helen asks, knowing full well that this is Lewis Preston's daughter. The height, the hair, the faded denim blue eyes, is an exact copy of her father in a feminine package, however her bloodshot and enlarged pupils tell the story of a life of drug abuse.

The trio stand looking at each other for several moments before they hear, "Come on. Get your ass back in here," from a deep male voice within the apartment.

"Who are you? What do you want? I'm kinda busy right now," the girl giggles as she starts to close the door, not waiting for an answer before Alicia puts her foot in the doorway to stop it from closing.

"What's going on in there? Are you OK?" she asks the young woman.

Izzy pushes against the door but is unable to understand why it's not closing. "Something's wrong with the door, Cody," she says over her shoulder.

"Are you Izzy Preston?" Helen asks again, as a young man appears behind the woman. His glaring eyes, as dark as night, are riveted on the intruders. He's naked except for a towel wrapped around his slight waist. His gaunt boney chest and hair are wet as if he's just come out of the shower.

"What the fuck!" he demands, pushing the girl back and looking down at Alicia's foot in the doorway. "Get your goddamn foot out of the way," he demands. "Whatever you're selling, we don't want any."

"We need to know that the young woman is OK before I do that," Alicia advises, as she pulls her badge from her pocket. Shock registers on the man's face quickly, his mouth opening slightly, his eyebrows arching, his eyes widening.

"She's fine. Tell them you're fine, Izz," the young man tells the girl as she tries to hide behind him, as if he is her knight in shining armour, as if he's there to protect her.

"Tell them, Izz," he demands again, as he steps back from the door and both detectives move into the room, taking in the chaos and mess of clothes strewn about the floor, the couch, the half-full bottle of whiskey, two glasses of the golden liquid with several joints on the scuffed ancient coffee table.

"What do you want? We've done nothing wrong," he utters as if trying to convince himself, as he takes another step back, Izzy cowering behind him.

"What is that?" Alicia asks, moving into the living room, and nodding towards the coffee table.

"You can't just come in here," the young man advises. "This is a private home, and we weren't doing anything wrong," he says forcefully, clutching the towel around his middle.

"You're right. We can't just come in. But we were concerned when Izzy answered the door. We just want to make sure she's OK," Alicia says, leaning sideways to look around the man.

"Izz. Tell them," the man demands.

"I'm OK," she says, peeking around his shoulder. "Who are you? What do you want?"

"We're with the Barrie Police. I'm Detective Hodgins and this is my partner, Detective Anderson. We want to talk to you about your father."

"My father is dead," she says quietly.

"We know and we are so sorry, but we have a few questions we would like to ask you."

"I don't think so," the young man says, putting his arm up in a shielding manner, keeping the girl behind him. "I know about this kind of stuff. If you want to ask Izzy questions, either get a warrant or make a formal request and she can come to the police station," he says protectively, probably knowing the finer points of law from his many clashes with the police.

"Well, Barrie is pretty far for Izzy to travel to, and we were in the city to talk to Rand, so we thought we'd drop by."

"You saw Rand?" the girl whispers.

114

"We did. And he didn't seem to have a problem talking to us," Alicia says, looking directly at the young woman. There's a pause before Alicia continues, "Up to you. Talk to us now. Or come up to the Barrie precinct."

Izzy's eyes open in shock at the suggestion, before she moves her attention to her boyfriend. "Can they do that?" she asks.

Not waiting for the young man's reply, Helen answers as if the question was directed at her. "We can and we will," she says plainly.

Izzy's eyes move back to the detectives, weighing the time and effort it would take to get to Barrie versus continuing the fun she was having with Cody. "Give us a couple of minutes to get dressed," she finally decides, turning and leaving the living room area, pulling her male companion with her.

Chapter 38

Izzy

As soon as the condo door closes behind the detectives, Izzy runs into her bedroom and flings herself on the unmade bed. Big fat tears blur her vision as she pulls the blankets over her head, gasping for air as she cries.

She lays there, limp, strung out and wracked with guilt, guilt for what she's not sure, but she could have been a better daughter, could have been closer to her father, could have listened to him more.

Cody sits on the edge of the bed beside Izzy, reaching out and rubbing her arm through the blanket. "It's OK, Izz. They were just fishing. They've got nothing," he advises, before adding, "Fucking cops."

Izzy flings the blanket off and stares at her boyfriend. "That was fucking wrong. They shouldn't have come here," she yells, tears dripping down her face.

"I know, I know," Cody agrees sympathetically before adding, "Where the fuck is our food? Fucking Uber. Probably left it in the hall with all the bullshit going on with the cops. I'll go see," he announces, jumping up from the bed, leaving Izzy alone.

She lies back on the unmade bed, wrapping the blankets tighter around her slight body. *My dad is gone, and he's worried about his fucking stomach.*

I can't believe Daddy's gone. The last time I saw him wasn't good. I thought he'd help me out. Told him I needed some money for marketing, to buy some more equipment for my videos. I studied in advance and used technical language that I thought would impress him, and that he could relate to. But no, the bastard simply refused. Fucking guy. Called me some bad stuff, told me I was immature. Called me juvenile. Said I couldn't look after myself. That I was high on drugs. Asshole. Said I was just there to mooch off him. Mooch off him? What the fuck! I'm his bloody daughter.

I was pissed off and when he turned away, I dropped a hit of valium in his drink. I was just trying to mellow him out. Thought he was going to have a freaking heart attack he was so stressed.

And what the fuck was he doing in the kitchen anyway? It was like he was making dinner or something, maybe expecting someone to come over. Mom was away. Who the hell would he be expecting?

But he was OK when I left. Wasn't he?

Hey, maybe Daddy left me some money. He wouldn't give me any the other day but I'm sure he would have put me in his will. If he had a will? What am I thinking? Of course, he had a will. Fucking Mr. Organized, Mr. Always-Be-Ready-Just-In-Case, Mr. Always-Have-Money-Set-Aside- For-An-Emergency.

Yeah, he had to have a will and even though he's been a prick to me ever since I left that godforsaken town and came to the city, he wouldn't forget me. Would he? No, no, he wouldn't. I'm his only daughter.

Yeah, I'm sure he left me something. He was worth millions. Or maybe he gave it all to his little darling, Rand. My God, I should have had him give me lessons on how to play the old man. Rand had him wrapped around his little finger. He gave him a fucking condo in the city. Paid for everything. Even paid for some fucking coach to teach him how to play football. All for his ego. For his own satisfaction.

But he wouldn't help me at all, and he had all the money in the world. Thought I was crazy trying to be an influencer. He didn't even understand what it was. And he wouldn't listen to me when I tried to explain how hard a job it is. But I'll do it. I'll show him that I can stand on my own and pay for my own stuff. I just need a little time to get my shit together. And if I have to turn a trick or two or three in the meantime, then so be it. If it gets me to where I want to be, then who the hell cares?

Fuck, I'm going to have to call Pam at the service, tell her I need to go out on more dates, that I need more money. I

don't want to do it, but I have to. I have to pay the fucking
bills. And I need money so I can go to exclusive, fun places
so I can rate their service, and their food, though I can
usually only stomach a mouthful or two.

I'll show them. I'll show them all. I can do it all by myself.

I'm sure Daddy left me money in his will. Yeah, I'm sure
he would have thought to look after me. If I can just hold on
until the will is read, everything will be OK.

Chapter 39

Cody

Cody Bruno jabs the button for the elevator, waits a moment for it to get to his floor, walks in and pokes the button for the lobby. *Fucking elevator. Like everything else in this building. Only works for the fucking yahoos with the big bucks. Like it almost knows that I've got my last $20 in my pocket and it's fucking with me,* he thinks as he smashes the button again.

Izzy is going to have to go back to work. Tonight. This fucking mourning bullshit is over, especially if the cops are down here asking questions about the bastard.

I'm sure there's a huge list of who wanted the asshole dead. He was such a dick, threw me out the only time I went to his house. Thought his daughter could do better. Had the gall to even say it out loud.

But look at you now, dickweed. Gone.

And if you are the father that Izzy seems to think you are, I'm sure you put her in your will. I hope you left her a big chunk of money, cuz I could really use it. I've played this game a long time, waiting for something to come of it and it looks like the time is ripe.

Wonder how long it takes to get a will read? The guy's dead. And Izzy needs the money. I need the money. She's going to have to turn some tricks until they read the damn thing. Her fucking influencer shit isn't working but hopefully Daddy looked after his baby girl.

The elevator doors slide open into the apartment's lobby, and Cody slips smoothly out, a shit-ass grin on his face.

Yup, everything is going to work out just fine. Izzy will get the money, and she'll be able to keep me in the style I deserve. She'll have to learn her place a bit better, not all of this influencer shit. She needs to look after me, service me, and pay to keep me in the style I've always dreamed about.

Chapter 40

Alicia

"Well, that was a hell of a day," Helen comments as she steers the police SUV up Highway 400 towards home.

"What did you think of Rand?" Alicia asks.

"Arrogant, callous, little shit," Helen answers succinctly.

"Yeah, his attitude, his demeanour, all very entitled," Alicia agrees. "A narcissist in the making."

"In the making? I would say already made," Helen pauses. "And that condo. Wow. The twenty-eighth floor, facing the lake, what an incredible view. And the furnishings. I would say Daddy employed an interior designer."

"Yeah, it was gorgeous. Preston would have had no problem selling it when the kid's done with it. Rand seemed to be forthcoming when we asked about who bought it, who owned it, who paid for it."

"He didn't seem to know much about his sister, if she got the same help from their dad, for school, for her condo."

"Yeah, I don't think they are close at all. Rand is an athlete, going off to university on a scholarship, while his sister is a want-to-be influencer, with a drug problem. They don't seem to have a lot in common, other than coming from the same house. And both of them seem to have interesting alibis. I'll follow up on them tomorrow," Alicia states as Helen pulls into the fast lane and passes a couple of slow-moving cars.

"What did Rand share with you? I didn't see," Helen asks.

"He gave me the names of two female friends that were at his place for the whole weekend," Alicia tells her partner, a smirk on her face.

"The whole weekend? He didn't have any time to drive to Barrie, visit his father, or give him something? Maybe he did it before his friends came over? Wanted them there for the weekend as his alibi," Helen suggests.

"I'll call them. See what time the festivities began," Alicia pauses, before changing subjects. "And then there's Izzy."

"Wow, just wow," Helen starts. "Coming to the door with nothing on."

"She had something on, some old t-shirt, ten sizes too big for her," Alicia corrects.

"She looked pretty high to me. I'll check when we get back – see if there are any drug charges on her record."

"Check for solicitation and prostitution."

"We didn't get much from her. She's a lost little girl, trying to make it in the big city, trying to be an influencer but doesn't have the experience, the life, or the money to make it happen. I think she's fallen on hard times and from what she said, her father wasn't about to help her."

"And what an alibi. Said she was at an alumni weekend with the rehab centre she went to last year. That should be easy enough to check."

"Never heard of an alumni weekend before," Helen comments.

"Alumni programs are pretty common for people who have completed treatment but still face challenges in their sobriety. The therapists get together with a group of patients who have completed the program to provide more tools to help them cope as they transition back to the real world. However, I have never heard of a weekend retreat."

"We'll have to check out Greenwoods. Sounds like it might be up north. Maybe she drove by and stopped in to see Daddy. Had enough time to give him something to end his life. And I'm not sure that she's really kicked the habit. Maybe it wasn't pre-meditated but done on a whim. When he wouldn't give her any money, when he didn't react the way she wanted, she simply shared some of her stash anonymously with him."

"Possible. We're still waiting for the final word on the cause of death. I'm assuming some kind of drug, but we'll have to wait and see."

"What did you think of that guy with her? Cody Bruno," Helen asks.

"I would say he also has some drug issues. The shakes, his pale skin, his eyes darting all over the place like he was looking for a way to escape. And the way he looked at the half-filled bottle of whiskey when we were talking to Izzy. Looked like he wanted to pick it up and guzzle the whole thing back."

"Yeah. They both looked pretty dependent on each other, with her hiding like he could protect her from us, like he was made of steel or something."

"He said Mr. Preston didn't approve of him, threw him out of his house."

"He's obviously aware of who her father is, knows that he owns a big company, big house. Maybe they plotted to get rid of Preston for his money."

"That's if Preston left her anything. He treated those kids like polar opposites. Rand talks about his father, almost like he was a saint. He bought the condo and put him in the city so a scout would find him. And when they did find him and offer him a scholarship, he bought him another condo in Austin."

"For a guy with so much money, you think he could have simply paid the kid's tuition," Helen suggests.

"Yeah, but maybe he wanted the kid to work for it, wanted to make sure he was a real contender before he laid out all that money. It would have been interesting to see what would have happened if he hadn't got the scholarship. Would Preston have paid for his tuition?" Alicia asks before continuing. "We need to check on the family. See if there were any police visits or any history of physical or mental abuse by Lewis Preston. Find out what went on in that mansion."

"Hmm," Helen replies, her mind thinking about the possibility of charges against such a community leader before adding. "Both of them seem to think he has money. What if his company is all smoke and mirrors? Maybe he's running day-to-day, waiting for funds to come from jobs they've completed to pay their bills, to meet payroll, with no backup funds?"

"Or what if the company isn't a proprietorship like the Mrs. thinks? Maybe there are partners that have lost big dollars and decided to kill him so they could sell off the company."

"Nico and his financial forensics team are looking at the books and I'm sure they'll be able to give us some answers."

"The differences in the way he treated his kids is unbelievable – the coddling of Rand, moving him into a condo in the city, giving him an allowance – is a stark difference to how he treated Izzy. Why? Why treat them like night and day?"

"I don't know. But maybe Izzy had enough. Maybe she was jealous of her brother. Wanted her share of Daddy's money. Thought getting rid of him was the only way she could get it."

"Possibly," Alicia replies.

***

"I just want to check my email before I leave," Alicia advises her partner pulling her phone out of her pocket as Helen parks the police SUV at the Barrie police precinct.

"Good idea," Helen answers, turning the key off and watching her partner move through several screens on her phone.

A couple of moments later Alicia advises, "Preston's body is being released next week. We'll have to find out exactly when and where the funeral is going to be so we can get the team set up for pictures."

Chapter 41

Luke

"Can I help you, sir," the store clerk asks the man looking intently into the display of diamond engagement rings.

The customer looks up and smiles. "They're beautiful. All of them."

"They certainly are. Would you like to look at any of them closer? Are you looking for white-gold or yellow-gold? Or perhaps rose-gold?"

Luke stops for a moment, a quick frown crossing his face as he pictures the love of his life and her taste in jewellery, before looking up and telling the salesperson. "Yellow gold, definitely. That's all she wears."

Chapter 42

Kandis

Kyle is sitting strumming his guitar, a half-full glass of Captain Morgan's black label rum and coke on the end table beside him. Alex is sitting mesmerized as Kyle's fingers glide over his guitar, listening to his newest composition.

Kyle looks up when he's completed the melody, a look of anticipation on his face.

"That's great man," Alex says. "Powerful, moving. Play it again and I'll add some bass to it."

The two men are jamming together, when the side door of the garage opens and Kandis steps into the space. She watches and listens as they work on harmonizing the two instruments, neither noticing her until Kyle lifts his head to make a comment about the notes in the chorus to his friend. He stops instantly, which catches Alex's attention, and he stops mid chord.

"Kyle. What's going on?" Kandis asks, not looking at Alex.

"We're just playing," he offers, giving no additional detail.

Alex, aware of the tension between the two, steps forward. "I wanted to come over and talk to Kyle and Abbie, and you about what happened the other night. I'm truly sorry about the misunderstanding with Abbie. I definitely didn't mean to upset her or give her the idea that I wanted anything other than a hug. We used to hug," he continues, "but I guess that was a long time ago and she's all grown up now and I shouldn't have," he finishes, as if running out of words.

Kandis has turned to listen to the man's explanation, watches for a moment for some sort of sincerity before pushing. "You looked pretty fucking guilty when I came in here and Kyle confronted you."

"I knew immediately that I upset her. She ran like hell out of the room and when you came in here, pulling the cords out, yelling at the top of your lungs, I knew it was going to go bad," he offers, lowering his eyes as if truly sorry.

Kandis stands for another moment before asking, "And what did Abbie say to your apology?"

"She was good with it," Alex offers. "Said I scared her. Said I caught her off guard. Said that she was over it," he ends watching for Kandis' reaction, but she's silent until Kyle breaks in.

"She's OK, Kandis. I talked to her too and she's fine," he offers.

"She might be fine. But I'm not. She's in a delicate place. You know that, Alex. You can't simply pretend that she's five years old anymore. She's a teenager with some issues and I don't want you," she looks pointedly at the bass player before swinging her head to her husband, "Or anyone upsetting her."

The threesome stand for a moment, quiet, the men unsure what to say and Kandis contemplating the situation before she notices the opened bottle of rum. "And what's that?" she asks Kyle angrily, pointing at the intrusive intoxicant. "I thought you quit. I thought you weren't going to drink anymore. I thought this was a new start for us," she says bitterly, her voice escalating.

"Don't worry, Kandis. It's just a little to help with my creative juices," Kyle says trying to placate his wife. "Did you hear that song? I wrote that after just a couple snorts. It could be the one. Could be the one that hits the big time," he adds enthusiastically.

Kandis shakes her head as she walks out of the garage, knowing that Kyle's Mr. Hyde is rearing his ugly head again.

Chapter 43

Alicia

The detectives carefully descend the stairs to the main level of the Preston Construction building, after spending the last six hours interrogating the VPs, asking questions about Lewis Preston as a President and CEO, asking about the company's financials including outstanding loans, investments, possible shareholders, any animosities and hostilities that he may have had in and outside the company. They asked specifically who would benefit from his death and got very personal, inquiring about his relationship with his wife and children, as well as asking about his succession plan in the event of his death.

They stop at the main reception area and sign out, dropping their temporary IDs before leaving the building.

"A lot of playing it safe," Alicia quips, as she climbs in the police SUV and buckles her seat belt.

"What did we learn?" Helen asks, as she manoeuvres the vehicle to the parking lot exit.

"Well, they didn't seem to know about his succession plan. It will be interesting to hear what his will says. Maybe he put it in there. Would he leave it to Rand or Izzy? Not sure either of them are qualified or even want the company."

"Money is always a motivator. Preston Construction could sell for tens of millions of dollars. Great incentive to kill if he left it to only one of them and the other knew. Or maybe one of them decided it was time to get rid of dear old Dad, assuming that they would split the company between them. Or maybe it was the Mrs. She was tired of playing second fiddle to him and wanted it all. Or she was just tired of him, and their marriage, and decided that killing him would give her the freedom to do what she wants with the company she says she helped build."

"Wouldn't it have been easier just to get a divorce?" Alicia asks. "She'd get half of everything."

"Depends. Maybe there was a prenup."

"Possibly, but they'd been married almost 20 years. And she said they didn't have much when they started out."

There's silence in the vehicle as they travel a couple of blocks. "What did you think of the VPs?" Helen asks.

"The IT guy, Gavin Ferguson, definitely looked the geeky computer nerdy part with his thick, black-rimmed glasses and curly dark hair. I think he exists in his own little world. Unless the issue is specific to their internal computer software, the billing system, or creating customer quotes, he's blind to what's going on."

"I could be wrong, but he seemed sincerely broken up about Preston's death. Bowed his head for a moment when he said his name like he was praying for him or something."

"You're probably right. Sounded like they had a long history, and his only job was to support Preston's vision and be ready when he expanded the company, launched new initiatives, whatever they do in a construction company," Alicia says.

"Yeah, and his story about the weekly meeting seemed to jive with the rest of them, though he did offer that Lewis talked about tightening the purse strings, that he wanted to get more involved in the money being spent."

"How about the HR lady, Fallon Shipley?"

"Shipley said there wasn't any ongoing HR issues, no grievances that she was aware of. She was forthcoming with his admin's name and address. She didn't have any idea who would want Preston dead, in fact, was taken aback when we told her it was homicide."

"Marketing? Cory Mercer?"

"He talked about the importance of the marketing department, how his department had grown the business by promoting the company, its quality of work, their Canadian-ness. He didn't offer anything substantial. Truly, I don't see him involved with fraud or embezzlement or a coup to take over the business," Alicia offers.

"What did you think of Jake Beckham, the VP of Finance and Elijah Greco, the VP of Operations? Do you see either of them killing Preston to take over the company?"

"Possibly. Preston Construction is worth about $100 million, with an annual revenue of about $30 million. That's a lot of money. It can make people do desperate things. And there was that talk of Preston getting closer to how the money was being spent. Greco is the Ops Manager, in charge of all the work that goes on, hence the bills, the contractors, and the materials, while Beckham is in charge of the money. I would think the CEO wanting to be more involved would reflect directly on their jobs, their responsibilities, something that probably neither of them liked."

"Wonder what that's all about? Nico's financial forensics team will have to go over the books with a fine-tooth comb and find out what's going on."

"Or at least what Preston thought was going on. Hey, did I miss the part about the company being worth $100 million? They didn't give us those numbers, did they?"

Helen smirks before answering. "No, they didn't give us those numbers. I did a little bit of googling last night. You can get almost anything from Google. Nothing is sacred anymore."

"Beckham has been with Lewis for years. Maybe they had a falling out? Or he thinks he's entitled to a bigger piece of the pie," Alicia suggests.

"Another possibility," Helen agrees as she guides the vehicle through the city streets. "It will be interesting to see what Nico finds when he looks at the financials. Is anyone getting their pockets lined illegally? It could be as small as having friends and relatives added to the payroll without even working. Could be as big as overbilling on jobs. Or maybe billing for a job that doesn't even exist. I would think the VP of Finance or even Operations would be able to do something like that, don't you?"

"So, you think Beckham and Greco are working together?"

"I don't know. Just throwing out ideas. Some possibilities. Beckham's been with Preston Construction for years, but Greco is fairly new, about six months. Maybe Beckham and Greco have some personal history. Maybe Greco approached Beckham with an idea to scam the company. Or maybe it's all Greco. Maybe Beckham suspected that Greco was submitting bogus invoices and he told Lewis."

"I thought it was interesting that Beckham talked about the animosity between Preston Construction and Rizzo Enterprises. Sounds like construction is a cutthroat industry."

"It sounds like Preston has been stealing some of Rizzo's biggest clients, possibly sparking a war between them."

"Maybe Rizzo got tired of losing business to Preston. They did have a meeting the week he died," Alicia states.

"Lots of maybes."

Chapter 44

Jake Beckham, VP of Finance

The heavy-set middle-aged man stands at the window of his corner office watching the parking lot as the detectives get into the police vehicle and slowly pull out onto the road.

Shit. They knew about our meeting with Lewis. Knew that Elijah and I had separate meetings with him, not the weekly team meeting. Thank God Elijah and I got our stories straight. Told them we were going over several major requests for bids, which typically doesn't involve Lewis, but these were big, these were important, so he wanted in on it.

We've been careful. Really careful. But Lewis was sniffing around, and he was getting close, wanting to check out all the bills, the contractors, fishing for something, but he's gone now and I'm running the company. Not really sure what his will says, but whatever it is, they'll need someone to run the place, and I've been looking after it for years anyway, even when Lewis was still alive. He never made a succession plan, at least that he talked about with the Board, so that gives me leverage.

But we need to stop. That fucking Elijah needs to stop – stop gambling, stop spending money like it's water. The cars. The trips. The fucking house. What is he thinking? Just spending like a drunken sailor and then using me to bail him out. Used my position here. Used London as an excuse. Well, it's got to stop. Up to now, we've been lucky, but it's got to end.

What the fuck was London thinking marrying that asshole Elijah? I told her he wouldn't come to any good. What the hell did she see in that arrogant, opinionated, self-centred piece of crap?

Chapter 45

Gavin Ferguson, VP of IT

Gavin Ferguson dashes down the hallway to the IT offices, late for a meeting that he had called with his Directors. *I friggin hate to be late. We need to get moving on the updates for the billing software. It's a huge build, and we need to get going now to keep Preston Construction at the forefront of the industry in Canada,* he thinks as he jerks open the door to the IT boardroom.

"Sorry I'm late," he apologizes. "Where are we?" he asks his second in command, as he collapses into the chair at the head of the table.

Chapter 46

Elijah Greco, VP of Operations

Elijah Greco slams his office door shut before skulking across the expansive office to drop into his ergonomic chair behind his oversized desk. He sits upright, tense, his hands gripping the armrests as he wills himself to calm down, to regulate his breathing, to lower his heart rate. *Jesus H. Christ! What was that all about? Lewis' death is being investigated? First, we hear it was a heart attack and now they're saying it was homicide? They were closed mouth when I asked them what had changed. Asked how he died. Like they didn't even know.*

Calm down. Calm down. Jake will be the acting president, and he's got your back. He'll always have your back when his delicate little flower London is involved. If he only knew what a know-it-all bitch his daughter really is. Never happy. Always wanting more. Always comparing herself to her mother, forgetting that her parents had 30 years to get to where they are today.

She's the one that drove me to gamble. I couldn't cope with her shit. Always wanting more. Spending more. So, I had to make more, and I thought I could play the odds and win.

I made a good income as Director at Rizzo's and I'm a VP here, but it is never enough for her. We have to have only the best. What will people think if we don't have a Tesla? And then we had to have two! Do we really have to save the fucking world all by ourselves? Same with the house – a showy, ostentatious mansion on acres of property.

She doesn't understand that you have to work your way up in the world. You don't start at the top. She doesn't understand that I've actually done well, maybe not good enough for her fucking standards, but well in the real world.

He looks around his office, at the large solid maple desk in front of him, the desk that London had insisted he tell

Lewis that he had to have when he took the job. He eyes the walls, painted dark green, a brilliant backdrop for hanging pictures and degrees that his wife had also said was a requirement for a VP's office. *Fuck. She's here. I can't even get away from her at work. She created this space. Wouldn't even let me do that without her interference.*

He pulls his cell phone off the desk, and searches for the odds on the horse races going off in an hour.

Chapter 47

Fallon Shipley, VP of HR

Fallon Shipley, smiles and greets staff as she walks calmly down the hallway towards her office. She smiles at her assistant but doesn't stop to talk, just breezes past her, closing her office door firmly behind her.

They asked about Lewis' assistant. Asked about how close they were. How long she'd been at Preston Construction. What was I supposed to say?

I had to tell them that she and Lewis were close, but I didn't tell them anything else even though they drilled me on it. They'll know the whole story soon enough. I can't be sure that her baby is Lewis' but come on, they were inseparable. And Lewis gave himself that bonus just before she got that new house. And all the office gossip points in that direction.

She smiles to herself. *Yeah, I do know. I saw them together at Windermere House when Garrett took me there for our anniversary last year. Very romantic. Very exclusive. Great place to get away from real life for a while, especially when you're screwing around on your wife with your admin.*

Could she have been involved in Lewis' death? Is that why they were asking who she is? Maybe they had a big fight. Maybe she wanted more. Maybe she threatened to tell everyone about the baby, tell everyone about their affair, and things went wrong. I wonder how he died. They are saying it was murder but weren't forthcoming with the details.

I'm staying out of this. I need to toe the company line and not disclose personal information unless legally obligated.

Chapter 48

Cory Mercer, VP of Marketing

Cory Mercer walks to the back corner of the second floor, into the open marketing area. He stands still for a moment, watching his team as they work to bring Preston Construction to new heights of success. *The team might be small, but they are mighty. Lewis didn't want to invest in marketing, thought word of mouth and history would bring in enough business. And he was right for a while. But then he brought me on, and we created a mind-blowing website, started promoting the company on social media, created a digital marketing team and started taking meetings in advance of bids and tenders. Got the Preston name out there. Blew the competition right out of the water.*

Yeah, that Rizzo never saw us coming. Took a lot of his business. Proved to his past customers that we were the new game in town. All because of marketing. All because of this team, he radiates, watching as his squad works busily.

Chapter 49

Jake

"Get in here now," Jake yells, slamming down the phone. *What do the cops know? They know that we had a meeting with Preston the day he died. They don't know what it was about. They might think they know but as long as Elijah held his ground and told them the same thing we discussed, we should be OK. But knowing him, knowing his arrogance, his egotism, he probably went rogue.*

Jake stands, walks away from his desk and paces his luxurious office a dozen times. He looks at his watch and huffs, before moving to the large window and looking out over the parking lot again.

Where the fuck is he? Thinks he can keep me waiting after all I've done for him?

Frustrated, the man turns and strides across his office, about to place his hand on the door as it opens inward. His son-in-law is standing in front of him, towering over him, his soft blue eyes shining, a silly grin growing on his face.

"Get your ass in here," Jake growls, standing back and allowing the VP of Operations to enter his office.

Elijah saunters in, crossing the office as if on a summer stroll in the park, before sitting down in one of the luxurious visitor chairs facing the desk.

Asshole. Walks into the place like he owns it. I want to push him. Get him on the floor and smack some sense into him, Jake thinks as he moves behind his desk and sits down.

There's silence until Jake finally asks, "Well?"

"Well, what?" Elijah replies. "Are you asking about the meeting with the cops?" He waits for a couple of seconds, taking in his father-in-law's furrowed brows, his puckered lips, his flared nostrils, and his scowl, watching as his anger continues to grow. Elijah raises his hand in surrender. "Jake, we're good. I told them exactly what we discussed. Just a typical meeting to talk about operations – the projects that are underway, where we're ahead of schedule, where we are falling behind, and issues with stock. Everything we talked about," he ends, a smile gracing his lips.

"You're sure? Did they question you further? Did they believe you?"

"They asked a couple of questions, like which projects, what stock, things that I was able to answer. They seemed to accept it, and they moved on," Elijah said, trying to pacify Jake's worry.

"Tell me exactly what you said."

"Really?"

"Really."

The pair spend the next 15 minutes with Elijah repeating the conversation that he had with the detectives, the dissertation peppered with questions from Jake, that he is quick to answer until Jake is finally satisfied.

"This has to be over, Elijah. We can't do this again," Jake demands, when Elijah is finished.

Elijah hangs his head, looking at his hand as he holds his phone, noticing that he has just received a text from his bookie. He moves to open the app.

"What the fuck, Elijah! Aren't you listening to me? Is there something more important on your phone than our future here?" Jake asks, through a clenched jaw, trying to keep his anger and voice in check.

Elijah stops clicking through screens on his phone. "No, I'm good," he murmurs, as he moves his phone into his pocket, looking up into his father-in-law's face. "I hear you, but we can't stop yet."

"What? You've made over $2 million on this invoice scam. What do you mean we can't stop yet?" Jake grumbles, standing up and starting to pace the office again.

"I don't know what to tell you, Jake. Did you never teach your daughter economics? She's overspending, buying everything she sees. I've tried to talk to her, but she seems to think she's in a race with her mother, with Preston, with whoever has all the money. She wants only the best, gets it and then gets tired of it."

"You need to talk to her, Elijah. You need to rein her in before she ruins you. And me."

"I've tried," he replies simply.

"You need to try again. You need to show her your salary versus her charge card statements."

Elijah simply shrugs at this suggestion.

"It's not all London. You and I both know that. You need to stop gambling. You need to stop thinking you're going to win big. You need to get in touch with the reality of the situation."

Again, Elijah simply shrugs his shoulders.

"You need to deal with this, Elijah. Up to you how you do it, but I'm not going down with you," Jake summarizes.

Elijah moves to the edge of the chair, his pale blue eyes glaring, his lips pouting. He pauses for a moment before standing up and stalking out of the office, slamming the door in his haste and anger. He stomps down the hallway to his office, ignoring his admin who is holding out a folder for his review, before stepping into his office and slamming the door closed viciously.

Chapter 50

Elijah

Elijah feels the vibration as he slams his office door, the tremor reverberating as he strides toward his desk. He looks at his desktop covered with files, invoices, his calculator, and several pens. He stands for a couple of seconds before taking his arm and runs it across the table, cleaning all his work paraphernalia off it. Everything crashes to the floor, and he steps back to take in the mess that he's created. His office door opens suddenly, and his admin stands there, a shocked, shaken look on her face, her mouth open in disbelief as she takes in the mess.

"Are you OK?" his admin asks innocently, standing in the doorway in case the violence moves towards her.

Elijah moves his eyes from the mess to his admin and sees the fear in her eyes. He raises his hands in surrender. "I'm sorry. I didn't mean to do that," he tries to explain, his hands still raised.

"Do you want me to clean it up?" his admin asks, not moving from the door.

"No. No. I'll do it," he advises.

The two stand and watch each other for moments until he finally adds, "I'm good. I'll fix it. You go back to whatever you were doing."

"OK," she agrees, backing out of the office, and pulling the door closed.

"Fuck," Elijah whispers to himself as he moves towards the mess of papers on the floor and begins to throw them on top of the desk. *I need to get a grip. Can't show emotion. Can't give them anything to talk about. Especially can't let Jake see the stress, the pressure I'm under.*

He stands up, picking up the last of the papers and moves to sit down behind his over-sized desk. *Jake is acting so fucking high and mighty. We won't get caught. We've got all the bases covered. Preston was curious and thought he saw something, but he's gone. No one else knows or even suspects. I need more, lots more. There's no way we're done yet. And hey, if Jake really wants out, maybe it's time for him to go.*

Elijah slowly shuffles through the papers, putting them back into logical piles on his desk as he deliberates on ways to get rid of his father-in-law.

Chapter 51

Abbie

Abbie sits on the cold cement steps at Meridan Place, the large outdoor amphitheatre in downtown Barrie. She's watching the boats coming and going from the Bayview Basin marina, just across the street, her mind a million miles away.

Fucking asshole. I don't know how Mom puts up with him. Always playing his music at full blast. Always a bunch of people in the bloody garage drinking, taking drugs. All of the old dickwads ogling like I'm a piece of meat for sale. Like, I'm a prize to be conquered or something. And Dad doesn't do anything. Doesn't say anything. Just smiles like the pathetic old man he is. It's almost like he's laughing at them, knowing there's no way in hell they'll get a piece of me. That he would never let that happen.

I think this place will be my new home away from home. I'll go home after Mom gets home from work. When the scum in the garage wouldn't dare walk into the house. I'll take her flack for not starting dinner on time, but at least I won't have to put up with any of those poor excuses for human beings.

Does Mom even know what an asshole he is? Does she care? Maybe I should just stay here. Hardly anyone bothers me.

Abbie's phone starts to ring, and she pulls it from her pocket and looks at the call display. "Mom?" she answers the phone, nods a couple times. "Just at the library. I'll be home shortly," she tells her mom, before standing up to start her walk home.

Chapter 52

Alicia

The church is overflowing with mourners at Lewis Preston's funeral. The sun shines through the large stained-glass windows behind the tall man in robes at the pulpit as he drones on. The detectives stand at the back of the church, watching the proceedings and taking note of the guests.

Maeve Preston sits in the front row, her son Rand on one side, her daughter Izzy on the other. Rand sits stolid, his face expressionless as he looks forward. His sister's shoulder-length dark hair is messed up as if she'd just gotten out of bed, her eyes swollen with unshed tears, her lips pressed together as she struggles to get her emotions under control. Both of the young adults hold their mother's hands, staring straight ahead at the altar, and the casket that holds the last earthly remains of their father.

The large congregation includes friends, family and politicians from all levels of government along with a handful of who's who from the region's wealthy community. The back half of the large cathedral is filled with Preston Construction employees. A dark-haired woman, her head bent down, her hair covering most of her face as she noticeably shakes as if shattered, sits conspicuously in the middle of the Preston staff. She is flanked by two women who are trying to comfort her, putting their arms around her, holding her close, and speaking softly to her.

Alicia nudges Helen and nods in the direction of the woman. "Interesting," she murmurs. "She's more upset than the wife. Wonder who she is."

The service is long and drawn out due to the numerous eulogies delivered by friends and business associates, each recounting Lewis' finer points including his love and devotion to his wife and family, his love of the water and boating. Some talk about how he worked his way up in the construction business, learning everything about the industry until he started his own very small company, expanding it through the years, and how in the end, he was taken suddenly, unexpectantly from his family and friends.

Finally, after over an hour of tender and sensitive words about Lewis, his life, his family and numerous songs and prayers, the minister extends an invitation to the guests to visit with the family at their home to celebrate his life.

The funeral home attendants wheel the casket down the wide church aisle, the family following closely behind. Alicia and Helen move to stand just outside the doors of the church, watching as the coffin is pushed into the sunlight, and Mrs. Preston, still holding on to her children, walks solemnly across the narthex, and down the broad stairs. The detectives stand like sentries against the church's front brick wall as the visitors leave the confines of the massive chapel, and the casket is pushed into the back of a large black hearse and taken away. They listen to murmured conversations, eavesdrop for anything out of place, anything that might give them a clue to Lewis' true demise, knowing that there are a couple of cameras augmented with telephoto lenses nearby taking pictures of all of the guests, like a mafia funeral.

As the crowd from Preston Construction trickles out, the distraught woman whom they had seen during the service, is assisted out of the church by her colleagues and led to a car in the parking lot.

"Let's go back to the station and take a look at the photos. See if we can match some of the faces to the pictures on the Preston website. And figure out who the hell that woman was that was so upset," Alicia suggests as the crowd dissipates.

"I'm in," Helen agrees.

***

After hours of examining the pictures taken at the funeral, Alicia and Helen are able to match the VPs and some directors, however, they are no further ahead in identifying

144

the dark-haired woman who was so distraught during the service.

Chapter 53

Kandis

Kandis is exhausted after attending Lewis' funeral and helping Maeve ensure all the reception guests were well fed and always had a drink in hand. She gets out of her car in her driveway and looks around in surprise. *No guitars. No drums. Maybe the good Kyle has resurfaced,* quickly flitters through her thoughts as she trudges towards the side door of the house. Suddenly the quiet is interrupted with sharp, explosive sounds of crashing coming from the house. *What the hell*, she thinks as she opens the side door.

She walks up the three steps into the kitchen; the noise continues to escalate in volume as she steps into the room. Kyle is leaning into the kitchen counter, stretching up to the highest shelf, in the process of pulling out dishes and throwing them on the floor.

She stops for a moment taking in the ghastly mess around him - their dishes broken and scattered around the room, pots and pans part of the turmoil, silverware scattered in the shambles.

Kandis finally finds her voice. "What the hell, Kyle!" she yells. "What the fuck are you doing?"

He hasn't heard her come in and jumps slightly at her unexpected, thunderous voice, before pulling his hand from the cupboard, clasping a teapot. His face is crazed, his eyes are wide and unblinking, his jaw is clenched.

He looks at his wife. His mouth pulled back into a snarl as he demands, "Where the fuck have you been?"

Kandis is silent for a moment before moving forward to grab the delicate white teapot rimmed with a blue floral pattern around the scalloped edge. But before she can grab it, Kyle drops it, smashing it into pieces on the floor.

"My mother gave that to me," Kandis blurts out, looking at the pieces around her feet, before her eyes move back to her husband who is smiling viciously. "What the fuck, Kyle!"

"Where were you? I came in looking for dinner. And nothing. No wife. No kid. No food on the table. What the hell did you expect me to do?" he asks, crossing his legs casually and leaning against the kitchen counter. "I decided that we didn't really need all these fancy dishes if you weren't going to feed me. So, I'm getting rid of them."

"Are you fucking crazy?" Kandis yells at her husband, looking around at the mess. "I'm a bit late. I told you I was going to Lewis' funeral."

"A funeral? All day? And half the night?"

"It's 8 o'clock, for Christ sakes. I stayed to make sure Maeve was OK and then came home."

"You're always at that bitch's beck and call. She says jump and you say how high. Your priorities are fucked. You should be here to look after me. To look after your kid, wherever she may be," Kyle rants.

"Abbie is at the library. Working on some project for school."

"So she says," Kyle snarks back.

"What the fuck are you saying, Kyle? Is something going on with Abbie that I don't know about?"

He stands, staring at his wife, disgust on his face. "You haven't got a fucking clue what's going on with her. With me. With anything that goes on in this house," he taunts.

"Then tell me. Tell me what I'm missing."

Just as Kandis finishes her sentence, the pair hear the side door slam, and they both turn to see their daughter walk into the kitchen. She looks around at the mess, looks at her parents who she's heard yelling as she walked up the driveway. "What the fuck," she mumbles as she turns, strides down the hall, goes into her bedroom and slams the door behind her.

"Satisfied?" Kandis asks.

Kyle pushes off from the counter, stomps through the debris, crunching the china as he moves. He walks down the three stairs, slamming the exterior door violently. Moments later, Kandis can hear blaring music from the garage, the whole house vibrating with the noise as she collapses on the floor amidst the chaos and starts to cry.

Chapter 54

Alicia

Alicia is sitting at her desk, with a scowl on her face, looking intently at her laptop when Helen enters the Detectives' Den and makes her way across the crowded room, acknowledging their colleagues as she walks past their desks. She deposits her briefcase on the workspace beside her partner and exclaims, "Good morning," as she sits down. "What are you working on?" Helen asks, looking over Alicia's shoulder towards her laptop.

"We got a couple of acceptances from the Security Camera Program, and I've looked through them. Most are too far away with no line of sight to Preston's house or driveway, but there's one from the neighbour's feed that may be promising. I'm just opening it."

Helen pulls her chair closer to Alicia as the document opens on her screen, and the pair have a view of the entrance and driveway of the Preston home, from the guard house of their next-door neighbours.

"Perfect view. This is the morning that Preston left the office early. Let's fast forward until we see some movement."

The detectives huddle around the computer as the video jumps through the morning until 1:07 pm when a car leaves the estate. "Looks like a white jeep, maybe 10 years old. Can you zoom in on the license plate?" Helen asks.

Alicia clicks on the picture, expanding it so they can see specifics of the car, writing down the license plate number, car details and time on her pad of paper. "I think that's Janie, her maid, servant, whatever she calls herself."

"You're probably right."

Everything is quiet for a while until a car pulls into the driveway and into one of the garages – a brand-new silver Lexus SUV. Alicia looks at her watch – 2:15pm and zooms in on the license plate.

"Betting that's Preston," Helen says.

"Probably."

"Here comes another vehicle," Alicia says, zooming in on an old beat-up red Honda hatchback. She writes down the license plate information and 2:45pm before continuing the video, fast-forwarding, and stopping it 23 minutes later when the car drives away from the house.

The pair continue watching the video, fast forwarding through the screens with no activity until another vehicle pulls into the laneway at 4:25pm, a black 2020 Mazda CX30.

"Busy place," Helen comments as Alicia writes down the license plate and time.

The detectives continue to watch the video, streaming through over four hours in 10 minutes, until the black Mazda leaves the estate.

They continue to fast forward until the time stamp advises 8 am the next morning, with no more movement.

Alicia picks up her phone and calls a contact at the Ontario Ministry of Transportation, giving them the specifics of the cars in question. She hangs up the phone, a smile on her face.

"Well?" her partner asks.

"The white jeep leaving the house at 1:07pm belongs to Janie Dewan."

"The housekeeper," Helen adds, as Alicia nods.

"The silver Lexus SUV belongs to Lewis Preston."

Helen nods.

"Here's where it gets more interesting," Alicia says. "The beat-up Honda Civic belongs to Isabella Preston."

"The daughter who hasn't seen her father in weeks?" Helen asks.

"The same one."

"And the Mazda?"

"The Mazda belongs to Dominique Guillaume."

"I think it's time we met this assistant," Helen suggests, as Alicia shuts down her laptop and stands up.

"Definitely," Alicia agrees.

"We also need to follow up with Izzy. Find out why the hell she didn't tell us she was at the house," Helen adds.

***

"Nice place," Helen comments as she pulls into the double driveway of the brand-new single-family home in a contemporary subdivision in the southern corner of the city. "She must be doing well for herself," she adds cynically.

"There could be lots of explanations," Alicia counters, as she unbuckles her seatbelt.

"I agree. She could come from money. She could be married and have a second income. She could have invested well before the stock market took its latest dive. She could be mortgaged to the hilt or maybe the boss owns this little love nest."

Alicia snickers at the possibilities. "Don't sugar daddies normally buy love nests in high-rise condos downtown? Something a little less family-oriented than a new housing development where there will be lots of nosy neighbours and young kids running around."

"Just saying," Helen finishes, as the pair mount the three stairs to the front porch of the two-storey brick home and ring the doorbell.

They stand for a moment, waiting, listening but there is no answer, no movement from within the house. Helen rings the doorbell again, waits and then leans on it until a voice is heard from inside. "I'm coming, I'm coming," the woman yells, before Helen pulls her finger off the buzzer.

A full minute passes as the detectives stand waiting. Helen's finger is poised to push the doorbell again, just as they hear movement on the other side of the door, and it opens just a crack, revealing a medium-height female with a perfect figure wearing a low skin-tight t-shirt and skinny jeans. The woman's long dark curly hair falls almost to her waist. Her dark chocolate brown eyes are speckled with gold, but they are bloodshot and puffy, as if she has been crying or has a hell of a cold. *Probably crying. This is the woman who was sobbing and needed to be propped up by her friends at Preston's funeral,* Alicia thinks.

"Yes?" the woman asks the unwelcome visitors.

"Dominique Guillaume?"

"Yes. And you are?" she asks, still standing inside the house, her hand on the door, holding it open only enough to allow the detectives to see a sliver of the white entranceway.

"I'm Detective Helen Hodgins and this is my partner, Detective Alicia Anderson," Helen offers, holding her badge out for inspection.

The homeowner sighs at the introduction but still holds the door firmly with one hand.

"Can we come in?" Alicia asks.

"What is this about?"

"We would like to talk to you about Lewis Preston."

The woman stands still, as tears begin to cloud her eyes, and one rolls down her cheek before she can wipe it away with the back of her hand. "What do you need to know? He's dead," she finally offers, as copious tears run down her smooth high cheekbones.

"We understand that you were his administrative assistant," Alicia starts.

"Yes, I am," she stutters before rewording her answer. "Yes, I was. We worked together."

"You seem to be taking his death rather hard."

Dominique's attitude and beaten-down stance change instantly, and she turns offensive and physically straightens up, making her almost two inches taller. "I don't see what that has to do with anything. We worked together. He was like a brother to me," she finishes.

"A brother?"

"Yes, a friend. We talked. We listened to each other. We gave each other advice. Friends. You know what friends are, right?" she replies crisply.

"And you considered yourself a friend of Mr. Preston?" Alicia asks.

"Isn't that what I just said? We were friends." She stops and swipes at her face, pushing the tears away. "What does any of this matter? He's dead. He died of a fucking heart attack."

"Who told you that?" Alicia asks matter-of-factly.

Dominique seems to crumble, her shoulders curve inwards making her smaller as she bends her head in mourning, The three stand on the porch for several moments before she looks up. "That's what his wife is telling everyone."

"He did not die from a heart attack," Helen pronounces.

Dominique's shock is evident on her face. "He didn't?" she whispers quietly. "Then how? How did he die?"

"The coroner is running tests to determine exactly why Mr. Preston died. At this point, his death has been ruled a homicide," Helen answers simply.

"A homicide?" Dominique parrots. "What the fuck are you talking about?" she asks, her tone and velocity increasing, as she looks from one detective to the other.

"Maybe it would be better if we came in and talked," Alicia tries again, just as they hear a baby's cry from inside the house.

Dominique freezes for a moment unsure of what to do, before asking, "Do you have a warrant?"

"For your arrest?"

"Yes, for my arrest," Dominique answers, as the baby screams again.

"No, there's no warrant for your arrest, unless you have something to tell us." Everyone falls silent until Alicia says, "We just want to make sure we have the whole story, understand your relationship and the situation surrounding Mr. Preston's demise and I would think a friend would want to see that happen," she reasons.

"I have nothing else to say." The young woman looks back into the house, her attention waning as the child continues to cry. "Now is not a good time. I have to go," she says, stepping back into the house.

"I understand you need to take care of your child, but we need to talk to you. Is there anyone else that can look after the baby, and we'll go down to the station so we can ask you a few questions?"

Dominique pauses for a moment, a look of fear on her face. "No, no, there's no one else here to look after Paige." She pauses for a moment before adding, "If you need to ask me questions, I'll come down to the station. I'll bring my lawyer."

"One more question," Alicia says. "Your car was seen at the Preston estate the day Lewis Preston died. Why were you there?"

Dominique's mouth opens in awe, surprise on her face before she can collect herself. "I don't know what you're talking about."

"We have a video that shows you coming and going from the estate," Alicia reiterates succinctly, holding out her business card to the woman, who grabs it quickly as if she's just been burned, before stepping back into the front foyer of the house, her hand on the door ready to slam it closed in their faces until Alicia asks innocently, "Is it a boy or a girl?"

Dominique smiles at the question. "A girl. She's nine months old," she glows before closing the door in the detectives' faces.

"Aah, such a great age," Alicia adds as the detectives stand alone on the front porch of the new home.

***

"Interesting," Helen says as she starts the police vehicle.

"Very," Alicia agrees looking out the front windshield at the house before Helen pulls away. "I would like to know who the father is."

"Are you thinking what I'm thinking?"

154

"If you're thinking that it's Lewis Preston, then my answer would be yes."

"It's a bit of a jump, but if they were having an affair, it's possible."

"She was pretty distraught at the funeral. Maybe they were just friends. Maybe we're barking up the wrong tree. Looking for something that's not there."

"Possible, but I still would like to know who the father is. The hospital, assuming she had the baby here in the city, won't give us any info unless we have a warrant. And there's no way of accessing marriage licenses to see if there's a Mr. Guillaume."

"The Ontario Land Registration System might tell us who owns this place. Could be Lewis; could be her; could be her and her husband, if she has one."

There's silence for a moment as the detectives contemplate the system, before Helen says, "So, let's say that the baby is Preston's and he bought her the house. A place for her and the kid to live. Somewhere they could be together, somewhere they could be a family."

"Or maybe he bought it to shut her up."

"Or he is showing responsibility for the kid. Making sure the baby-momma and the kid have a home to live in. If Preston bought it, Nico will be able to find it when he looks at Preston's finances."

"Probably under the business. Hide it so the wife doesn't see it."

"Maybe. And what if the wife knew about the assistant, knew about the baby, knew about the house? Mrs. Preston may have had her husband killed while she was away, so she didn't have to put up with Lewis' new family."

"It will be interesting to see how long it takes Ms. Dominique Guillaume to come in and talk to us," Alicia muses, as Helen drives the police vehicle through the upscale new subdivision. "Hey, you know the monthly income that Rand talked about?" she turns her head to her partner.

"Yeah, what about it?"

155

"Maybe the kid knew about Dominique, and he was extorting his dad. He threatened to tell Mom unless Dad ponied up the money for the condo so he could go to the city, have some fun and get discovered by the big leagues."

"Possible. Anything seems possible with this freaking family."

"Did you see her fingernails? Not sure how she can look after a baby with those claws. They must have been at least two inches long," Alicia says, looking down at her own chewed nails.

Chapter 55

Dominique

Dominique collapses against the inside of the door, short of breath as if she'd been trying to suck air in through a straw. *Get out. Stay out. You want to come in here, into my house and make me feel guilty for loving him, for needing him, for having Paige. I don't think so.*

I should have stayed with him that night. He said he wasn't feeling well and that he wanted to get some sleep before the meeting the next morning. He complained about his stomach and thought he ate something bad. He was so calm, so cool, like he always is, was. How could I have known? I should have stayed the night. But I needed to get home. I'm still breastfeeding Paige, and I didn't leave an extra bottle for her.

A loud wail emanates from upstairs, and Dominique looks at her watch. *Guess nap time is over. How the hell am I going to tell her that her daddy is gone? No, I'm not going to say anything to her. She's young, too young to understand life and death. But she will miss his smiles, his touch, his attention, and their playtime together. I'll have to do all of that now.*

She probably won't even remember him when she grows up. Hell, she's only nine months old. She's my responsibility now and I will make sure that she has only the best, and if I have to play both Mommy and Daddy until I find someone else, then so be it. She at least met her father. We know who he is, unlike my father who left within hours of creating me, she thinks before launching herself up the stairs to get her daughter, wanting to keep her safe from the chaos, and the lies that the detectives wanted to bring into their home.

Chapter 56

Kandis

Kandis pulls her rusty old beater car into the driveway, gliding it to a stop before turning the engine off, which continues to shake for several moments until it dies out. She shakes her head as it goes through the throes of a slow death. *It's going to give up on me soon. Probably sooner than later. I would love a new car but that's definitely not in the cards. Could I swing a used car, something not quite as used as this one?*

She shakes her head again, clearing car thoughts out of her head and looks towards the closed garage doors, silence in the air. *Hey, listen to that! Silence. No music. No cars in the driveway. He had the guys over the last couple of nights but maybe he's taking a break. Maybe he's going to play and party in moderation, like we talked about. Maybe this is the new Kyle. Maybe he's going to reform and be part of this marriage, part of this family, try and make up for all the shit he's done,* she thinks stepping out of her car and slamming the door, it rattling on its hinges, as she walks towards the front door of their bungalow.

She steps into the foyer, and notices Abbie's shoes and books tossed on the floor, "Abbie, I'm home," she yells, kicking her shoes into the same pile as her daughter's. "What's for dinner?" she asks, moving into the empty kitchen, seeing that dinner has not yet been started. "Abbie?" she repeats questioningly, moving into the living room and seeing her daughter sitting glued to the TV, watching some boy-band video.

"I thought starting dinner was one of your chores? If you want an allowance, you have to do some stuff around the house to help me," Kandis says, but there is silence as if she hadn't uttered a word. She moves and stands in front of the TV, blocking her daughter's view. "Dinner," she repeats succinctly.

Silence.

"I'm talking to you," Kandis says, her hands on her hips waiting.

"Mom, I just got in from the library. I just sat down for a minute," Abbie huffs, as she slides to the edge of the couch.

"And where's your father?" Kandis asks.

"Haven't seen him," Abbie mumbles, as she moves past her mother on the way to the kitchen.

Kandis stands in the living room for a moment. *What the fuck. Where could he be? It's so quiet in the garage. He'd at least be playing his guitar if he was in there,* she thinks as she moves down the hallway to the side door, and the entrance to the garage.

She puts her hand on the doorknob for the garage, stops and takes a deep breath, unsure which Kyle she'll find – the man that she loves, that treats her like a queen or the self-centred, drunk that inhabits the garage and treats her like shit.

She quietly opens the door and steps into the remnants of a party, empty beer bottles, half-full glasses left on the floor, overflowing ashtrays with ashes and butts spilling about, bottles of pop and a sleeve of plastic glasses on a makeshift table made from an old piece of wood laying across a couple of sawhorses. As she looks around the mess, she spies Kyle's guitar stand but it is lying sideways on the floor, like it has fallen over. *What the fuck went on here. That's not like Kyle.*

It's Abbie's job to clean up the goddamn mess. Something else she hasn't done. No allowance for her this week.

"Kyle," she says quietly, looking around at the wreckage, almost turning to leave the carnage before her eyes spot the lower half of a body stretched out on the cold cement floor, behind the drum set.

She moves towards the inert body. "Kyle? Are you OK?" she asks, thinking that he must surely be drunk again or still sleeping it off from last evening's escapades. "What the fuck?" she mumbles, as she bends down and touches his arm.

"Kyle!" she yells, grabbing his arm, and nudging it forcefully. "Wake up. Wake up," she shrieks. She leans back

159

for a moment, watching his chest. *Is it moving? Is he breathing? Fuck, his chest is barely moving.* "Son of a bitch," she hisses. "Kyle wake up. Wake up," she repeats, slapping his face with her open hand, a little harder than is required.

"Ugh," she finally hears from her husband, still sprawled on the floor.

"Kyle," she repeats. "Open your eyes. Talk to me."

She waits another minute, but he is quiet, no sound, no movement. "Fuck, this is more than just passed out. Something is definitely wrong," she tells the motionless body as she pulls her phone from her back pocket and dials 911.

Chapter 57

Alicia

Jeff and Alicia had been out for the day, wandering around at the Waterfront Festival in Orillia, checking out the brand-new boats, looking at the numerous vendors selling a variety of items from accessories for boating, and fishing, to summer clothing, to local authors flogging their books.

Jeff drives steadily down Highway 11 towards home when Alicia asks, "So tell me why we spent the day looking at boats."

"Just looking," he replies, turning his head for a moment to smile at her.

"Are you thinking of buying one of those gigantic homes on the water?" she asks.

"Just looking," he repeats.

***

"Dinner?" Alicia asks, as Jeff manoeuvres his car along the exit ramp from the highway.

"I think I'm too tired for a restaurant. How about we order in?"

"Chinese?"

"Sounds good," he replies.

Minutes later, he turns the corner onto Alicia's street, and she sits up straighter in the car seat. "Is that Luke's car?" she asks, eyeing the ancient Toyota Corolla sitting in front of her house.

"Looks like it. Were you expecting him?" Jeff asks, as he puts the signal on to turn into the driveway, looking straight ahead so she can't see his smile that will give away the surprise.

"If I was expecting him, we wouldn't have spent hours looking at bloody boats," she replies. "I wonder how long he's been here."

"Good question. Let's go in and ask him," Jeff suggests as he parks the car.

Alicia jumps from the car and makes her way to the side door of her house. "Luke," she yells, not waiting for Jeff to follow her. "Luke. Are you here?" she asks, as she moves through the kitchen and into the living room to see her son and his girlfriend, Annie, standing in front of the window.

She sees the broad smiles on both their faces before she looks down to Annie's left hand which she is extending towards her. Alicia grabs her hand and looks at the single diamond on her ring finger before she looks up at her soon-to-be daughter-in-law, who has the largest grin on her face that she's ever seen. Her eyes travel to her son's smile as he says, "Surprise. We wanted you to be the first to know."

He steps forward and hugs her tightly, whispering in her ear. "I know you think we're too young, but we're not." He pushes her away to see her face as he continues. "We'll wait for a bit, wait until we both have jobs, but it just felt right," he finishes, pulling Annie in beside him.

"Welcome to the family," Alicia says to Annie, reaching out to give her a hug.

Chapter 58

Alicia

"Son of a bitch," Alicia mumbles, as she hangs up the phone.

"What's going on?" Helen asks.

"That was Trina Gomes from Preston Construction. She was thinking about Preston's calendar and realized that he had an off-the-cuff meeting that wasn't documented. Seems his son Rand showed up unexpectedly. She didn't hear what the conversation was about, but voices were raised and when the kid left, he slammed the door and was muttering under his breath."

"Rand didn't mention he was in the area," Helen declares.

"Guess it slipped his mind. Just like Izzy forgetting to tell us she was at her parents' that day."

"Freaking kids. Tells us the kind of people they are."

"Liars, self-centred, maybe killers."

"What do you want to do?" Helen asks. "Go to the city and ask them what the hell they were thinking lying to the police?"

Alicia thinks for a moment before asking, "Do you know anyone in 52 Division?"

Helen hesitates before offering, "I might. Not sure if he's still there. Why? What are you thinking?"

"We get 52 to pick both of them up and take them to the precinct. Put them in separate rooms, let them know that they're both there but don't let them talk to each other. Let them sweat a bit. Then we go in and question them, threaten them a bit, make sure they know how serious this is. Their father's been murdered for Christ's sake."

Helen smiles. "Give me a sec," she says as she picks up her cell phone, scans her phone contacts and presses a button. She has a quick conversation before hanging up. "We are good to go. Bruce just needs to know where and when to pick them up. He needs an official ask with why we want them picked up to cover his ass with his Chief. Said an email from one of us would suffice."

"Perfect. How about you do that, and I'll set up a meeting with Antony Rizzo? We'll go down tomorrow morning – see Rizzo if he's free and then go over to the precinct and have a conversation with Izzy and Rand."

"Works for me. Today I'd like to take some time and do some online research on the family."

"Definitely. I'll look at the police databases and you take the social media stuff."

***

The detectives spend the rest of the day at their desks, their eyes glued to their computer screens. Time flies by as the two work diligently, getting up occasionally to grab a coffee, a sandwich for lunch from the precinct cafeteria, saying a couple of words to their associates, before they return to their desks and get back to their search for information on Lewis Preston and his family.

Just after 4pm, almost in unison, they sit back in their chairs, exhaustion on their faces.

"Now?" Alicia asks.

"I just want to grab something to drink. Something cold. I'm coffeed out," Helen replies, standing up and stretching.

"Sounds good," Alicia agrees, standing up and following her partner out the double swinging doors of the Den.

***

When they return, Alicia starts her dissertation first. Lewis Preston was charged with public intoxication causing a disturbance in a bar in Orillia, Ontario, when he was 19 years old. Both he and the other person involved in the altercation

164

were charged, leading to a night in jail to sober up and a fine of $1,000 plus restitution to the bar for chairs and tables damaged in the fight. There are no other charges or mentions of Lewis Preston in any of the police databases.

Maeve Preston, previously Maeve Ellis, has no charges, and no arrest history, however her father, Donald Ellis has numerous notes on his personal record including police intervention in domestic disputes, allegations of sexual offences against his wife and two daughters, as well as assaults causing bodily harm. Donald and Mildred Ellis were divorced in 1995 when another flurry of notes were made on his record – domestic disturbances, sexual assaults, harassment, public intoxication and public mischief – none of which extended into charges, probably because of the patriarchal society of the time.

It's around this time that charges start to appear on Pearl Ellis' registry, Maeve's older sister - petty theft, underage drinking, and hitchhiking.

Rand Preston has no police record, and only one note in the police database regarding drug possession, which was later dropped when Judge Mitchell vouched for the teenager.

Isabella Preston has a long list of legal troubles. She has no specific soliciting charges, however there are a couple of notes suggesting the possibility. There are a number of drug possession charges, all of which were reduced or pleaded down to a misdemeanor with the intervention of Judge Mitchell, resulting in monetary penalties - $100 to $10,000 except for the last incident, when she was mandated to attend an elite drug rehab centre in Muskoka, just north of the city.

Cody Bruno, Izzy's boyfriend, has been in trouble since he was in diapers with charges ranging from petty theft to break and enter to car theft to drug possession. He was in and out of youth justice facilities, out long enough to commit another indictable offence, be tried, found guilty and returned to the system. As an adult, he continued to be on the police's radar with pending indictments for drug possession, as well as notes about possible involvement with the Pacino group, an extended mob family in Southern Ontario, with ties to drug trafficking, cigarette smuggling, extortion and gambling.

Preston's VPs have no police records or pending trouble or accusations against them.

Alicia sits back in her chair and looks up from her notes at her partner.

"The notes on possible solicitation are interesting," Helen comments, pausing a moment before she begins her social media analysis including Facebook, Instagram, X, Bluesky, Reddit, Snapchat, Tumblr, YouTube, WhatsApp, Discord, Thread and Mastodon.

Both Lewis and Maeve Preston, typical of people in their 40's, have Facebook pages, but both are private, showing only their name, a profile and cover picture. That's it for Lewis; however, Preston Construction has social media profiles on Facebook, Instagram, X, Bluesky and TikTok, all specific to the business and its capabilities.

Maeve also has accounts on Instagram and Bluesky, which are private.

Rand is much more liberal and has all his accounts open to anyone who wants to take a look at Facebook, Instagram, Bluesky and Snapchat. His posts are mostly about football, from playing it to practicing it to being drafted by the University of Texas. He also posts about the clubs he's been to, including a plethora of pictures of different women in a variety of circumstances and conditions – from dancing at clubs to clinking glasses and guzzling what looks like alcoholic drinks.

"Pretty active at the bar scene for a senior in high school, don't you think?" Alicia says, before Helen continues.

There are a couple of pictures with his friends Kim and Bree, all three barely clothed and enjoying themselves in a hot tub.

"Probably taken the weekend he told us about," Alicia offers.

Izzy's Facebook, Instagram, X, Bluesky, Snapchat, YouTube, Tumblr, WhatsApp and Threads are all open to the public. All posts are specific to her business of being an influencer with reviews of restaurants, nightclubs, theatre productions, concerts, several exclusive stores and fashion designers.

All the open accounts carry the same information, pictures, and recommendations. The number of Izzy's followers vary on each of the sites from less than 100 on Threads to just under 2,000 on Instagram, making her, by definition, a micro-influencer, with such a small audience.

The Preston Construction VPs – Jake Beckham, Elijah Greco, Fallon Shipley, Cory Mercer and Gavin Ferguson – all have accounts, mostly on Facebook, Instagram and BlueSky, but all are private and inaccessible.

"Hmm," Alicia comments. "What about Izzy's boyfriend? Anything there?"

"His social media access is limited to Facebook, Bluesky and Discord. All private access."

"Discord?"

"Basically, a gamers' site where you can play games, talk and stream with others, either individually or in group chats, while playing games, or watching a show together."

"Hmm," Alicia replies.

"Yeah, not much there but it was worth looking. You just never know when someone slips up or is simply arrogant and doesn't make their messages private," Helen answers, before leaning back in her chair.

Chapter 59

Jules

The coroner sits at her desk after a long day on her feet conducting four separate autopsies. *What a freaking day that was,* she thinks, slipping her shoes off under her desk. *I'll just check my email before I pack it in for the day. See if there's anything important before I go home and hit the hot tub.*

Her computer opens slowly, as if it too had an exhausting day and she clicks on the email icon. Jules glances through the numerous online correspondences, deciding what needs to be opened today and what can wait until tomorrow.

One stands out from the rest – a note from John Richardson, entitled 'Lewis Preston'.

She moves the pointer on her computer screen, clicks on the title and begins to read John's summary.

"Son of a bitch," Jules says to no one in particular as her eyes skim through the memo.

Sodium nitrite. I'll be damned. I've never had a death from sodium nitrite before. I was right. It definitely was a homicide.

Look at the levels, My God they're high. Very high. His MetHb test came back with 50% concentration of methemoglobin in his blood. And that's after sitting in the water for three days, where some of it would have dissipated. The valium and alcohol didn't help his situation, but it was the sodium nitrite that killed him.

Wonder where the hell the killer got it. Not something that you can simply buy at a store. Probably online. I hear you can get everything online.

I'll send John's email directly to Alicia and Helen. I'll have to go tell Mrs. Preston the results of all the tests in the morning. Wonder if Alicia and Helen have their sights set on her for the murder?

Chapter 60

Maeve

Maeve stands for a moment at the door to Kyle's hospital room, taking in his prone body, the multiple tubes weaving in and out of him, the plethora of monitors filling two separate poles behind the bed. She clears her throat and Kandis looks up.

"Hi, Maeve. Do you want to come in?"

"No. I think we should talk. Can you come out here for a couple of minutes?" she asks, continuing to look at her friend's husband, watching as his chest moves up and down with the help of a respirator.

"Sure," Kandis replies, standing up. turning off her tablet and placing it on her vacated chair. She moves to the door and reaches out for a hug from her friend. After a moment, they part and she suggests, "Coffee?"

"Sounds good," Maeve agrees, as she turns and leads the way to the elevator.

***

"Are you OK?" Kandis asks, as the two women sit down at a small table in an empty corner of the large cafeteria, coffees and donuts in front of them.

Maeve blows on her coffee for a moment, before she looks up at her friend and whispers, "What were you thinking?"

"Thinking?" Kandis parrots back to her friend, unsure of what she's asking.

"The police are still investigating Lewis' death. Hell, we just buried him. They know we're friends. Once they hear about Kyle's death," she puts her hand up to stop her friend from commenting. "Sorry, his imminent death, they're going

169

to be looking at you. They always look at the wife first. And that will lead them back to look at me for Lewis."

Kandis is quiet, listening to her friend's stress and anger. "Maeve, I don't know what to say. I didn't do anything," she finally admits, her hands open on the top of the table in innocence.

"What? You didn't do anything?" Maeve asks in a stern, soft voice as if speaking to a wayward child.

"The doctors aren't sure what's going on with Kyle, but I didn't do anything," Kandis adds emphatically.

"If you didn't do this, then what happened?" Maeve hisses quietly.

"I don't know. Alcohol poisoning. Drug overdose. They're checking a lot of stuff."

Maeve sits staring across the table, unsure if she should believe the woman she's called her friend for over 20 years. "Alcohol poisoning? Drugs?" she asks skeptically. "Why would this happen now? He's been doing both for so long. I would have thought his body was immune to the abuse."

"I don't know. The doctors are still trying to figure out what's going on," Kandis repeats.

What the fuck! She talked about getting rid of him. She was researching how to do it for Christ's sake. She had every right to kill the son of a bitch, but she says she didn't do it. He just happened to get deathly ill all by himself? Bullshit, Maeve thinks as she sits back in the rigid, uncomfortable chair, staring at her friend.

Chapter 61

Alicia

Helen is engrossed with something on her computer when Alicia walks into the Detectives' Den, stopping along the way to say hello, and talking to a few of her colleagues, before making her way to their workstations. She places her purse on her desk and asks, "So what's so interesting?" before sitting down.

"Jules sent the results from the toxicology tests."

"Excellent. Do we have a definitive answer?"

"Sodium nitrite," Helen breathes.

"Now that's unquestionably premeditated."

"Definitely," Helen pauses before adding, "Do you remember that case that was in the news not too long ago?" Helen asks, without giving Alicia a chance to answer before continuing. "I was just googling it. A guy in Mississauga is accused of sending at least 1,200 packages of sodium nitrite to people in more than 40 countries. He was originally indicted for 14 charges of counselling or aiding suicide, but it has recently been upgraded to include 14 counts of second-degree murder."

"Fourteen counts? From the 1,200 packages? Sounds like there should be a hell of a lot more victims than that."

"Well, that is 14 charges in Canada and they're still working on the case, so there will be more. Not sure how many charges will come from other countries."

"We need to talk to whoever is heading up the investigation," Alicia says, as her partner nods in agreement.

"The case is being managed by Peel Region. I'll call down and get a name and set up a meeting."

"They must have some kind of information on who he sold to, a list of customers, some way to trace a purchase to someone on our list of suspects," Alicia adds.

"You would think he'd have some kind of records. Just give me a sec to make a couple of calls and we'll go down to

171

Toronto. We're meeting Rizzo this morning. Bruce is going to pick up the kids at 12 noon and we'll see them this afternoon."

***

The detectives stand in the front lobby of the skyscraper in downtown Toronto, waiting for the security guard to grant them access to the private elevators that go up to the penthouse offices of Rizzo Enterprises.

Finally, the watchman looks up. "Sorry for the delay, detectives. The elevator is all yours," he says, nodding towards the dark wood-clad doors.

"What floor?" Helen asks.

"That's the company's private elevator. Just push the up button," he smiles. "It stops at the reception area for the firm, and they'll be able to direct you to Mr. Rizzo's office."

The two march across the Carrara white and grey marble floor to the now open elevator doors. They step inside, and Alicia pushes the button.

The elevator rises quickly to the 54th floor and the door opens onto a bright reception area with sunlight streaming through the floor-to-ceiling windows. A receptionist sits to the right of the expansive view and greets them warmly as they walk out of the elevator.

"Ms. Santoro will be with you in a moment," she tells them, as the door behind her opens. "Oh, here she is now," the receptionist finishes, as a woman walks into the reception area.

"Welcome to Rizzo Enterprises. Mr. Rizzo is just finishing up a phone call. If you follow me, I'll take you to our executive boardroom and he will join you in a couple of minutes," she says, holding the door open for the detectives.

The tall dark-haired woman, wearing a very expensive made-to-measure pantsuit, leads the visitors to the opposite end of the floor to a large boardroom with more floor-to-ceiling windows overlooking the city. The boardroom table, positioned in the middle of the room, is at least five metres in length, able to seat at least six people comfortably on either side. A built-in kitchenette sits at one end of the room, including a fridge, stove and a fully stocked bar. The other end of the space hosts a comfortable living room-type area with a sofa and a couple of matching chairs for more intimate meetings.

The two detectives move to the windows to take in the view as Ms. Santoro walks to the kitchenette. "Can I offer you a coffee or tea?" she asks, before both detectives turn her down politely.

"No problem. I'll just go see how long Mr. Rizzo's going to be," she explains, as she moves towards the outer door.

Alicia and Helen continue to look out the windows at the cityscape and Lake Ontario. "Nice view," Helen comments, "though I'm not sure I would want to work this far up in the clouds."

The door softly opens behind them, and a tall, slender gentleman, with dark hair and piercing almost-black eyes, dressed in a dark blue suit, with a light blue shirt and a red tie with white polka dots, strides into the room, his hand outstretched to the two officers. "My name is Antony Rizzo. I was very sorry to hear of Lewis' passing. How is his wife doing?"

"As well as can be expected," Alicia answers. "Quite a shock when something so unexpected happens."

"I'm not sure how I can help you, but please sit down," he greets, moving to the informal area of the meeting room.

He sits in a large bucket chair facing Alicia and Helen, who sit across from him on the couch. "Thanks for taking the time to talk with us," Helen starts. "We understand that Preston Construction was one of your major competitors and that there was animosity between you two."

Antony Rizzo smiles at the statement, shaking his head. "Lewis did a great job with his company, but I wouldn't say it was one of our major competitors, though he was becoming a bit of a rival with his expansion into the commercial segment, but you have to understand that type of construction is only a small part of Rizzo Enterprises. We also do residential subdivisions, condo buildings and infrastructure work such as highways, bridges, and water treatment plants. One of our biggest projects right now is working with the City of Toronto on the subway expansion." He pauses for a moment, looking from Alicia to Helen before continuing. "Preston Construction is a good company but on a small scale compared to Rizzo Enterprises."

"We heard that Preston stole a couple big contracts out from under you," Alicia suggests. "The new Amazon distribution centre in Scarborough for example."

Antony chuckles before answering. "You're right. Lewis did take a couple of Amazon plants from us. We built the majority of their warehouses in Canada and probably got a bit sloppy with some of our quotes. No worries. We were reminded that there's competition out there and we reviewed our in-house processes and costing and hit back and got the contract for the two million square foot fulfillment centre being built in St. Thomas. All's good," he says.

"How long have you known Lewis Preston?" Helen asks.

Antony's eyes move to Helen at the question, a smile gracing his face. "Years. I've known Lewis forever. He learned the trade from the bottom up, moving from company to company, progressing up the ladder as he went. He worked for us for a while when my father was still around, probably 20 years ago. I didn't have any contact with him back then."

"When was the last time you saw Mr. Preston?" Alicia asks.

"Probably at the Canadian Construction Awards last year. Rizzo Enterprises won an award for Excellence in Innovation for the work that we did for the Ontario Government."

"You had a meeting with Mr. Preston the day he died. What was that all about?"

Rizzo stops for a moment like he's reaching back in his mind before he answers. "Lewis and I touched base every once in a while. We talked about our upcoming projects, how the new tariffs would impact us, and the shortage of concrete. Stuff like that."

"Rivals talk about the business?" Alicia asks suspiciously.

"As I said earlier, we weren't really rivals. We were in the same business, but our clientele and the size of our projects were very different. We tried to keep it friendly. Our meetings were a bit of a fishing expedition to learn what the other was up to."

"Where did the meeting take place?"

"It was a phone conversation. One thing that Covid taught us is all meetings don't have to be in person," he grins.

"Do you know Dominique Guillaume?"

The man is silent for a moment before admitting, "The name is familiar. I believe she worked for us a couple of years ago."

"What position did she have at your company?" Alicia asks.

Rizzo hums and puts his hand to his chin like he's thinking deeply before answering, "I believe she worked in marketing. HR could tell you for sure."

"Where were you the day Lewis died?" Helen asks.

Antony Rizzo is silent for a moment before pulling his phone from his pocket. He swipes through several screens before looking up. "As you know, I talked to Lewis in the morning. Then I left here about noon for a flight to the Bahamas. My wife and I went down for an extended long weekend. Just a short trip to celebrate our tenth wedding anniversary," he advises, closing his phone.

There's silence for a moment before the tall man stands up, towering over the detectives still sitting on the couch. "I have another meeting in five minutes so if there's nothing else," he says dismissively, waiting for the investigators to stand up.

As if on cue, Ms. Santoro opens the door to the boardroom and steps in, watching her boss intently. "Please show the detectives out," he directs, as he treads across the room and out the door.

"This way, please," his assistant says, holding the door open for the detectives.

***

"Thoughts?" Alicia asks, as Helen manoeuvres the police SUV through the traffic in downtown Toronto, moving slowly towards 52 Division precinct.

"Interesting guy. Arrogant. Showy. Sure of himself. Had all the right answers. Even had a great alibi of going to the Bahamas with his wife."

"Yeah, good for them celebrating ten years together."

"He was very nonchalant about the conversations with Lewis. I don't think I've ever heard of competitors having a friendly conversation just to catch up, especially when one of them took business from the other. Rizzo would have lost millions of dollars in that build. I wonder who lost their job over that error."

"But was a couple of contracts enough for Rizzo to want to get rid of him?"

"Maybe it was just the start of Preston Construction taking away business. Maybe Preston was expanding and was going to cut Rizzo out of a lot of other big stuff. I would guess working with Amazon would be a feather in Preston's cap and if he's on the hook to build a couple more centres, what's saying he couldn't become the prime contractor going forward for Amazon?"

"Money. It all comes down to money. A good motive if I've ever heard of one."

"And what about Dominique? Working for Rizzo, then moving up to Preston Construction and working so closely with the president of the company?"

"Strange that Rizzo knew her, don't you think?"

"Maybe he knows most of his employees. One of those fuzzy family-oriented leaders."

Alicia laughs at the thought. "I don't think so, Helen," she replies. "He tries to give the air that he's a caring kind of guy who knows his staff, but I would say it's all a façade. He's all business. It's all about him. All about his money. All about how it looks."

"Yeah, you're probably right. Just look at his office. In downtown Toronto, no less. A construction company? What's that all about? Probably the only one in the centre of the city."

"The meeting with Preston was over the phone. How would he have administered the sodium nitrite to Preston?"

***

Helen pulls the police vehicle into 52 Division and parks in one of the two visitor parking spaces. They walk through the double set of doors into the public reception area of the precinct and move up to the bay-style window. They wait for several moments before an officer comes to the glass partition and asks, "Can I help you?"

Helen introduces herself and Alicia before asking for Constable Bruce Brunswick. The officer behind the glass smiles. "You must be the detectives from Barrie," he says. Both nod their heads in the affirmative before he continues, "I'll tell Bruce that you're here."

"Thanks," Helen says, before she turns around and wanders over to the recognition wall, her eyes moving over the awards for bravery, for contributions to law enforcement and the community, for long-term service and leadership within the department, as well as memorial plaques for two police officers killed in the line of duty.

As she looks at the accolades on the wall, she hears a door open behind her and the voice of an old friend. "Hey, Elle.

177

It's been a long time," he announces as Helen turns around. She takes in Bruce's highly developed muscles, his sculpted body, his broad smile, his bright green eyes, his chiseled face, no different than when she met him three years ago at a mandatory first aid course sponsored by the police association.

"Hey Bruce," Helen replies, stepping into his outstretched arms. "It is great to see you. How are you? How's Amelia?" she asks, stepping back.

"Good. We're good. She's not in the field anymore. Decided after the baby that an office job was better for her. She's been working in communications for a while now."

"Good for her. And how's the baby?"

"He's fantastic – walking, talking, though we can't really understand half of what he says," Bruce laughs. "I could bore you with pictures, but your suspects are waiting," he says, as he opens the door to the inner offices of the precinct.

"Thanks for picking them up for us," Helen says. "This is my partner, Detective Alicia Anderson," she adds, nodding at Alicia, who is now standing beside her.

Bruce Brunswick nods his head, waits for the two women to enter the inner sanctum of the precinct before stepping into the area, and closing and locking the door behind him.

"Any issues picking them up?" Alicia asks.

"Some. Rand Preston was at his apartment. He asked a lot of questions about why, did we have the right, did he need a lawyer, but he finally agreed to come with us peacefully."

There's a slight pause before he continues. "Izzy Preston was erratic, agitated, yelling, didn't want to cooperate, didn't want to come to the precinct. We had to use a bit more force with her, had to put her in handcuffs. She wasn't alone when we got there. Not sure if the guy was a friend; he seemed more like a trick. He hightailed it pretty quick when he saw the uniforms. A guy was hanging around the lobby when we went in, and he was still there when we came down with the suspect. He went a little crazy too, asking where we were taking her, and what was she charged with. He came in just after we got here, wanted to see her, wanted to sit with her until we questioned her. We said no."

"Do Rand and Izzy know they are both here?"

"They do. We moved Rand when Izzy was coming in. They definitely saw each other across the office. Didn't say anything to each other though," Bruce reports.

"Let's talk to Rand first," Helen suggests, before the detectives follow the patrolman through the dispatch area and down a stark corridor with pairs of steel doors every five meters.

"We have eight interrogation rooms, each with a viewing room," Bruce explains, as he stops at the second set of doors. "Rand Preston is in this one," he says as he opens the solid steel door for the detectives. He nods as they enter, closing the door behind them before opening the adjacent door to watch their interrogation.

As the door opens, Rand Preston's head jerks up. He closes his phone and places it on the table. "Was this really necessary?" he asks with anger in his voice. "I'm missing school because of this bullshit."

"It was necessary. Did the officer read you your rights?" Alicia asks, moving into the room and sitting across the table from the young man.

"Rights?"

"Yes, your Charter of Rights."

"Why the hell would you need to do that? I've got nothing to hide," Rand answers.

"If you have nothing to hide, then it shouldn't be an issue," Helen says before reciting the well-known words – why they have brought him in for questioning, his right to speak to a lawyer and the right to remain silent.

Rand agrees to the conditions before asking if he should have a lawyer with him.

"Do you need one?" Helen asks.

He thinks for several moments before confessing, "No, I'm good. I didn't do anything wrong. Ask your questions,"

Rand says, moving forward in his chair as if listening to something important from the other side of the table.

"Why were you in Barrie the day your father died?" Alicia asks, sitting straight in her chair.

"Barrie?" the young man parrots.

"Barrie," Alicia repeats.

"Why do you think I was in Barrie?"

"Let me ask again. Why were you in Barrie the day your father died?" Alicia says with intensity.

The young man thinks for a moment before laying his hands flat on the table as if he's going to push himself up. "I don't understand why you need to know. My father was found in the lake. I was nowhere near the water."

"One more time, why were you in Barrie the day your father died?"

Rand sits for a moment in silence, weighing his options, unsure what the officers already know before he finally concedes, "I'm sorry. I didn't know the specific date of my father's death last time we talked. He was missing for a couple of days before he was found. And he was found in the lake. I was nowhere near the lake, nowhere near the house, so I didn't think it was important." He looks down at his hands and moves them into his lap, almost humbling himself at his error. "I did see my father at his office that day. I came in for a quick conversation with him before my weekend with Kim and Bree," he smiles wickedly.

"Why did you drive all the way up to see your father?"

"I wanted to talk to him."

"Must have been important. No appointment. Just barged in expecting him to be free to see you. What did you want to talk to him about?"

Rand looks down at his lap for several moments before looking up at the detectives. "I called him a couple of times. He was always too busy to talk so I went up there. I thought he couldn't slough me off if I was right in front of him."

There's silence in the room as the detectives wait for the rest of the story. "I needed more money. He gave me a pittance to live on, and I needed more." He pauses momentarily before continuing, "We had a heated conversation, and I left."

"Then what happened?"

"I left."

"Did you hit him?"

Rand is silent for another moment before he finally confesses, "There was a bit of a scuffle. He shoved me like I was five years old. He said some nasty stuff; said I was taking advantage of him and his precious money. He said this was the last time that he would up my allowance, that I needed to learn fiscal responsibility," he huffs. "He has no clue how much it costs to live in the city, to have a life," he explains, running out of steam.

"Did you hit him?" the detective repeats.

"I might have shoved him. He fell, might have hit his head on his desk," he quietly confesses before adding, "But he was OK when I left. He got up, shook it off, even put his hands up like he was going to hit me. But he didn't. Told me to get the hell out of his office," he grimaces.

"What did you put in his drink?"

"His drink?"

"Yeah, his coffee, his water, whatever he had on his desk."

"Nothing. I swear."

"Did you kill your father?"

Rand looks into her eyes, his face the epitome of seriousness before answering, "I did not. I swear I did not hurt my dad."

"Why should we believe you? Especially knowing that you were there, that you hit him and that you lied to us."

The young man hangs his head and mumbles, "I swear I didn't do it. I've told you everything."

There's silence in the room for a moment before Rand asks, "Why is Izzy here? Was she up there that day? Did she see my dad? Did she do this?" his voice escalates as he continues his questions to the detectives. "Son of a bitch! Did she kill my dad?"

Chapter 62

Kandis

"You should come with me," Kandis tells her daughter as they sit at the kitchen table, eating their dinner of grilled cheese sandwiches.

Abbie dips the edge of her sandwich into the ketchup on her plate and moves it to her mouth, taking a bite.

Kandis waits until her daughter has chewed the mouthful and swallowed it.

"Abbie, are you listening to me?"

There's silence for a moment as Abbie dips the sandwich again into the ketchup and raises it to her lips.

"Abbie, answer me, please."

Abbie looks across the table at her mother. "I am not going to see him," she states.

"Why? Why aren't you going?" her mother pushes.

"Why? You're asking me why? What the fuck, Mom."

Kandis sighs loudly before replying. "There's been a lot of chaos in the house. A lot of crap over the years and I'm sorry that you've sometimes been caught in the middle. But your father is sick, and he needs our support right now."

"Bullshit," Abbie replies. "Bullshit. Nothing has changed. He's still a drunk, who hangs out with assholes. He lets dickheads come into our house. He doesn't care about us. He parties all the time; he doesn't work, he doesn't help you, he doesn't even talk to me most of the time and when he does, it's to yell at me for something I didn't even do. He creeps me out, Mom and no, I'm not going to see him."

"This is serious Abbie. The doctors don't know what's going on. He could die," Kandis adds, trying to guilt her daughter into doing the right thing.

"I don't care. He deserves to die," she tells her mother, as she gets up from the chair matter-of-factly and stomps to her bedroom, slamming the door behind her.

Chapter 63

Rand

The teenager pushes the front door of the police precinct open viciously, so hard that it slams into the brick wall of the building. He hurries across the front portico and down the three stairs before looking around. *Where the fuck am I? 52 Division? I'll just call an Uber,* he thinks as he pulls his phone out of his pocket, his finger poised, ready to input his access code.

Shit. Izzy is still in there. God knows what she'll tell the cops if she's high. She'll go on about the family, how cruel they were to her, how they favoured her little brother, how he got all the help from dear old Dad. If she'd only learned how to manage the asshole or at least had Mom on her side against him. Nope, she just did her own thing, didn't give a thought on how to tap into Dad's resources and look where she is now, turning tricks and getting high as a kite with her asshole boyfriend.

I better wait for her. Make sure she didn't tell them anything that would put me in their bright lights. She's stupid enough to just spout stuff without thinking. He stands still on the sidewalk in front of the precinct for a moment as thoughts of his sister fly through his brain. *Yeah, I'll just wait and have a conversation with big sister when she comes out*, he thinks, moving back towards the precinct and sitting on a bench in front of the busy entrance.

Chapter 64

Alicia

Bruce opens the door to another interrogation room, holding it open as Alicia and Helen enter, before closing it softly. Izzy Preston is sitting at the table, her head bowed, her face wet with tears. She jerks up quickly when she hears the click of the door as the two detectives enter. The detectives focus on the young woman - skinny as a rail, dark circles rimming her eyes as if she hasn't slept in days or is on a shitload of drugs.

"Izzy Preston, did the officer read you your rights?" Helen asks.

"My rights?" she parrots, similar to her brother earlier.

"We need to make sure that you know your rights. You are in a police precinct and being questioned about a murder," Helen says before she recites the words of the Canadian Charter of Rights and Freedoms. When Izzy is asked if she understands, she is silent but nods in the affirmative.

"Please say yes," Helen tells her. "We need verbal confirmation."

Izzy takes a moment before uttering, "Yes. I understand."

"Why did you go to your parent's home the day your father died?"

The girl is silent for a moment, her eyes on the door, as if someone will magically appear to help. Her eyes finally move to the detectives. "I was on my way to Huntsville. To a weekend retreat."

"A retreat?"

"I went to rehab last year, and they have follow-up sessions after you get out if you're struggling. I went up for the weekend."

"Are you struggling with your addictions?"

Izzy doesn't answer immediately. She tilts her head to one side like a dog listening to its master before answering, "Life is a struggle at times."

"Why did you stop at your parents? Did you know your mother wasn't there?"

Izzy thinks for a moment before answering. "I knew Mom had left on her trip."

"Why did you stop there?" Alicia asks for a third time.

"I just wanted to see my father. I hadn't seen him for a while," Izzy replies.

"Why did you want to see your father?"

Izzy hangs her head, her long stringy hair covering her face. There's silence in the interrogation room for several moments before she lifts her head. "I went to ask him for money. Times are tough and I need a bit of help," she finally admits.

"What did your father say to that request?"

"He said no."

"Because?" Alicia leads.

"He always used the old saying about making your bed and lying in it. Said if I came home and went back to school, he would help me out."

"Did you hit your father?"

"No way. He was bigger than me and he would have hit me back."

"What did you put in his drink?"

"His drink?" she repeats.

"Yes, his drink."

"I didn't put anything in his drink. Why the hell would I do that?"

"Did you have any drugs with you when you went into your parents' house?"

Izzy hums for a minute, swaying back and forth in her chair, as if in pain before she answers. "I had a couple hits of valium. I was going to take them before I got to the rehab centre."

"You were going to rehab for the weekend, and you took valium?"

Izzy simply shrugs her shoulders, saying nothing.

"Did you put valium into your father's drink?"

Izzy looks around the room for a moment before finally confessing, "Yeah, OK. I did. He was freaking out, running around the kitchen like a mad man, putting dishes out on the counter, pulling stuff out of the fridge. Looked like he was going to have company or something."

"And?"

"I just put half a tab in his drink. I thought it would calm him down a bit. Calm him enough so he would listen to me. He was ranting and raving, not listening to me. He said he was ashamed of me. Blaming me for being broke. He didn't understand that I had a bad year, that I needed money to make money. He didn't understand my job. He didn't want to understand what I do for a living."

"Why didn't you tell us you were at your father's when we interviewed you at your apartment?"

"I didn't think it was important. He was alive when I left."

"What else did you give your father?

"Nothing. I didn't give him anything else. Just a little valium to calm him down. That's all I had on me. I was going to rehab for Christ's sake. They would have searched me before I went in." There's silence in the room for several minutes before Izzy adds, "I swear."

"Did you kill your father?"

"No."

"Why do you think someone would kill him?"

Izzy thinks for a moment before telling the detectives, "Probably for his money. He's got lots of it."

"Who do you think killed your father?"

Izzy shrugs again. "Someone that wanted his money. Someone that he pissed off. Someone that thought they could get away with it."

"One more question, did you go there alone? Was your boyfriend with you?"

"Cody was there, but he stayed in the car."

"Why didn't he go in with you?"

"Daddy hated Cody. Thought he was a loser because we met at rehab. No, he stayed in the car. We thought I'd have a better chance of getting money from my dad if I went in alone, though that didn't happen."

Chapter 65

Rand

Rand squirms on the cold metal bench as he waits. *What the fuck is taking her so long? Probably that asshole is blowing everything up. He probably has a rap sheet as long as Highway 401. The guy has no ethics, no morals, living off my sister. If he really cared, he would help her get off drugs, help her make it in the influencer world, and get a fucking job for Christ's sake.*

He continues to sit for what seems like hours before Izzy finally staggers through the double glass doors, followed closely by her boyfriend, who is yelling at her.

"What the fuck, Izzy. Those fucking cops know what's in the bloody will. They get to see it as soon as someone dies," he blathers, knowing nothing about death, wills or investigations. "They know what the hell is going on. They're all in it together," he continues, until his eyes fall on Rand, sitting on the front steps. "What the hell are you doing here?" he asks, as Rand stands up and brushes his butt off.

Izzy isn't listening, can't concentrate on anything through the fog in her brain from the extra hit of coke she did in the police precinct bathroom, just to calm her nerves. She still hasn't seen her brother as she teeters down the stairs on her four-inch stilettos, her denim skirt just long enough to cover her underwear.

Cody follows her down the stairs, taking her elbow as if to steer her away from her brother, when Rand says, "Izzy."

Izzy doesn't hear him, as she pulls her arm away from Cody. "Leave me alone. I'm not a grandmother. I can walk by myself," she growls as she reaches the bottom step, turning and almost running into her brother.

"Izzy," Rand says again, louder this time.

She looks up as her brother's voice penetrates through the fog surrounding her brain. She smirks at him before she asks, "What the hell are you doing here?"

189

"Are you kidding me?" he replies.

She turns to the precinct building before turning back to her brother. "Did they question you too?" she asks in amazement.

Rand reaches out, grabs his sister's arm and pulls her close, hissing in her ear, "What the fuck are you on?"

"Hey man," Cody says, pushing between the two. "Leave her alone."

"This has nothing to do with you," Rand growls at the man.

"That's where you're wrong, asshole. It has everything to do with me."

Rand doesn't reply but clasps his sister's arm tighter, dragging her away from her boyfriend, away from the front of the police precinct. "We need to talk," he growls, as Izzy protests weakly, wobbling on her pretentious shoes.

"Where the fuck are you taking her?" Cody asks, following closely behind.

"Away from the fucking police station for starters," Rand snarls over his shoulder. "The cops are watching us," he adds, as he continues to guide his sister away.

Cody stops and looks up at the glass doors they've just walked through, looking for someone watching, seeing only shadows of people, possibly of someone stepping away from his view. "Son of a bitch," he mumbles as he turns to see Izzy and Rand moving up the street. He runs after them, falling in step beside Izzy. "You're right. They were watching us," he claims, taking Izzy's other arm as if he too is guiding her.

"Fucking right. This is not my first rodeo," Rand declares.

The threesome march up the street at a clip, Rand and Cody practically carrying Izzy away from the large concrete and glass building filled with Toronto's finest. When they can no longer see the façade of the precinct, Izzy stops dead, forcing her brother and boyfriend to stop as well. "Where the fuck are you taking me Rand?" she asks before adding, "I'm tired. I want to go home."

"Not before we talk," Rand growls as he looks around the street. "There's a Tim Hortons. Let's go in there," he instructs, pulling Izzy by the arm, passing a couple of storefronts and into the café.

He escorts his sister to a booth at the back of the coffee shop, her useless boyfriend following a half-a-step behind them. Rand pushes Izzy into the booth. "Back in a sec," he tells her, turning and going back to the front of the shop and ordering three coffees.

He takes the three covered cups to the cubicle and sits across from the pair, pushing two cups across the table at them. Rand pulls the tab on his coffee lid, blows on the hot contents before asking, "What did you tell them?"

Izzy is trying to open her coffee and is having difficulty freeing the small plastic spout, her fingers fumbling around on the top of the cup before looking up at her brother.

"I didn't tell them anything. I don't know anything," she confesses in one breath, as Cody reaches forward and opens the tab on her coffee cup.

"Yeah, man. I don't know what you're all pissed about. She didn't say anything. I was there with her the whole time," he declares.

Rand ignores Cody, his eyes focused on his sister. "Did you tell them Dad wouldn't give you any money to help with your business?"

Izzy nods slightly as she blows on her coffee.

"Did you tell them that you were there that day?"

"They already knew that," Izzy offers quietly.

"Did you tell them that you're addicted to coke, that you're probably an alcoholic, that you're a hooker?"

"I'm not a hooker," Izzy declares loudly, slamming her coffee on the table, hot liquid splashing out of the cup.

Rand puts his hand up in a stop motion. "Ssshhh," he instructs, looking around the shop for anyone that might be listening to their conversation. He turns his head back to the pair across from him. "I don't care what you call it.

Influencing, hooking, paying the rent, whatever. Do they know?"

Izzy is silent, looking down at the table, her finger drawing lines through the drops of coffee as if drawing a picture, a smile on her face as she starts to hum.

"What the fuck," Rand says, looking from his sister to the asshole sitting beside her for some type of answer.

"No, she wouldn't tell them how she makes extra cash," Cody offers. "But when they came to the apartment, there was a half bottle of whisky and some tokes on the coffee table. And then today, she was with a friend when they showed up."

"Fuck," Rand breathes.

"What's the problem, man? So, she drinks a little, she parties a little. So what?"

"My father died from some drug, sodium nitrite, I think it was called," Rand says. "Izzy," he nods towards her before continuing, "takes drugs." He pauses, putting his hand up in a stop motion before continuing. "Which means she has a pusher, a dealer, whatever," he continues, again putting up his hand as Cody is about to refute what he is saying. "Which means she has the means to get the drug that killed our father. Which means she's now a suspect."

"Is that why they pulled her down here?"

"What the fuck do you think, asshole?" Rand snarls.

Rand leans back in the booth for a moment, watching as his words are sinking into the jerk across from him, but not his sister who is humming to herself as if she's somewhere else and they are not talking about the death of their father and her possible involvement. He crosses his arms before it finally dawns on him. *Hey, why the fuck should I care if they think she did it? This could be a good thing. If they pin it on her, it leaves me free and clear. And then I won't have to put up with her, this asshole and their constant asks for money, which will never stop even if Dad left her some. Nope, this might actually be a good thing for me. Fuck her. I tried to help. Tried to be her brother but it's not worth it. Let the*

192

cops think she's involved. Yeah, let them look at her and not me. I'm out of here.

Rand stands up suddenly and moves from behind the table, leaving his half-finished coffee.

"Where are you going man?" Cody asks, looking at Rand.

"I'm done," Rand tells him.

Cody nods his head, before he asks, "Do you know when they're reading the will? Do you know when Izzy will get her money?"

Rand shakes his head before leaving the table, leaving the store and begins to walk back to his condo. "Stupid bitch," he mumbles to himself.

Chapter 66

Bruce

Alicia and Helen look up as Bruce Brunswick walks into the interrogation room while the detectives are discussing the cross-examinations of Rand and Izzy Preston. There's silence for a moment before Bruce offers, "I followed them out to the lobby, watched them leave. The brother was waiting The boyfriend was going on about the will, the money and when he'll be able to get his hands on it."

The detectives nod at his information.

"If you want to look at their drug use and who they get it from, I can hook you up with narcotics, see if they have some time to watch these two, find out who's dealing to them, lean on the dealer, find out specifically what he's sold them, see if they've asked about sodium nitrite."

"That would be helpful, Bruce," Helen answers. "Not sure pushers would have sodium nitrite but it's worth a try."

"Give me a few minutes. Let me see if Billy is around. See what he can help you with," he pronounces as he moves towards the doorway.

***

A short, slight man in his mid-30's with disheveled dirty blond hair, a scraggly beard and moustache walks into the interrogation room wearing grimy, ripped jeans and a faded soiled t-shirt, a grin on his face. "Ladies," he greets the detectives.

Alicia and Helen are speechless for a moment, before the man offers his hand to the pair. "Billy Elliott," he says. "Bruce thought I might be able to help you," he greets before sitting down. "I work in narcotics, on the street most of the time. Bruce says you were asking about dealers in the Distillery District. Something about sodium nitrite?"

"Yeah. We have a dead man; coroner is ruling it homicide from sodium nitrite. His daughter and boyfriend were just here for questioning, and she was as high as a kite. We haven't been able to track down where the sodium nitrite came from and Bruce suggested maybe she got it from her dealer," Helen explains to the undercover police officer.

"Honestly, I've never heard of any of the dealers selling sodium nitrite. It's extremely potent. Too dangerous, too risky for a dealer to sell. They would be losing customers, not growing their potential sales. But with that said, some pushers do sell poppers, which are inhalers that contain amyl nitrite. Gives the user a rush. Different than sodium nitrite but the same family of drugs," the narcotics officer tells the detectives.

"Interesting," Alicia offers, "But our coroner is sure that the victim was killed with sodium nitrite."

"I hear you. And a coroner would definitely know the difference between the two chemicals. Have you reached out to the cops investigating the Suicide Killer? They might be able to help."

"Jasper Huntley is heading the investigation out of Peel. We're meeting with him next week," Helen says.

Billy Elliott nods. "Give me their address. I'll hang around, watch and find out who they're buying from. Maybe have a conversation with the dealer. Ask what they buy, how often they call him, find out if they've ever asked about sodium nitrite or anything else that could kill someone."

"That would be helpful," Helen answers. "Bruce taped the interrogations so you can take a look at Izzy Preston and her boyfriend, Cody Bruno. We'll give you her address. Anything that you can do to help us track down how they got the stuff would be appreciated."

"Has she ever been charged with drug possession?" Buying or selling drugs?"

"She's been charged with possession a couple of times, all reduced to misdemeanors, all with monetary consequences except the last incident, when she was sent to rehab. Her boyfriend, Cody Bruno has been charged with everything under the sun, including drugs."

"OK. Well, if she's still using, I'll find out what she's buying and who she's getting it from. I'll get back to you," Billy advises confidently.

"Thanks," Alicia says looking at the scruffy agent, hoping that he will be able to help them.

Chapter 67

Kandis

Kandis stands in the hospital hallway, her eyes downcast looking at the scuffed, worn floor, as the doctor tells her that Kyle is dead. She is stunned, not sure what to do, not sure where to go, so she continues to stand there, unable to move.

I feel sad for the Kyle I first met, the man that I fell in love with. But he changed, became bi-polar or something, became someone I didn't know half the time, someone that was hard to love. And now he's gone. The bullshit, his friends, his music, his drinking, his forcing himself on me, his fists – all gone. Even with the occasional reprieve, life with Kyle was a struggle. I will miss him, miss the Kyle I knew and loved, but now I can breathe and not worry about what I'm going to find when I come in the house.

He must have drunk himself to death. I guess he got what he wanted in the end and I'm off the hook. And we are free to live a normal life without him.

***

Kandis stands on the sidewalk in front of the hospital, exhausted from spending so much time playing the always supportive wife. *So, what do I do now,* she wonders as she watches the people entering the hospital through its revolving doors. She stands for a moment, unsure which way to go, before she is nudged by someone trying to enter the hospital. "Sorry," she says automatically and moves to the side of the entranceway, still perplexed about her next steps.

She slowly takes her phone out of her pocket and calls her best friend. *She'll know what to do,* she thinks as she listens to the phone ring.

"Hi Kandis," Maeve finally answers after the fifth ring. "What's going on? How's Kyle?"

Kandis is silent, unable to put the words together to form a sentence.

"Kandis, what's wrong?" Maeve asks.

"Kyle is dead," she tells her friend, sadness in her voice. There's silence for a couple of seconds before Kandis adds, "I'm just leaving the hospital."

"Fuck Kandis. What happened? No, no don't say anything. Cell phones aren't secure."

"He did this himself. Alcohol poisoning probably."

"Alcohol poisoning?" Maeve questions. "Are you sure?"

"No, I'm not sure. But what else could it be?"

Both are quiet for a second, both deep in their own thoughts until Maeve mutters, "Alcohol poisoning? Drunk in life. Drunk in death."

"He'd been drinking for four days straight. I don't think he slept. I think it finally just caught up to him and killed him."

Chapter 68

Elijah

The fusion red sport model Tesla speeds along the country roads. The driver, a younger version of Brad Pitt, smiles as the race car-like vehicle glides past the million-dollar mansions on his way to his own grandiose home which sits back from the roadway, on ten acres of land in the rurals outside out of the city.

The car slows down as he pulls his foot off the accelerator and stops at the iron gates. He touches the button on the visor, and he watches as the entrance gate opens. His foot hits the gas again as he drives past the manicured lawns, through the row of mature trees towards the sweeping stone façade of the multiple level home and his five-car garage.

What the fuck, he thinks as he eyes a van parked in front of the house, his once-carefree smile dissipating as he takes in the brightly coloured advertisement on the side of the van, transforming the simple vehicle into a mobile billboard. *Home decorating. What the fuck decorating can she be thinking of? The whole house was just done when we moved in.*

Elijah parks the car and jumps out, a frown taking over his face, his eyes squinting, his forehead wrinkling, his eyebrows furrowed. *She must think money grows on trees. We've had this conversation. What doesn't she understand about being satisfied with what we have? She never fucking thinks about how the hell we're going to pay for anything. Leaves that all to me,* he thinks, as he stomps to the front door of his mortgaged-to-the-hilt home.

He throws open the door to the massive front foyer, a waste of space in his mind, but a grand, sophisticated entrance in his wife's world. He stops for a moment and listens, hears his wife's voice deeper in the house. He follows the sound of her twittering laughter and finds her sitting in

199

their family room, the floor-to-ceiling windows at the back of the house letting in brilliant light from the cloudless sky.

She looks up as she hears his footsteps, the conversation suddenly going quiet.

"Elijah, you're home," his wife London says, after a moment's silence. "I wasn't expecting you," she adds, looking at the large clock on the dining room wall.

Elijah doesn't say anything as he eyes the pile of fabric swatches, the deck of paint strips, and the numerous books of wallpaper samples sitting in front of his wife.

Aware of the stillness and the silent stares between husband and wife, the decorator, a trim, middle-aged woman with her hair tied into a tight face-pulling bun, stands up, straightening her light blue cotton shift dress. She nods towards her partner, her complete opposite, dressed in a bright yellow jumpsuit, with long kinky hair highlighted with sprays of blue and purple.

"Hello Mr. Greco," the decorator says. "We'll get out of your way," she continues, starting to gather her paraphernalia together. "We can get meet later this week, or next. Whatever works for you, London," she says, as she picks up a pile of wallpaper books, stacking several paint swatch cards on top, while her partner shoulders the rest of their materials.

The pair almost run to the front door, London following behind, apologizing for her husband's intrusion. She opens the glass wrought iron doors for their escape, agreeing that she will call them to set up another conversation about updating the main floor. London stands at the door, watching as the women load the colourful van, and waves as they drive towards the gates.

"What the fuck Eli?" London yells, as she slams the door, the glass shaking in its frame.

"What?" he retorts angrily. "I didn't say anything."

"The look on your face. Your stance. The huff. It told the whole story. It was the same as actually throwing them out of the house."

"What the fuck are they doing here anyway?" he asks, looking around. "There is nothing left in this house to decorate."

"Eli, you just don't get it. This," London dramatically points to the walls, the couch, the drapes, "is all out of style. Last year's colour. Last year's materials. All last year," she finishes, putting her hands on her slim hips and looking pointedly at her husband.

Elijah sighs, looking at his wife like she's crazy and doesn't have a grip on their reality. "London, we've talked about this. You need to slow down on spending. You need to stop trying to have the best, the latest, the most stylish thing in the magazines," he tells her, looking at the mass of glossy magazines still sitting on the coffee table.

"Yeah, like you've slowed down on betting the ponies," she counters. "If you stopped wasting money on the hags that have no chance of winning, we would have money for the necessities in life."

"Necessities in life? Are you kidding me?"

"Didn't you see my mom's face last time she was here? She walked around the room, shaking her head like she was abhorred by it. We need to do this."

"For God's sake London. We were talking about Lewis' whore. We were not talking about the décor," he counters.

"You weren't even part of our conversation. You might have been talking to my dad about Lewis' girlfriend, but Mom and I were talking about her new living room, how she blew out the window and made a double walk out to the deck. How she changed the colours of the room to accent the water and the lawns. You never hear what's going on around you. You never really see what's right in front of you. You're too wrapped up in your own little world and can't see what others see," London continues, her intensive bright green eyes narrowed, her coiffured brows furrowed, her normally smooth, gentle jawline clenched.

"We've talked about this, London. We can't do it now," Elijah says, not willing to give in.

201

"And are you going to stop gambling? Stop wasting our money?" she counters.

Elijah looks down at his feet for a moment before replying. "I have stopped betting on the ponies."

"When?"

"It's been over a week," he says with certainty.

"Really?" she asks, her eyebrows raising, her eyes widening.

"Really," he says again, a smile gracing his lips. *Except for that bet yesterday, the one with the 21/1 odds. Damn nag almost made it too. Came in third but I placed the bet to win. Next time I'll get her and then we'll be in the money big time,* he thinks as he opens his arms to his wife.

"I'm proud of you," London replies, taking a step forward, her facial expression lightening, a mischievous grin taking its place.

"Yup. I'm a changed man," Elijah says, as she comes into his arms, and he kisses the top of her head.

They stand for a moment in silence, before London moves her hand to her husband's crotch, and starts to massage him.

"Mmm" he whispers in her hair as he becomes hard.

"Mmm," she agrees, knowing that she will win the fight to redecorate the house.

***

An hour later, the pair are lying in their luxurious king-size bed, the sheets and blankets tossed around from their intense and highly pleasurable sexual encounter.

"Mmm," Elijah sighs, looking at his slumbering wife. "So, we're good?" he asks, rubbing her back. "No redecorating," he clarifies.

"Mmm," the blonde beauty replies arching her back to his touch.

"No redecorating," Elijah offers again as he moves his hand around to her stomach, stroking her soft skin as his hand continues down between her legs. He watches as she reacts to his touch, knowing that at this moment, she'll agree to anything.

"No redecorating," he says again, watching as her legs part and her breath starts to catch in her throat.

"London," he says, pulling his fingers away from her heat.

His wife opens her eyes. She looks at him directly. "No ponies, no redecorating," she offers before he moves on top of her, entering her, watching desire and pleasure cross his wife's face.

"Mmm," he murmurs, as he thrusts harder, faster, his body following its own path while his mind is a thousand miles away. *Jake says he won't sign any more bogus invoices. Maybe it's time for him to go. That would leave his job open. What an opportunity that would be! Give me free run at Preston. No Lewis. No Jake. Just a little sodium nitrite and it could all be mine.*

And I'm sure London is in his will. Sure, he'd leave the house, and most of his money to Stephanie, but he wouldn't forget his little girl. Probably leave her the condo in St. Maarten. That's worth a pretty penny.

Or perhaps I'll change the amount on the invoices. Yeah, lower them so he doesn't even have to sign them. But that would put the responsibility solely on me. Mmm, I'm going to have to think about this, he thinks, as a moan of pleasure escapes his lips.

Chapter 69

Alicia

Alicia sits back in her chair to contemplate next steps on the Preston case when her phone rings. A puzzled look crosses her brow as she looks at the call display. *The Chief? She doesn't usually call. Charlotte always sets up meetings or makes requests. This can't be good if she's calling me directly.*

"Detective Anderson," Alicia answers the phone.

"Alicia. It's Margaret O'Malley," the Chief starts, hesitating a second before continuing. "I just got a call from Jules. She says there was a suspicious death at the hospital and that she's been asked to investigate by Dr. Lee. She thought we should be involved."

The Chief pauses and Alicia fills in the silence. "I know Dr. Lee. I've dealt with him a couple of times. Seems to know what he's doing."

"Can you and Helen follow up with Jules and the doctor? Check out what's going on and brief me on the situation. I understand you're busy with the Preston case, but this could be important."

"We can definitely do that," Alicia replies.

"Thanks," is all Alicia hears before the line goes dead.

She looks to her left, her eyes falling on Helen's empty desk. *She's not far. All her stuff is here. Probably just gone to get a coffee,* she thinks as she stands up and spots her partner walking through the double doors to the detectives' workspace, two coffees in her hands.

Alicia waits for her partner to work her way across the room. As Helen reaches their work area, she hands her a coffee cup and asks, "What's going on?"

"We just got a call from the Chief. Seems Jules was called by one of the doctors reporting a suspicious death. She's asked us to find out what's going on and report back."

"Sounds interesting but aren't we a bit busy with the Preston case?"

"I agree, but this is coming from the Chief," Alicia justifies.

Helen simply shrugs her shoulders. "I guess the boss thinks this is important. Did you get the doctor's name?"

"The Chief said it was Dr. Lee."

"You know him pretty well, right?" Helen asks, giving Alicia a moment to nod her head in the affirmative. "Why don't you go see him and I'll talk to Jules to see if she has any preliminary findings and find out when she's doing the autopsy."

"Good idea," Alicia agrees, before shoving her computer into its bag and picking up her purse.

***

Alicia walks through the main doors of the emergency department at the hospital and moves towards the nurses' station. She asks for Dr. Lee. "Is this an emergency?" Nurse Sally asks before adding, "He's probably with a patient."

"It's not a medical emergency, but I need to talk to him. He reported a suspicious death to the coroner," Alicia advises, showing the nurse her identification.

"Give me a sec. I'll find him for you," the nurse tells her, before she hurries from behind the desk towards a hallway of closed examining rooms. She knocks on a door about halfway down the corridor, opens it and has several words with the occupant before closing the door and returning to the nurse's station. "Dr. Lee is with a patient, but he has asked that you wait for him. He's going to grab a coffee after he finishes," Nurse Sally says, gesturing back towards the patients' waiting room.

Alicia nods at the nurse. "Thank you," she says, before moving towards the overcrowded waiting room. She looks around the area, each chair filled with someone waiting to

205

see a doctor or a nurse; a teenager with long scraggly hair
cradling his arm to his chest, another resting their ankle on
their partner's lap as a lone running shoe sits under the chair,
a mother sitting in the corner rocking a baby with a soother
in their mouth, an old man holding the hand of an old woman
whose hair is dramatically pulled back from her red face, a
nasal cannula feeding her oxygen from the portable oxygen
tank in her lap. Alicia's eyes continue to move around the
room, until she spots the empty hallway just beyond,
typically used for patients being brought in by ambulance.
Alicia moves into the doorway of the hallway, strategically
standing where she has a view of the entire room and the
hallway leading to the nurse's station within the emergency
department.

After 15 minutes, Dr. Lee appears, speeding through the
waiting room towards her. "Coffee?" he asks, as he continues
towards the cafeteria, expecting to be followed.

After ordering coffee in the hospital's eatery, they sit at a
small table off to the side of the large open eating area.

"Thanks for meeting me," Alicia begins. "I understand
that you contacted the coroner's office about a suspicious
death."

"I did," Dr. Lee replies, blowing on his hot coffee. "Mr.
Kyle Sheridan."

"What can you tell me about him?"

"He came in with problems breathing, so we immediately
gave him charcoal, in case it was an overdose of something.
He was conscious at that point. He was slurring his words,
nauseous, vomiting, uncoordinated and complained of being
exhausted. We did a physical exam, listened to his heart and
his lungs and then he blacked out, became unconscious. We
did a bunch of tests – blood, chest x-rays, CT scan of his
lungs, ECG to look at his heart, all the while giving him an
IV of electrolytes, sugars, vitamins, and antioxidants," he
answers, stopping for a moment to take a sip of his coffee.
"Then we noticed that there were longer spaces between
breaths, that his breathing was noisy, and when we used an

ophthalmoscope to look at his eyes, they appeared glassy, which indicated a possible overdose. We'd already tried charcoal to counteract a drug overdose, but there was no change, so at that point, we gave him fomepizole, which is an antidote for some poisons. We also pumped his stomach, assuming that whatever was causing his issues was ingested. We drew more blood and checked for liver and kidney functioning and that's when we discovered that his organs were beginning to shut down."

There's silence at the table as the doctor takes another sip of his coffee and looks around the dining hall as if ensuring that no one is trying to overhear his conversation with the detective.

"We put him on a ventilator, moved him upstairs, did renal dialysis for the kidneys, trying to prolong his life, while still trying to figure out what was going on. I rushed more samples of blood and urine to the lab, but we lost Mr. Sheridan a day later before we could figure out what was going on. The symptoms were unusual. It's not natural for the entire body to be impacted so quickly and so severely."

"What do you think it was?"

"I'm not sure at this point, but I think he was poisoned. I ran tests but ran out of time. I've asked the coroner's office to complete the toxicology tests for the common homicidal poisons – arsenic, cyanide, thallium, strychnine, aconitine, atropine and antimony, most of which are easily accessible. If it's none of them, I've suggested they test for alcohol, bleaches, cleaners, insecticides, anti-freeze, and herbicides."

"How long will all this take?" Alicia asks. "How long to be sure that he was poisoned?"

"Well, that's the other problem. A lot of poisonous substances are difficult to detect as they are absorbed into the body within hours of ingestion. Some are even chemically converted to something innocuous already in the system." He stops and takes another sip of his coffee. "I'm 100% sure that he was given something. I believe this is not a natural death. That's why I called the coroner when the patient died."

The pair sit quietly for a moment, each deep in their thoughts until Alicia breaks the silence. "Is there anything else about this case that's suspicious? Anything else that I should know?"

Dr. Lee, who was looking at the table deep in thought, raises his head and looks into Alicia's dark brown eyes and confesses, "His wife was here, Kandis Sheridan. She brought her husband in. She was here most of the time. The only other visitor he had was her friend, but she didn't stay long."

Alicia waits for more, waits for the doctor to complete his thoughts, and voice his concern.

Dr. Lee drains the dredges of coffee from his cup before continuing. "I recognized her from all that hoopla on the news."

"Hoopla?" Alicia parrots questioningly.

"Yeah, the body they pulled from the lake," he answers. "The wife's friend was Maeve Preston. I saw her on TV a couple of times, doing interviews after her husband's death." He stands for a moment, before declaring, "I've got to go. Emerg is crowded today. Busy every day really. Let me know if there's anything else I can help with," he finishes, before scooting away from the table, striding across the public space towards the hallway to Emerg.

Alicia sits for a moment, mulling over Dr. Lee's suspicions. "Hmm," she murmurs before getting up and throwing her coffee cup into the recycle bin.

Chapter 70

Helen

"Any thoughts on Kyle Sheridan?" Helen asks Dr. Jules Diamond as she moves piles of bulky file folders off the visitor's chair, setting them on the window ledge, which is already brimming with stacks of paper. She sits down, facing the colourfully dressed red-haired coroner, waiting for an answer.

"Thanks for moving that stuff, Helen. My admin is on maternity leave, and I haven't had a chance to get a replacement for her. I can't believe how much work April used to do, and I didn't even notice," the coroner declares as she moves her mouse around the paper-strewn desk to activate her computer. "She'll definitely be getting a raise when she gets back," Jules smiles. "I called the Chief on this one. Dr. Lee was the one who flagged him. Mr. Sheridan came in a couple of hours ago, but we haven't had a look at him yet. Dr. Lee worked on him, tried to figure out what the hell was going on, but he lost him before he could figure it out."

"When do you think you'll have a chance to take a look at him?"

"Well, we need to get him in within 48 hours, before the organs and other body tissues deteriorate even more than they already have," Jules advises as she makes a couple of clicks on her computer screen and studies it. "I was thinking first thing tomorrow morning. I'll come in and start by 7 am. Probably take a couple of hours to complete," she raises her hand in a stop motion before continuing. "I get you are anxious for the results. I'm moving out a couple autopsies already booked to accommodate this victim."

"How long for results?"

"Depends on what we find. If there are no drugs present in his system, four to six weeks is standard. However, with what Dr. Lee suspects, it might take longer, six to eight weeks, for the necessary confirmation of the type of drugs present."

"Shit," Helen mutters under her breath, knowing that if this man was killed, two months will give the murderer time to cover their tracks and get rid of any incriminating evidence. "How flexible are those timelines? Anything you can do to shorten them up?"

Jules smiles at the detective sitting across from her, knowing the pressure that she and her partner will be under to solve the case, if in fact the man was poisoned. She pauses for a moment, moving tasks around in her head before finally announcing, "I think I've got a bit of overtime left in the budget. I'll fast-track the tests. See if I can get them done within four weeks."

"Four weeks?" Helen repeats, knowing that the coroner is doing her a huge favour, while still hopeful that the results could be obtained even quicker.

Chapter 71

Alicia

Connor looks up from his computer as Alicia and Helen walk into his team's meeting. He smiles at the detectives.

"Welcome, welcome," he says, motioning towards a couple of empty chairs for the pair to sit in. "Perfect timing. We were just about to start."

"Thanks for the invite," Alicia tells the forensics team lead as the pair sit down.

"I'll summarize our findings for the file, but I thought it would be nice for you to hear the team's work directly," Connor says, looking around at his people as they nod their heads in agreement.

Connor looks down at his computer screen before diving into their results to-date in the Preston case. "The warrant allowed us access to anything that belonged to Preston in the house, on the boat and in the boathouse, from computers and phones to guns and any weapons or tools, books or papers, clothes, basically anything that we thought could be pertinent. There's a full list of all the items we took on our shared drive." He pauses, looking around the room before his eyes fall on a nondescript tall, bald man dressed in a simple, plain white shirt and dark pants, sitting across the table from Alicia and Helen.

"Drew, talk to us about the cell phones," Connor asks, acquiescing to one of his experts.

"As you know, Mrs. Preston's phone was cloned," Drew starts, "Allowing us to construct a list of calls, both incoming and outgoing for her phone. The telecom provider supplied the call info for Mr. Preston's phone once they got the warrant. We are still tracking all the numbers down, but there are tons of calls on Mr. Preston's phone to and from Dominique Guillaume."

"We're aware of Lewis' assistant and their so-called friendship," Alicia advises.

"Calls between the two were constant - all day, all night. Most of the calls were relatively short. An average of about 20 calls per month over the last year during business hours but then it skyrockets to an average of 75 calls after hours," Drew explains. "We weren't able to get a current location on Lewis Preston's phone, probably because it's at the bottom of the lake," he smiles. "I can confirm that Mrs. Preston's phone was in Mexico at the time of her husband's death." He takes a sip of his coffee before continuing. "And I told you about the mSpy app she had on her phone so she could track exactly where her husband and kids were at all times."

"Unbelievable," Helen mumbles under her breath.

"Yup. Interesting mothering, I thought," he pauses and smiles at the people in the room. "The app told me that both her son and daughter were in the neighbourhood the day that Lewis Preston died," he concludes.

"You're right. An interesting technique for mothering. A little controlling, I would say," Alicia replies. "We know that both kids were in town that day. Rand went to the office and Lizzy was at the house. We found a camera at one of the neighbours' houses that had a good view of the driveway. It showed Izzy first and then Dominique Guillaume, Preston's admin, going to the house that afternoon."

"We've talked to both the son and the daughter again and are checking their alibis. We met with Ms. Guillaume and are expecting to talk to her again," Helen clarifies for the team.

"Cool," Drew replies. "I can tell you that Izzy was around Huntsville for most of the weekend, while Rand was only in the area from about 10 am to 12 noon, before heading back to Toronto," Drew adds.

"That syncs up with what they are telling us," Alicia says simply.

"We didn't have authorization to get specific cell phone info from Preston's VPs, but the warrant did include security card logs for the company," Drew smiles. "I can confirm that all five VPs," he looks to his computer before reciting the names, "Jake Beckham, Gavin Ferguson, Elijah Greco, Cory

Mercer, and Fallon Shipley were at Preston Construction, all in by 8 am, the first of them leaving at 5:30pm the day Preston died. None of them left the building at all that day. Preston checked in about 7 am and left at 1:05 pm," he finishes, looking up at the team.

"Maybe the sodium nitrite was given to Preston before he left the building," Helen suggests, making the members of the team pause once again.

"That's possible. Jules couldn't be specific on how much he ingested or the timing because he was in the water for so long allowing for some of it to dissipate," Alicia answers.

"How about the laptops?" Connor asks, moving the conversation back to forensics.

"We took two laptops, one that belonged to Lewis Preston, the second that belonged to his wife, which Preston could have accessed," he clarifies. "We also found an iPad, which was the Mrs., but again, Mr. Preston had access to it." He pauses for a moment, before continuing. "I haven't completed a full analysis of the computers yet, but I can tell you that I didn't find anything directly pointing to the death or murder of Mr. Preston. No out-of-line or out-of-character emails on either computer. No searches on either computer on how to kill someone. I did a search of Mrs. Preston's deleted cache, including websites, emails, and cookies. Nothing. Then I used our special tool that can recover documents, information that was supposedly permanently deleted, but again nothing of value," he concludes.

"Anything on the iPad?" Connor asks.

"I believe it was only used as an e-reader. The device was connectable to the internet, but the access was turned off. I would guess that Mrs. Preston simply bought books, downloaded them onto the iPad, and then turned the internet access off. I couldn't find any other documents or apps on the device."

After several minutes Connor moves the discussion forward again. "Thanks, Drew. Eddie, what about the guns? Were they registered? Who did they belong to?" Connor asks, as all eyes move to a tall, bearded man with clear-framed glasses sitting beside Drew.

"There were two guns – one an antique, an 1889 Colt double action. It was passed down from his father. The second is a Smith and Wesson 9 mm, model 986. Medium size," Eddie advises.

"Are they registered?"

"Yes, both are registered to Lewis Preston."

"Does he have a gun license?"

"He does."

"So, they are legal?"

"As far as I can see, I would say yes, it is legal for him to have both guns in his home."

"Had they been used lately?"

"No, there was no gunshot residue on either gun. Neither gun contained bullets. Both were clean," the technician finishes.

There's silence in the room for a moment before Helen asks, "Anything else about the stuff taken out of the house?"

"We're still sifting through their personal effects, but nothing else to report yet," Connor says before adding, "Oh yeah, we also took a look at the cabin cruiser at the dock. It was decked out with food, water, alcohol, the gas tank was full and looked like it was going to be used in the near future."

"Sounds like he was planning to use the boat while the wife was away. Maybe with his friend, Dominique Guillaume."

There's silence in the room for several moments, everyone taking in the comment about the dead man's plans to use his boat before Alicia tells Connor and his team, "Thanks for all your work on this case. And just to keep you guys up to date, the coroner has ruled that Preston died from sodium nitrite. We are working on finding its source and hopefully will be able to tie it back to one of our suspects. But keep up the good work. Anything you can find that will help us narrow it down and find the culprit will be greatly appreciated."

"How about we get together again once you've got more results," Helen suggests. "And if we find something, we'll let you know too."

Chapter 72

Luke

"Hi Mom," Luke says whispering into his cell phone, as he gets up from the table that he and Annie are sitting at in the College's library. "Everything OK?" he asks, as he walks towards the exit.

"Everything is good here. How about there? I haven't heard from you in a while," his mother says, worry creeping into her voice.

"We're good, we're good. We had a bunch of papers due and now we're getting ready for exams," he explains, knowing that he should have reached out, knowing that she worries about him, knowing that she only means well.

"Exams? Already?"

"Yup, it's amazing how time flies," Luke replies automatically as he leans against the exterior brick wall of the building.

"Well, then I won't keep you," Alicia concedes. "Say hello to Annie for me and call me when you're done," she instructs her son.

"Will do," he agrees. "Love you," he adds before disconnecting the line.

Chapter 73

Kandis

Kandis looks around her bedroom, an empty box in her hand. *Where to start? I know I shouldn't have taken notes when I was at the goddamn library. Fuck, I need to get rid of everything, anything that might make them think I had anything to do with Kyle's death, just in case they come looking. They won't believe I was just dreaming of getting rid of him, that it was just wishful thinking, that I didn't have the nerve to really do anything. In the end, he died the way he lived – drunk.*

She opens the top drawer of the bedside end table, picks up a notebook, turns to the first page and starts to read the list of the most common ways to kill someone. She throws it into the box and continues to the second drawer. *Fuck, I took way too many notes. And a lot of good they did me. They should have added alcohol poisoning to it. I guess it could have been included under poisoning.* She smiles as her mind sees Kyle reading the list and deciding to do himself in with alcohol. *Impossible. No fucking way he did this on purpose. He just pushed the envelope one too many times and didn't make it back.*

She moves to the double dresser and looks through each of her drawers, throwing in a couple of novels about murder, the box getting heavier as she moves along. After searching all the drawers, she moves onto the closet and goes through the pockets of each of her dresses, pants and jackets looking for any stray notes that may be incriminating.

I should have listened to my father. Don't write anything down. Never admit to anything. Make them prove it.

After the closet, she gets down on her hands and knees and looks under the bed, just in case anything fell and was accidentally pushed out of sight. *Nope, nothing there,* she thinks, getting back on her feet, looking around at the almost-cleaned room.

217

How the hell am I going to get rid of this, she thinks, as she looks at the box brimming with papers and notebooks. *If I had a fireplace, I could burn them, but it's the middle of the summer. That would be awfully suspicious. I could take it to the mall and throw it into one of their garbage cans, but what happens if someone sees me?*

I know. I'll take it to work. There's a shredder there. I'll work late and when everyone is gone, I'll shred it all. I'll put it in a couple different bags, mix it with stuff from work and put it in the recycling bin. No way will they find it there.

Just as she's about to leave her bedroom, Kandis stops in her tracks. *My disguise. I need to get rid of that. I need to package it up and drop it back at the second-hand store. Wonder if they have cameras there? I'll do a drive-by first and if there is no camera, I'll drop it. If there are cameras, I'll go to the Salvation Army store. And if they have cameras there, I'll go to another one. There has to be at least one in the city that doesn't have cameras.*

Shit. I shouldn't have started down this path. I knew I wasn't going to be able to do it, but no, I wanted to live in that fantasy world that I was going to be strong. I was going to be free from all his shit, all his baggage, all his Jekyll and Hyde bullshit.

Kandis closes her bedroom door behind her as she carries the heavy box up the hallway to the kitchen and out the door to her car. She slams the lid closed after putting the box in the trunk and looks around suspiciously, looking for anyone watching.

It'll be OK. He's gone. Life is going to turn around and be good for Abbie and me. Abbie will be able to concentrate on her sobriety and get her shit together, Kandis thinks as she walks back to the house.

Chapter 74

Alicia

"Your 10 o'clock is here. With her lawyer," the receptionist advises Alicia.

"I'll be right out," she replies, standing up as she disconnects from the call.

"Is she here?" Helen asks.

"Yup. Apparently, she's brought her lawyer. I'll get her. Meet you in Interrogation Room #1," Alicia advises, before moving towards the door of the Detectives' Den.

Alicia moves down the hall quickly, as if on an important mission. She rounds the corner into the reception area and spies Dominique Guillaume standing just inside the double doors of the foyer. A tall, very well-groomed large-framed man in a very expensive tailored grey, pinstriped suit, stands beside her, looking at his phone. As the detective moves towards the pair, he looks up, his dark brown eyes alert, a gentle smile on his face, as he pockets his phone and nods.

"Ms. Guillaume," Alicia greets, offering her hand, which is ignored, before Alicia turns to the man beside her.

"Detective Anderson," he greets. "I'm Sutton Fox. We've met before," he says, as they shake hands.

"Mr. Fox," Alicia acknowledges. "Please come this way. We have a room where we can talk privately." Alicia turns back to the hallway that she has just exited, takes a couple of steps before glancing back over her shoulder to ensure the pair are following her.

The room is several doors down the passage and Alicia can hear the clicking sound of the woman's three-inch heels on the tile floor. Alicia stops at the door, opens it, and stands back allowing Dominique and her lawyer to enter. Helen is standing just inside the room and smiles, motioning for the visitors to sit in the chairs on the opposite side of the table, across from the two chairs reserved for her and Alicia.

"Please have a seat," Alicia instructs before adding, "You remember, Detective Helen Hodgins?"

The dark-haired woman nods her head curtly at the question and moves to the opposite side of the plain metal table as her lawyer offers his hand and says, "Sutton Fox."

Helen nods in acknowledgement. "Thank you for coming in," Helen starts. "We just had a few questions that we wanted to ask you about Lewis Preston."

The woman doesn't say a word but nods her head in acknowledgement.

"Can you tell us about your relationship with Mr. Preston?" Alicia starts.

"You already know that," Dominique sighs, not even trying to mask her frustration with the process and the questions, as she turns her head to her lawyer.

"Yes, you told us you worked for him. For about three years, correct?"

The young woman nods her head in agreement.

"And your personal relationship?" Alicia asks.

"Not sure that's pertinent," Sutton Fox answers on behalf of his client.

"Friends?" Alicia asks.

"No comment," the lawyer answers.

"What's your baby's name?" Alicia asks.

"Her name is Paige. She has nothing to do with this," the woman answers firmly.

"Who's her father?"

"I don't see why that's relevant to this conversation," the lawyer protests, putting his hand up in a stop signal.

"Her parentage has nothing to do with why I'm here today. Next question or are we done?" the woman asks, ready to leave.

"If Paige's father is in fact Lewis Preston, then his death will have far-reaching ramifications for her."

The woman is quiet, looking across the table, her eyes moving from one detective to the other, her lips pursed together.

"Next question," Sutton Fox coaches.

"You realize that, don't you?" Alicia says, ignoring the lawyer. There is silence in the room until Alicia leans towards the pair and asks, "Did you kill Lewis Preston?"

Defiance blooms on Dominique's face, the golden flecks in her eyes sparkle as she uncrosses her legs and leans forward, mirroring Alicia's stance. "Why would I kill Lewis? He was my boss. My friend."

"Why were you at his house the night that he died?"

Dominique looks at her lawyer, pauses as he nods his head and answers, "Yes, I was there."

"Why? You're not working right now. You're on parental leave. Not sure why you would be at your boss' house."

"She's answered your question. Move on," Fox tells the detectives.

"Has she? She's agreed she was there but hasn't answered why," Alicia pushes before adding, "I understand that you don't want to answer our questions. But if you didn't do this to Preston, then I would think you would want us to find out what happened, who did this to your friend," she says the last word sarcastically.

The room is quiet for several minutes while Preston's assistant thinks through her options before she puts her open hands on the table. "Do you know what killed him yet? It was ruled a homicide but there was no cause ever given."

Alicia pauses before answering, "You're right. The coroner initially ruled it as homicide and brought in a forensics pathologist to determine the cause. The toxicology reports show beyond a shadow of a doubt that Lewis Preston died from sodium nitrite poisoning."

Dominique's face crumbles with the news as she looks across the table at the detectives. "Fucking bitch," she seethes.

"And who is that bitch?"

"His wife, of course. She was jealous of me. Angry, resentful that Lewis had finally decided to leave her, so we could be together. She's a bitter, malevolent old shrew that saw her life of luxury slipping away."

The lawyer reaches out and puts his hand on his client's shoulder to get her attention. She turns to look at him as he shakes his head.

"You are suggesting that his wife did it?" Helen asks. "You say she knew about your relationship with her husband, and that she wouldn't give him up. All that makes perfect sense, but she was out of the country when Lewis died. She was in Mexico. And there are witnesses."

"You're positive? Are you sure that she didn't stage that somehow?" Dominique asks, ignoring her lawyer.

"We have substantiated witnesses, proof that she was 5,000 kilometres away."

"She could have paid someone to do it. That would be something that she would do. A great cover being out of the country. Makes everyone think that she's the poor widow, when in fact, she poisoned that marriage. That's what you need to investigate. How she killed him from Mexico."

Sutton Fox squeezes his client's arm as he says, "My client has been forthcoming and is helping you find the person responsible for Mr. Preston's demise. I think we're done here."

There's silence in the room as Fox helps Dominique to her feet. Helen asks, "What do you mean poisoned the marriage?"

Dominique stops moving towards the door, turns around and crosses her arms across her chest. "I have nothing more to say," she says stubbornly.

The detectives pause for a moment before Helen offers, "If you didn't do this, isn't it better to tell us what you know, tell us about the wife, their relationship, tell us about the kids, talk to us about his business?"

Again, Dominique is silent as Fox has his hand on the doorknob ready to leave the interrogation room.

"No comment," she finally spits out.

"Mr. Preston must have been sick when you were at his house. Why would you leave him if he was so sick?" Alicia asks, trying to shock some answers out of the woman.

Dominique, standing by the door, shakes her head. "He said he was tired and didn't feel well. Said it must have been something that he ate. That his stomach was upset. I wanted to get him something – Pepto Bismol or Gaviscon or something, but he said no, it wasn't that bad. So I left. I didn't really think much of it. I'd had a hard couple of days with Paige. She's teething, and Lewis suggested that we call it a night."

"And then what happened?" Alicia asks.

"I went home. The next morning, I wanted to call him but knew he was in a meeting. Knew that when he was working, he didn't like to be disturbed unless it was urgent," she replies still standing at the doorway with her lawyer.

"And then what? You never called him?"

"Please Ms. Guillaume. I think we're done here," Fox says, opening the door.

But Dominique doesn't listen. "I waited for him to call. I waited until after 5 pm, thinking that the meeting took longer than he had thought it would, and then I called him. But he didn't answer. I left a message. I called an hour later, but again no answer. I tried every half hour for a while and then I had my mom watch Paige and I drove over to his house. I pounded on the door, but he didn't answer. I walked down to the water and the boat was there. I didn't know what else to do so I went home."

"You loved him? You say you were going to have a future together and all you did was call him a couple of times, go to the house, look around and then left? That's it? Sounds a little fishy to me, not like someone who says she was in love with the guy," Helen comments.

Dominique's head jerks back, the golden flecks in her eyes quivering in anger as she focuses on the detective. "You're right. I didn't handle it properly. I should have looked for him. I should have found a way to get into the house. I should have called the police and reported him missing. I should have called the hospitals. I kick myself every day that I may have been able to save him," she pauses for a moment, looking at the detectives facing her with frowns on their faces. "But don't you ever say I didn't love him. He was my everything. My life. My baby's father. We were going to be together," she finishes, her voice strong, a river of tears cascading down her face.

Fox tries to manoeuvre his client out the door as the detectives continue to question her. "What was the situation between Lewis and Maeve?"

Dominique shakes her head at her lawyer before answering. "Lewis and Maeve had a marriage of convenience. It had been that way for years. Lewis had other women in the past, he told me that, but when I started working for him and we got together, he said we were different. Said we had a future. That we loved each other and then we had Paige. And he said Maeve had changed. She had grown cold, distant, only spoke to him when the kids were around or they were out for some business function."

"Was that around the time that you two started your relationship?"

She thinks for a moment and shakes her head again. "No, it was after that. Probably around the time that I became pregnant with Paige."

"So maybe she knew about you two, knew about the baby."

Dominique continues to shake her head before putting up her hand up in a stop motion. "No comment," she finally chokes out before turning to her lawyer. "I'm done here," she says, as he fully opens the interrogation room door.

***

Alicia walks the two to the front door of the precinct. She watches as Dominique almost sprints to Fox's Jaguar, before she heads back to the interrogation room.

"Interesting take," Alicia says as she walks into the room where Helen is still sitting at the small table, a pen and paper in hand, making notes from the recent conversation. She pauses for a moment before continuing. "There's so much to unpack with her. Does she love him? Who knows? Does she need him? Not really. She could always get another job and raise the kid by herself. But kill him? I don't see any motivation for doing that unless he was breaking up with her, telling her that it was over. His death was premeditated, not something last minute or done during a fit of anger like pushing him into the fireplace or off the dock."

"I have a shit load of questions that I would have liked to ask her," Helen announces, sitting down across from her partner.

"Such as?"

"I would like to have pushed more on why she left him that night. Really? He was tired? He had a stomach-ache? He had an early morning meeting? None of that makes any sense. They had the house to themselves. They were in love. I'm sure he was probably in lust too. Makes no sense to me. And then the next day, she calls him a couple of times, she comes over but then basically that's it? What the fuck! I think I'd be a little more concerned if my boyfriend went missing. Seems too vague, too one-sided to me."

"Yeah, she's with him just before he dies. She says they had no issues but what if he was finished with her? Maybe they had dinner at his house so he could get rid of her quietly. Maybe he bought her the house as a parting gift, something to make the breakup softer. Maybe she knew what was coming and brought the sodium nitrite and sprinkled it on his dinner when he wasn't looking."

"Maybe he fell into the water. He was a big guy, no way she could get him out, so she just let him float away. Banked on him drowning if the sodium nitrite didn't get to him."

"Possibly. And cleaned up everything before she left."

"I would have liked to ask her about the house. Did Preston buy it? We still don't know. But if he did, look at the difference between her house and the freaking estate Preston had with his wife. Hundreds of thousands of dollars different. Was she really satisfied with an 1,800 square foot house when she could have had the palatial waterfront castle?"

"Maybe she couldn't take being second fiddle anymore, so she killed him. No one was supposed to know she was there. And then she comes here and tells us that his wife did it, trying to throw us off the scent."

"I think it's time we find out where the sodium nitrite came from. It's not like it's something you can buy at Shoppers Drug Mart."

Chapter 75

Dominique

Dominique slumps in the passenger seat as Sutton Fox walks around to the driver's side of the car and gets in.

"They tried to turn everything around. Said that I did it. Said that I wanted him dead," she sniffles.

Fox sits for a moment before telling his client, "I told you this was a bad idea. I told you that you didn't need to come here," he pronounces quietly, as if talking to a wayward child.

"I told them I would come in. And they kept calling me. I had to," she replies, tears running down her face. "They were brutal. They accused me of killing him," she almost screams.

Fox is still, watching his client. He hesitates before asking, "So what did you learn?"

"Learn?"

"Yes, I agreed that we would come today if we could question them. If we could find out as much as possible about Preston's death."

Dominique sits for a moment, her eyes looking out the front windshield, her mind remembering their conversation before she entered the police's lair. *He's right. That was his caveat when I forced him into talking to the detectives.* She's quiet for another couple of moments before she offers, "Lewis was poisoned."

"Yes, that's new," Fox states. "And sodium nitrite isn't something that is common in any household," he states. "Do you have any at home? Did you buy any recently?" he asks.

Tears leak down her cheeks, and she starts to shake. "I thought you believed me. I didn't kill Lewis," she chokes out.

Fox starts the car and slowly pulls out of the parking spot. "Calm down. Big breaths. We'll talk about it at the office, where we can discuss the whole situation, what they think,

227

what they know, what really happened," he directs, silence falling between them quickly.

Bloody hell. Sodium nitrite! What the fuck! They think I gave him sodium nitrite! That I wanted him dead! I would never do that to him. I loved him.

That fucking Maeve. She knew about us. Had to. Maybe she found out about Paige too. Found out about the house that Lewis bought for me. For us. Lewis said she was a conniving bitch and had ruled the house with an iron fist for years. And when she thought she was going to lose it all, she killed him.

But how could she have done it? She was in Mexico. She could have put the sodium nitrite in something that Lewis used all the time. Maybe in the sugar? The saltshaker? I didn't use either of those. Or maybe changed out his cholesterol pills with the fucking drug.

But why would she kill him? Wouldn't she be afraid that the cops would find out what she did? Lewis always said she was smart, and shrewd, kept the family afloat when they had next to nothing, helped him build the business in the early days.

Fuck. I was in the police station a long time. For something that was only supposed to take 15 minutes, it took almost an hour. Mom is going to have a hissy fit when I get home. Think she could look after her only granddaughter, always so afraid that I'll take advantage of her. Take advantage of her? When she's living in my house, living off of me.

She sure liked Lewis. Would have liked to have him for herself but I saw him first. She's probably more his age but I could make him feel good, make him feel young again, and I did. I captured his heart, his mind, his body and now what do I have? He talked about updating his will to include me and Paige, but I don't think he ever did.

Well, at least I have a house that's paid for. And a baby with no father. I'm going to have to fight for some of Lewis' money for Paige. I have proof that he's the father. Made him take a blood test when she was born just in case Maeve came and tried to make trouble for us. And his name is on her birth certificate. Maeve will probably offer me money to make me go away. She's like that. But it has to be big. It's got to be enough to take care of me and Paige. Enough so I don't have to go back to Preston Construction. Fuck, the looks I got before I left, those holier-than-though assholes watching my belly grow and whispering behind my back. No, I can't go back there. Maeve is going to have to cough up enough money for me to go away quietly.

Chapter 76

Alicia

Alicia watches the steady stream of traffic as Helen guides the police SUV down Highway 400. Her long chestnut-brown hair blows about her shoulders from the wind through the slightly opened sunroof and she pulls a hair clip out of her purse to tie it back.

"What do you know about this Detective Jasper Huntley?" Alicia asks.

"I did a bit of research on him. He's been with the force almost 35 years and he's been on this case since the UK notified Canada of a problem. Seems a post office box in Mississauga was included in a coroner's report in England, a mailbox where sodium nitrite was shipped from and that's what started the whole investigation."

"And they were able to link the box to this Kenneth Lawlor?"

"Yup. Along with five websites where he sold his goods."

"What a sicko."

"Sometimes the deviousness of the human mind is incredible," Helen agrees before a comfortable silence settles between them.

***

The meeting with Detective Jasper Huntley lasts about three hours and the detectives learn about the growing case against the accused, the things that can be proven and the craziness that they are still learning about this monster's unsavoury business of selling lethal drugs. Huntley is willing to share everything available from the five companies – sales information, email correspondence, shipping addresses, financials including payment information.

The pair decide to wait out the heavy rush hour traffic and have dinner in the city to talk about what they have learned. They sit across from each other in a small, Italian restaurant, menus in front of them.

"What looks good?" Alicia asks over the top of her menu.

"Hmm," Helen sighs while reviewing the menu. "I always seem to order the chicken parm," she answers, putting the menu on the table in front of her. "And you? What looks good to you?" she asks, smiling.

"I'm going to try the seafood pasta."

The two place their order with the waitress and sip their glasses of water, both in deep thought. "So, what do you think? Do you think the drugs that killed Preston came from this asshole?" Helen finally asks.

"It's possible," Alicia answers. "Could take us a while to prove it one way or the other."

"This guy sold drugs through five different company names. It's going to take a while to go through all the data to see if we can find a link to one of our suspects."

"And what if whoever the culprit is created a private email account? Something cryptic. Something we can't trace."

"I doubt that they would use their 'regular' email to buy sodium nitrite to kill someone. But if we can at least find a suspect email trail, we could get a warrant for the IP address."

"We can check credit card information. We have that info for Mrs. Preston, but not for anyone else. But if it was her, she's smart enough not to use her everyday credit card which could be tracked back."

"Could have used a virtual credit card?"

"Or gift cards. They're used in a lot of scams."

"What about cryptocurrency? No trail whatsoever."

There's silence as the waitress sets their dinners on the table. They pick up their knives and forks ready to dig into the scrumptious dinners. "Need any cheese?" the woman asks, waiting as both nod.

She leaves the table, returning quickly with a cheese grater and proceeds to add mounds of pungent parmesan to the tops of their pasta. As she walks away, Alicia asks, "Is there a way to check the other suspects' bank accounts or credit cards?" Do you think the judge would open up the warrant to cover banking info for our suspects? Or at least the family?"

"If we find something that specifically incriminates one of them, we could definitely go back to the judge for another warrant, but we need something specific to get him to expand it."

The two tuck their heads down and eat their dinner, with oohs and awes escaping as they enjoy their meal.

Helen finishes first and moves the napkin that had been sitting on her lap onto the now-empty plate. "Well, I guess that leaves lots of work for us," she smiles across the table at Alicia, who is wiping the remnants of her dinner from her lips, nodding her head.

"Lots," she agrees.

"One more – how about Maeve's internet browser? Did she change it? If so, Drew needs to check all of them, just to make sure she's not hiding anything," Alicia adds.

"So, I'm thinking delivery address…." Helen starts, taking a sip of her water before continuing. "If I was trying to kill someone, I wouldn't have them deliver the drugs to my house. I would rent a post office box or send it somewhere that couldn't be traced back to me."

"We'll put that on the list too," Alicia agrees. "We might have problems tracing a post office box especially if she paid with cash or used another name."

They are silent for a moment taking in the breadth of the problem.

Chapter 77

The Chief

"So, what did you get? Is it a homicide?" the Chief asks her detectives, not even looking away from her computer as Alicia and Helen enter her office.

The two stand for a moment inside the door, hearing her question before they move forward in unison, each sitting on one of the luxurious chairs in front of the Chief's massive desk.

"Well, don't keep me in suspense," the Chief says, looking up at their solemn faces. "What's wrong? What aren't you saying?"

"Dr. Lee believes that the victim, Mr. Kyle Sheridan, ingested some type of poison. He ran a bunch of tests but was unable to keep the man alive long enough to pinpoint the culprit."

"I talked to Jules and the autopsy happened yesterday morning, but we haven't heard anything yet."

"That's great. Let me know what Jules finds," the Chief replies dismissively, turning back to her computer screen, while her detectives continue to sit in front of her. She clicks a couple of keys before turning back to them, and asks, "What else?"

"Jules is confident that the body will give her the information required to decide why Mr. Sheridan died. The problem is that test results, especially if drugs or poisons are involved, usually take six to eight weeks," Helen offers, raising her hand before the Chief can interrupt. "She has agreed to throw some overtime at it and thinks she can get the results in four weeks."

"What the hell! That's still a long time to wait. I thought she would be able to turn this around quicker than that."

"We hear you Chief and we're just as miffed as you are, but she says once they confirm that he ingested drugs or poison, it takes time to understand exactly what and how much," Alicia offers.

"How long to rule if the death was natural, accidental, homicide or suicide?" the Chief pushes.

"Usually about the same timing."

The Chief sits back and folds her hands on the top of her bare desk. "Dr. Lee seemed pretty convinced that this man was helped to his death. What do you two think?"

"I tend to side with Dr. Lee. He's a very competent doctor. He's seen it all, working in Emerg. He asked for all the right tests, did all the right procedures but he couldn't stop Mr. Sheridan from dying," Alicia offers.

"And he added an interesting tidbit. Seems the deceased's wife had a visit from her best friend, Maeve Preston," Helen adds.

"Hmm," the Chief mutters. "Nothing strange about a friend comforting a friend. But the timing is suspect. Both husbands die within weeks of each other, and both are suspicious." Again, she steeples her hands together, and leans back in her high-back executive chair, assessing the situation and their options, before changing the subject. "Talk to me about the Preston case."

Alicia and Helen give the Chief a quick summary of the forensics pathologist's conclusion that Lewis Preston died from sodium nitrite and their meeting with Detective Jasper Huntley, the lead on the Kenneth Lawlor case. They discuss the mountain of documents, emails and orders that they received and the effort it will take to sort through it, looking for something that could lead back to Lewis Preston's killer.

There's silence for a moment before the Chief leans forward in her chair. "I know you're busy with the Preston case, but maybe you could spend some of your spare time doing a background check on the Sheridans - find out if there are any priors for the deceased or his family, any police calls to the address, any neighbour complaints, collect hospital records including Dr. Lee's reports," she suggests. "We can't actively pursue this until we get word that it is in fact a homicide, but we can definitely be prepared for that day," she finishes, looking at the pair.

"We'll fit it in," Alicia agrees, nodding first at the Chief and then at her partner.

Chapter 78

Alicia

Alicia, Helen and Nico sit in one of the boardrooms in the precinct. Papers, charts and emails are scattered across the table. Nico, their financial guru, is in his element as he explains that the company is financially healthy and the estimate on the internet is valid, $100 million. He has reviewed the income statements, the balance sheets and the cash flows ad nauseam to the pair and finally concludes that Preston Construction has stable earnings, a great return on equity and is valued comparably with other companies of the same size and in the same business.

When asked about anything strange, Nico flips to a new spreadsheet on his laptop. He shows them that Rand Preston has been on the payroll for exactly 22 months, at a fairly decent salary, and he has just received a whopping 30% increase, a raise that took effect the day Preston died.

The detectives smile as Nico laughs, suggesting that he too would like a 30% increase.

Nico adds that Maeve Preston is also on payroll with Preston Construction, has been since its inception and that this is typical for smaller companies and is basically a tax dodge. He goes on to explain that there have been no large amounts withdrawn or deposited in Maeve Preston's personal account within the last year, however, there has been a lot of buying activity, more than usual, during the couple of weeks before her husband passed, but again explainable – clothing, shoes, new suitcases, the cost for the all-inclusive trip and a substantial purchase at a jewelry store in Playa del Carmen.

The forensics accountant expounds on Lewis Preston's wealth stating that he could have quit work, travelled the world and still left his wife and kids lots of money. His weekly pay cheque was excessive, even for the President and CEO of a successful company, and he also consistently gave himself a substantial year end bonus.

236

Helen asks about the two condos Preston purchased for his son. Nico produces a statement of company assets and Rand's condos are listed, confirming that they belong to Preston Construction. He then pulls up a separate document which states that Lewis gave himself a substantial bonus, enough to purchase a house in the Barrie market, around the time that Dominique gave birth to their daughter, Paige.

The financial wizard is asked about any issues, gaps, holes, or anything financial that stands out as a red flag. The young man smiles again, as he puts his head down and flips to another document on his computer showing them a list of invoices for amounts over $10,000 that Preston Construction has paid out within the last year. He filters the data for one company – London Construction – telling the pair that Preston Construction has paid this company almost $2 million within the last six months for services rendered. Alicia and Helen look at each other, wondering what they're missing before Nico advises that there is no such company in Canada and that the cheques have been mailed to a post office box in Barrie.

The detectives sit back, the magnitude of the situation growing in their minds. But Nico is not done yet and gushes as he tells them he pulled the invoices from London Construction, and that all of them were approved by Elijah Greco for work completed, and then subsequently signed by Jake Beckham, due to the substantial dollar amount. He advises that when he couldn't track down a company with that name in Canada, he reached out to Canada Post for information on the post office box. Exaggerating his position with the Barrie Police, he was able to get information on who rented the box. "Elijah Greco," he says breathlessly, a huge smile on his face.

"Great work," Alicia comments at the end of Nico's dissertation. "Greco and Beckham need to be charged with fraud. We need to get the OPP and FINTRAC, the Financial Transactions and Reports Analysis Centre of Canada, involved in this."

"The question is whether Beckham knew about London Construction? Did he help Greco set the whole thing up? Beckham would normally sign invoices for the large amounts that were submitted, but he could still cry innocent, that he just thought it was a company that was being used for work. But the number of invoices and the amounts – that should have been a red flag to him," Helen considers.

"No, he knew. He would have to," Nico offers. "When a new contractor is utilized, a full financial review is completed to ensure they are on the up-and-up before they are added to the company's vendor list."

Alicia moves to the edge of her chair, listening carefully before adding, "Maybe Preston found out about the payments and decided to do something about it. He was taking more of an interest in the banking, the money. Maybe his two VPs found out that he knew, and they decided it was time to take him out. Beckham said he always looked after the company when Preston was on vacation. Maybe he thought his death would give them free run to embezzle more money with fake invoices. Either way, this puts Beckham and Greco at the top of the list of murder suspects."

"Wonder what they were doing with the money? Beckham's been with Preston Construction for years. He must make a pretty penny. Greco is fairly new. Whose idea was it to steal from the company and why?" Helen asks as Nico sits back, a smile on his face, a lock of his hair escaping his man bun, falling across his forehead, his face almost glowing from excitement.

Alicia smiles at his enthusiasm. "Give it up Nico. What do you know?"

"Meet Mr. and Mrs. Greco," Nico announces as he pulls up a wedding picture on his laptop – a shot of a bride and groom in formal wedding attire, their parents flanking each of them. Alicia leans in to look at the photo, taking a couple of moments before recognizing the groom. Elijah Greco is in a black dinner jacket with matching pants, a stark white shirt with a bright red bow tie, standing beside the bride, who is in a classic white, floor length strapless gown, her long flowing blonde hair cascading over her shoulders. Alicia's eyes roam to the parents on either side of the couple, narrowing as she recognizes the bride's father, Jake Beckham.

"The bride's name is London." Nico's grin grows as Alicia and Helen connect the couple and the bride's father with London Construction.

Chapter 79

Kandis

Kandis stands in the middle of Kyle's garage and looks at the overabundance of musical paraphernalia - guitars, speakers, amplifiers, microphones and their stands, cords running everywhere, and music books strewn everywhere. *Fuck, what the hell am I going to do with all this? Is this all Kyle's? Who the hell paid for all this? Stupid question, Kandis. You did. You paid for all of this. He just bought anything that they needed. The boys simply brought their instrument and everything else was his. He never thought twice about spending the little money that we had. Never a thought for the impact to Abbie or me. He always wanted the best. Always wanted everything, just in case. Son of a bitch.*

You'd think one of his supposed friends, his so-called band members, would have at least volunteered to help me clean this up. Offer to sell this stuff or at the very least haul it away.

Maybe Eric can help me with it. Put it on Marketplace or take it to the music store in town. I'm not sure if it's even worth doing that.

Fuck!

I can't do this now. Too tired. Too stressed. Maybe tomorrow. Maybe next week, Kandis thinks as she turns from her husband's mess, walks to the door and slams it behind her, leaving everything for another day.

Chapter 80

Billy

Billy watches as Nick, the dealer who serves the Distillery District, runs across the busy downtown street to get away from his invasive questions about Izzy Preston and Cody Bruno.

Nick didn't know their full names, but he did know their faces. He sure knew the number of times they bought and the massive dollars that they spent.

I'll have to call those detectives. I knew it was a dead end, but it was worth a try, I guess. From what Nick says, they are crack heads. They smoke it, they inject it, they snort it, anything to get it into their system, the faster the better.

Said he's sold them some poppers if they couldn't find the bucks for crack, but it was only a stop gap until they got enough money for the real stuff. Poppers don't give a big enough high.

Said that the girl sells herself to get most of their money. She talks about having followers online that pay for her opinions, her suggestions, her recommendations but obviously that's not quite working out for her, and her body is what brings in the bucks.

They never asked him about sodium nitrite, or anything else that would kill someone. Nick said that he doesn't have any, that he's never been asked for it by anyone and wouldn't even know if he would be able to get it.

Too bad I couldn't help the detectives close their case. Hopefully they can trace the purchase of the sodium nitrite to that Suicide King guy.

Guess I've blown my cover in this part of town. Not sure I was able to help the detectives, but it is what it is.

Chapter 81

Helen

Helen places her fingers on the keyboard. *Think I'll start with my old favourite - Facebook. Then, I'll move on to Instagram, Twitter, oops I mean X. You never know what you can find and if there's time, I'll search for accounts on Pinterest, YouTube, TikTok, and Reddit,* she thinks as her eyes move to the clock in the lower corner of the computer screen.

Shit, I almost forgot Google. Let's see if any of the Sheridan family show up there, maybe a news article. Think I'll start with Kandis and then move on to Kyle. He probably doesn't have a big presence. Probably not a computer kind of guy, though he might have spent time chatting or in music or sports rooms. I bet the daughter chats a lot. All kids that age do these days. Helen moves a yellow pad of paper close to her laptop, aligns a pen beside it, and begins to type.

Five hours later, the clock on the computer screen reveals midnight has come and gone. Helen sits back in her chair exhausted. *Amazing, simply amazing what people reveal without even thinking about it,* she reflects as her eyes move to the extensive notes she has taken.

Kandis has a public profile on Facebook. Lots of old pictures of Abigail, who goes by Abbie – at a dance recital, a birthday party at the bowling alley, hitting a baseball, and a few pictures of a trip south – looks like the one that Maeve Preston talked about when we questioned her. Great alibi. The most recent picture of Abbie looks like her last birthday. In one of the pictures, she's blowing out the candles on a cake and her mother is standing beside her with a big smile, but the girl looks out of it. Her eyes are bloodshot, and the pupils are pinpoints.

Kandis only has 95 friends on Facebook, which is a lot lower than the average of 338. It looks like a lot of her contacts are from work. And of course, Maeve Preston is a friend. I can't see any messages between her and her friends. Facebook is too secure for that.

Doesn't look like she has an account on any of the other apps, except LinkedIn. Not much there but she does have a lot of contact with people from work, people in the industry. She's been with the company for almost 15 years and has worked her way up from call centre to secretarial to management. She doesn't post a lot of stuff but does comment on other's promotions and job changes.

Kyle has public accounts on YouTube and TikTok with posts about the band he plays with, including a couple of videos of the group doing covers of other people's music. No original songs. The ensemble doesn't seem to play gigs or go anywhere where fans could see them. More like a garage band that just wants to have fun. Nothing wrong with that, but maybe if they worked at it, they could have gone somewhere.

He spends a lot of time on dark sites looking at porn. Found a couple of sites where he added insensitive, ill-chosen remarks agreeing and egging the creators of the content to become more violent, and more graphic. Not the making for the Father of the Year award, and he didn't even have enough sense to make up a code name or a pseudonym.

Abbie has a huge social media presence on Facebook and Instagram. Everything she does, everything she sees, and every thought she has is put on at least one of the apps, usually both. Her posts give a blow-by-blow of the trauma and turmoil that goes on in her family home from the loud fights to the aggressive, physical violence between her parents. She blames her father, his attitude, his violence, his alcohol consumption, his drug use, as the reasons she left the house on several occasions, preferring to live on the streets rather than live with him. Poor child. Only 16 and has been to hell and back.

She talks about being back at home but is not sure how long she'll be able to stay.

Chapter 82

Alicia

Alicia pushes the lid on her laptop closed, sits back in her dining room chair and gazes across the living room to the large picture window looking out onto the street. *Everything is so quiet around here,* she sighs. *I sure miss Luke and that silly little dog, George. The cutest thing I've ever seen and oh so smart. And he knows it,* she smiles to herself as visions of the little black and tan miniature pincher standing on his back legs, twirling as if a ballet dancer, begging for just one more liver treat, dances through her mind's eye. *Can't wait to go down there in a couple of weeks for their graduation. Then they'll come home. Hopefully to stay, depending on the job situation.*

Alicia's eyes move from the darkness out the window to her yellow notepad sitting beside her computer, and the notes she has taken from the police databases – CPIC, the RCMP's Canadian Police Information Centre which is a national information-sharing system, ViCLAS, the Violent Crime Linkage Analysis System which reports family and domestic assault, missing persons, abductions and child luring, and the YCJA, the Youth Criminal Justice Act which records youth criminal activity across the country. She also accessed the Personal Health Information Protection Act which gave her access to hospital records and doctors' visits for the Sheridan family.

Well, it's been an educational night. Lots out there, if you know where to look, she thinks as she peruses her notes.

Kyle Sheridan was born on March 11, 1980, in Orillia, Ontario. No health problems until he hit high school. Seems he was part of the school's hockey team and suffered numerous broken bones – his wrist, his arm, his ankle – and a considerable number of concussions from fighting, so many that the team doctor suggested he had chronic traumatic encephalopathy which ended his possible illustrious hockey career. A year later, the once-promising hockey star was driving after a night of drinking when he drove off the road and hit an old oak tree. The tree fell onto the roof of the vehicle killing his best friend and hockey star Todd Sloan instantly. Kyle was charged with impaired vehicular manslaughter in an adult court, even though he was still a minor, and spent the next eight birthdays in prison before being released when he was 25 years old. Alcohol continued to play a big part in Kyle's life with several impaired charges over the next five years, culminating with the permanent loss of his license. During this time, Kyle Sheridan attended three separate rehabilitation programs, of which none helped him quit drinking.

Kandis Sheridan, family name Sweeney, was born May 25, 1985, in Barrie, Ontario. She had a tumultuous childhood, as her parents, Bob and Joan Sweeney, wrestled with their own alcohol demons. The Sweeneys divorced when Kandis was 10 years old. Neither parent seemed to get sober after that and the girl was bounced back and forth between them until she finished high school, and started work at a telecommunications company, where she's been ever since, slowly moving her way up the corporate ladder.

Whether the two knew each other before Kyle's incarceration or met after he was discharged from prison is unknown. They married September 10, 2009, five months before their daughter, Abigail Lynne, was born.

The married life of Kyle and Kandis was marred with many visits from the police, usually instigated by neighbours reporting excessive noise, music, and crowds of people at the Sheridan residence, whether in their small apartment in downtown Barrie in the first couple years of marriage or at their modest bungalow in an older subdivision in the city's south end later on.

Kandis has had numerous visits to the emergency department with broken bones, sprained ankles, and torn ligaments in her shoulder, which she always blamed on her clumsiness. The visits were not deemed suspicious by the medical staff and no follow-up was ever conducted.

Abbie visited Royal Victoria Hospital's Emerg with typical childhood maladies – a broken ankle when she was six years old, a few other bumps and bruises, plus a couple of urinary tract infections, pneumonia, strep throat, and other types of infections requiring medical assistance.

Alicia continues to scan her summaries, her eyes falling on the notes she made about Abbie's difficulties at school – from being suspended on several occasions for verbal and physical abuse of students and teachers, to smoking both tobacco and marijuana on school grounds to intoxication. There were no real explanations for her constant truancy other than her age and being friends with the wrong crowd.

The police records note that she was reported as a runaway half a dozen times, sometimes brought home by the police, sometimes going home on her own.

The kid sees everything, sees the mother and father struggle to get along, fight to put food on the table while only one of them works and the other parties, drinks, and probably does drugs with his friends. She internalizes it, dabbles with alcohol and drugs until it gets a hold of her, and she ends up living on the street. Wonder if there was anything else that drove her out of the house? There's no mention of physical or mental abuse, but the home situation would have been ripe for something like that to happen.

Alicia rises from the chair, leaving her laptop and papers strewn on the dining room table. She walks into the kitchen with her empty coffee cup, before pulling out the dishwasher rack and depositing it. She shuffles down the hall towards her bedroom, exhausted from a long day at work, tired from the hours she's put in researching the lives of Kyle and Kandis Sheridan, wondering what information Helen has been able to uncover.

Chapter 83

Alicia

"Finally," Alicia breathes, as she navigates the Barrie Estates Department website. "They've filed Preston's Certificate of Appointment. We'll be able to see it now."

"His what?" Helen asks.

"They've officially changed the name for probating a will to Application for Certification of Appointment of Estate Trustee," Alicia replies, her eyes glued to her computer screen.

"Wow. That's certainly a mouthful," Helen comments before moving her chair in closer to Alicia's shoulder, watching as she clicks through the website looking for the document. "Let's see who is getting what from the old man."

Alicia pauses after several minutes and sits back in her chair. "Well, the good news is that they have the document and it will go through the process. The bad news is that it hasn't yet been scanned. But never fear, I have a contact at the Barrie office. I'll just give her a call and see how we can get our hands on it sooner rather than later," she finishes, picking up her cell phone and scrolling through her contacts.

"Here it is. Let's see if Jan can help us out," she says, as the phone line rings to her old friend Jan Jerome.

Alicia's phone clicks as Jan picks up. "Look what the cat dragged in," her friend laughs into the phone as a greeting. "How the hell are you?"

Helen stands up, makes a drinking motion, as Alicia holds the phone to her ear and nods yes. Helen smiles as she leaves the Detectives' Den for the short walk to the cafeteria to give a couple of old friends time to catch up, and for Alicia to ask her friend for a favour.

***

Alicia and Helen sit at their desks in the Detectives' Den, their faces glued to their computer screens, the odd hmm and ah and uh-huh escaping their lips. Alicia finishes reading the document first, going back to several places to re-read, googling a couple of things included in the will before sitting back in her chair, her eyes closing as she contemplates what she has just read. Helen finishes shortly after Alicia and turns to her partner. "Well, that was interesting," she comments.

Alicia opens her eyes and nods her head in agreement. "Definitely."

"Very sad though, when you think of it. The guy has over $50 million in cash, bonds and shares, plus a company worth about $100 million and he's dead. Such a waste."

"Well, at least the will was updated after Paige was born and he confirms that he is the father of the little girl."

"He does. Interesting how he divided the money up."

"Yeah, $22 million for his wife, $22 million for his girlfriend," Alicia says.

"That's got to burn the wife's ass. She's put in over 20 years and gets the same as some floozy who just showed up a couple of years ago. I wouldn't be happy if I was Maeve Preston."

"I hear you. But he does give the house and cottage to her, which is valued a lot higher than Dominique's place."

"Yeah, still not enough. Three years versus twenty years. Somehow it doesn't seem right to give them the same amount of cash."

"And he certainly has some very specific rules for the kids to get their $2 million pittance," Alicia says.

Helen laughs, before adding, "Not sure if the guy was cheap or smart. Only $2 million per kid, when he had $50 million?"

Alicia smiles. "And the $2 million is contingent on his conditions. Rand's inheritance starts now and Preston was very clear that it takes the place of his ongoing allowance. He will get $100,000 per year for twenty years and after that, he's on his own."

"His rules for Izzy to get her money are a lot stricter. She's got to be drug and alcohol-free for six months before she gets her first installment and then like her brother, she would get the rest annually as long as she stays sober."

"Her boyfriend won't like that," Alicia says.

They sit for a moment, Cody Bruno's question of when Izzy would get her money ringing in their ears.

"Even with the 9-month-old, his terms are very specific."

"Yeah. Definitely put up some guardrails so it didn't get spent willy-nilly."

"Holding it until she's 18 years old is not a bad thing."

"Yeah, but he's very specific that it can only be used for her education."

"And if she doesn't use it for school, she can't have it until she's 25, barring any legal issues, arrests or drug, alcohol addictions."

"Wonder when he put this together? It must have been recent, especially with the specifics around Rand and his football scholarship."

"And Paige is only 9 months old," Alicia adds.

"Yeah. Scott Wolfe is all over this – from writing the will to administering it, to overseeing the personal assets to both the wife and the girlfriend, holding the funds for the three children until Preston's conditions are met. Wonder if Maeve and Dominique knew the specifics?"

"Certainly gives both of them motive. I mean $22 million is not a bad haul."

The two sit back in their chairs, contemplating Preston's will and how he continues to control his wife, his girlfriend, and his children, before Helen adds, "And then you have the company. He created a testamentary trust. Never heard of that before."

"That's what I was googling when I finished reading the bloody thing. Basically, Preston set up a family trust to run his company after he died. He named Scott Wolfe as the Chairman, someone who oversees the business while giving him leverage to hire a CEO to run the day-to-day. He also

249

appointed the current VP team to stay in place, less Jake Beckham and Elijah Greco. He's let them both go with the minimum severance possible."

"Interesting that he eliminated those two. Pulling both of them from the team on the testamentary trust would be a good indication that he either knew or had some inclination that something was going on."

"What if Beckham and Greco decided they needed to get rid of Preston before he found out about the thefts? Especially if Beckham thought he would get to run the place once Preston was gone. He could rape and pillage the place if he was sitting at the top of the company."

"So, who gets the company?"

"Preston has put the company in trust, which according to google can last for up to 21 years," Alicia replies glancing at her computer. "The company is technically owned by Maeve Preston, and it is being managed by Scott Wolfe."

"Interesting way to keep it functioning, while making sure that there's someone to run it."

"Wonder if the wife and girlfriend knew about this wrinkle?"

"The trust doesn't mention a salary or shares or money from the company for any of the family, but I'm sure that is something the Chairman can make happen."

"Which brings us to another big winner in Preston's death," Alicia starts before pausing, her mind racing before she adds, "Wolfe."

Helen pushes back in her chair, puts her hands behind her head, and looks towards the ceiling as if in deep thought. Alicia waits for a couple moments before asking, "What are you thinking?"

She pulls her hands back and puts them in her lap. "Preston's will is definitely interesting, but it doesn't really eliminate any of our suspects. And really, it's just given our suspects more motivation to end Preston's life." She stops and holds up her right hand, her index finger raised. "First, there's the wife. Will or no will, I would put her at the top of the list, even if she was out of the country." She adds her middle finger, holding up the pair. "Then you've got the mistress. She must have known about the will. Knew about the $22 million that she was going to get when he died. That is definitely motivation to off someone, even if he is her best friend, the father of her kid, and all the mushy things that she said," Helen smiles and puts up her ring finger and baby finger. "Then you've got the kids – I would say both of them. They both saw him the day he died. It could have been one of them or maybe they decided to work in concert to get rid of their father for the $2 million pay out," Helen stops and holds up her entire hand, adding the thumb. "And then there's Izzy's boyfriend, Cody. He was with her when she stopped at the house. She says he stayed in the car, but who knows. He didn't get the stuff from his dealer, but he might have got it somewhere else. He's hot for Izzy's old man's money."

Helen leaves her right hand raised; all fingers representing a suspect and raises her left hand putting two fingers in the air. "And then there's Beckham and Greco. Maybe Preston found out about them stealing from the company. Christ, Beckham has been there for years. He's got a reputation in the industry. Maybe Beckham killed Lewis before it all came out – a last-minute effort to save himself. And I would say the will adds Scott Wolfe to the list," she says adding another finger. "He's going to be in charge of Preston Construction, as much or as little as he wants and he will be drawing a salary, probably even bonuses whenever he wants."

"That's eight suspects."

"We need to connect one of them to the sodium nitrite. We need to go through all the orders, all the emails, everything that Peel shared with us from the Suicide King. One of them has to be there."

"Or they bought it from somewhere else."

Chapter 84

Alicia

"We had the chance to read both Lewis Preston's will and his testamentary trust," Alicia advises Scott Wolfe, but he doesn't acknowledge the comment.

"We were surprised to hear that you are going to be the Chairman of Preston Construction," Helen adds, but still there is silence on the phone.

"No comment?" Alicia asks, waiting through the silence before the lawyer finally answers.

"I'm not sure what you're looking for. I knew of Lewis' wishes. We worked together to put them on paper, both from a personal perspective and for the business," he finally admits.

"We would have thought he would have left more to each of his offspring," Helen suggests.

"Everything included in the documents were directives from Lewis," the lawyer repeats. "If that's all ladies," he says about to end the call.

"We do have a couple of questions specifically around Jake Beckham and Elijah Greco."

"Such as?" the lawyer asks.

"The testamentary trust specifically leaves these two VPs out of Preston Construction's new organization. Why was that?"

"That was Lewis' decision," the lawyer answers smoothly.

"Nothing else?" Helen asks.

"Such as?" Wolfe asks, not giving the detectives any unsolicited information.

"Our financial forensics team are examining the books for Preston Construction, and they have found several interesting payments to London Construction."

"Can you be more specific?" the lawyer asks.

"Was Mr. Preston aware of any issues with London Construction?"

Scott Wolfe pauses for a moment, knowing fully what the detectives have found in the accounts payable division of Preston Construction. "Mr. Preston brought London Construction to my attention, and I had my legal research team look into the company, its business, its owners, and the amount of invoices submitted."

"Could you give us more details?" Alicia asks. *It's like pulling fucking teeth,* she thinks to herself. *We are not the enemy here.*

"Well, if you're asking me these questions, I'm assuming that you've found out a little bit about London Construction as well," Wolfe answers evasively.

Alicia is fed up with the vagueness and raises her voice. "Mr. Wolfe, we understand that you represent the late Mr. Preston and that you are now Chairman of his company. We are trying to understand the puzzle, understand who wanted Mr. Preston dead, find the killer and make them accountable for their actions."

"Honourable. Very honourable intentions, but I'm not sure that any of Preston's business matters have anything to do with his death."

"And you know this how?" Helen asks.

"The man had been in business for years. And he always treated his employees, his contractors, his customers fairly."

"That could all be true; however, the man is now dead, and it has been ruled a homicide. And we are trying to find out who killed him. Hence, we are exploring a number of possibilities, including you becoming Chairman of the company and the London Construction situation." Alicia pauses for a moment for effect before adding, "Are you able to give us any insight into what Mr. Preston knew, and what you know about this company, this situation."

"Mr. Preston was aware of London Construction. The number of payments and their amounts were brought to his attention by one of his accounts payable managers, who was concerned with the number of invoices in such a short period of time and their excessive amounts."

"And?" Alicia leads.

"He asked me to have my legal research team take a look and we discovered the same thing that you did. The company, London Construction, doesn't legally exist in Canada."

"And what are you doing about it?"

"We have contacted the OPP and FINTRAC and they have opened an investigation for fraud."

"And?" Alicia asks again.

"The OPP will be charging Jake Beckham and Elijah Greco with fraud over $5,000. If convicted, they could each face up to 14 years in jail."

"Don't you think you should have mentioned this to us? Don't you think the possibility of 14 years in jail is motive to kill someone?" Alicia asks, astounded that the lawyer would not be willing to share such information.

"I wanted to tell you, but as Chairman of the company, it was inappropriate."

Alicia simply shakes her head at this explanation before there's an audible click as the lawyer disconnects the call.

"Unfreaking believable. Inappropriate? What the fuck! Preston is dead. Someone killed him. Doesn't that trump everything?" Alicia yells as she slams the phone down.

Chapter 85

Alicia

"Neighbours are interesting, don't you think? They see everything. They tuck it away in the back of their minds and when something like this happens, they just want to tell you everything," Helen says to Alicia, as they return to the police vehicle after several hours of knocking on doors in the Sheridan neighbourhood.

"You're right. Neighbours can be so freaking nosy, wanting to know what's going on all the time. I talked to one of the next-door neighbours," Alicia flips a couple of pages back in her small notebook. "Denise Grant had a lot to say. She's been neighbours with the Sheridans for over 10 years and she's never known Kyle to hold down a job. Says he loves to have garage parties with his friends. Lots of drinking and loud music. She's called the police on several occasions about the noise." Alicia pauses and looks up at her partner.

"What did she say about Kandis?"

Alicia nods. "Said Kandis was the breadwinner in the family, worked hard, worked for the same company for years. Manager, she thinks. Said sometimes Kandis would come out and pull the plug, literally pull the plug," she laughs before continuing, "on the party before she had a chance to call the police."

"Sounds like there was a lot of friction, but enough to kill him?" Helen offers.

"I also spoke to Jamal Malik. Lives across the road," Alicia offers, nodding at a small, neat bungalow directly across from the Sheridan home. "He said the same thing. Kyle was pretty rowdy and had lots of people over, loud music, and drinking in the garage. Also added that Kandis did all the outside work," she looks up at the neatly cut lawn, the trimmed hedges in front of the small bay window, the bright perennial flowers in the baskets hanging from the front porch.

The detectives stand for a moment before Helen says, "I talked to Asher Freeman. He lives on the street behind and says he's been to a couple of Kyle's parties. Confirmed that there was lots of drinking, lots of pot available to both enjoy and buy and probably other drugs as well. He said the wife never came out to party, always just Kyle and the guys. He also confirmed that the wife was not happy with the situation and that on one occasion that he was aware of, the two had a knock-down drag-out fight as she was trying to shut them down."

"Knock-down drag-out fight?"

"Yeah. Asher told me about the last time he was at one of the parties, probably a month before he died. Said she came out yelling to turn the music down, got in Kyle's face screaming, saying what an asshole he was, how he had no respect for her, for the neighbours. She physically pushed him. And he pushed back and then took a swing at her, a vicious swing that would have caused damage if he'd connected. The guys at the party had to get between them. Said it was the last time he came over, though he did hear the music after that."

"Wow," Alicia offers. "Sounds like two very different people in that marriage. Partying all the time with his friends. Cops coming around for noise complaints. Maybe she'd just had enough."

"Actually, Asher suggested that," Helen smiles.

"Really?"

"Yup. Said that he was surprised that she stayed with him. All he did was party and spend her money. He said he couldn't blame her if she did something to him. Thought she put up with a lot of crap," Helen finishes, as the pair look at the pretty little bungalow, wondering if the stories about the Sheridans' relationship were true and if Kandis Sheridan finally had enough of her lazy-ass husband.

Chapter 86

Helen

"Look at that view," Helen mumbles as she drives the police SUV around the U-shaped driveway to the Beckham home which sits on the Bay's shoreline. As she pulls the vehicle to the front of the luxurious oversized brick bungalow, the double glass doors open to Jake Beckham wearing a pair of cream-coloured khakis, a light blue golf shirt and tan leather sneakers.

He watches in silence as Helen parks the car in front of the house, and the detectives get out and walk towards him. He is still silent as the pair pull out their badges and re-introduce themselves.

Beckham doesn't move, doesn't acknowledge their greeting. "What do you want?" he asks simply.

"We would like to talk to you," Alicia says succinctly.

"About?" he asks.

"About Preston Construction for starters," Helen answers.

"No comment."

"No comment?" Helen parrots.

"On the advice of my lawyer, I have been told not to talk about the company or anything related to my position there," he advises, a malicious smile gracing his lips.

"Are you allowed to talk about Lewis Preston's testamentary trust?"

"No comment," he repeats.

"How about the fraud charges filed with the OPP and FINTRAC?"

"No comment," he repeats.

"Whose idea was it? Yours or your son-in-law's?"

"No comment."

"I bet it was his," Alicia continues, as if she hadn't heard his refusal to discuss the matter. "There didn't seem to be any issues before he showed up at Preston. Was he blackmailing you for something? Or maybe he needed the extra funds for your daughter? Needed it to keep her in the style she was accustomed to," Alicia presses as Beckham's smile falls from his lips.

"Maybe you're the one that needs the money. This is quite the estate. Mortgage payments must be big. And the upkeep would be expensive too," Alicia continues. "I would suggest you come clean now and we'll put in a good word for you."

Beckham doesn't reply.

"Mr. Beckham, we believe that your son-in-law killed Lewis Preston. Come clean. Tell us what you know, and you won't be charged with accessory."

Beckham turns his back on the detectives, opens his front door, and slams it closed behind him, leaving the detectives standing in the driveway.

"Guess he didn't want to talk about it," Helen smiles at her partner as they stand for a moment. "Bet Greco has the same reaction."

"Bet Beckham is in there right now calling him," Alicia counters, as they move back to the police SUV.

Chapter 87

The Chief

Alicia and Helen sit in the plush visitors' chairs in front of the Chief's large mahogany desk, watching as the boss holds up her index finger, indicating that she will only be on the phone another minute. The Chief continues to nod, finally speaking into the microphone. "Thanks for the call, Jules. Send the completed report to me and I'll make sure that Helen and Alicia get a copy." She looks towards her detectives as both nod their heads as she wraps up the call.

"The results are in," the Chief advises. "Jules and Dr. Lee concur that Kyle Sheridan died from ingesting ethylene glycol and methanol. The mixture is extremely poisonous, impacting the kidneys, lungs, brain and nervous system, with irreversible damage within 24 to 72 hours."

"So, she's ruled it a homicide?" Helen asks.

"Yes," the Chief answers succinctly.

"Does she have any idea what the substance was specifically?" Alicia asks.

"Said the poison was some kind of solvent. She suspects its antifreeze, windshield washer fluid, maybe some kind of cleaner or even acrylic plastic. We'll be able to run tests against her results once we find the actual substance that killed Mr. Sheridan."

"I'll work on a search warrant for the Sheridan property as soon as we're finished here," Alicia states. "With any luck, we can still find whatever caused this at the house after all this time."

"Were you able to do any research on the Sheridans?" the Chief asks.

"No police record on Kandis, but Kyle has been in and out of trouble since he was in high school. Did a prison stint for killing his best friend while driving drunk and was in for eight years. Small stuff after that – drinking and driving, drug charges," Alicia answers. "Lots of issues with the daughter,

Abbie. She runs away, comes home, repeats the cycle every couple of months."

"I looked at their social media feeds. Abbie comments a lot on family violence and alludes to firsthand knowledge," Helen adds.

"Did you talk to the neighbours?"

"We did. They all commented on the craziness in the house. He didn't work. Kandis Sheridan on the other hand, has been at the same company for years and has continued to work her way up the ladder. She's a manager now," Alicia says, as Helen nods in agreement.

"One of the neighbours wondered how she stood it for so long. Why she hadn't kicked him out or killed him before this," Helen adds.

"Interesting. OK. Keep me in the loop," the Chief finishes, before quickly changing subjects. "Where are you with the Preston case?"

"We have lots of suspects, all with great motives to want Lewis Preston dead, but we have not been able to tie anyone to the sodium nitrite."

The room is quiet until the Chief decrees, "Preston was a leader in the business world, and we need to find out what happened to him. I'm thinking that the Sheridan case might be related. The wives are besties and their husbands both die unnatural deaths suddenly. Keep working on both of the cases," the Chief concludes, watching as each of her detectives nod in agreement.

Chapter 88

Kandis

Kandis sits at the kitchen table with a steaming cup of coffee, lost in thought. *The funeral was small, only a few of his garage-friends, a couple of people from my work and of course, Maeve and Eric. The minister didn't know Kyle at all, and when he asked for some information for the eulogy, I drew a blank and was unable to remember anything positive about his life. The whole thing was exhausting and sad, and a miserable end for someone that once had such potential.*

"What the hell," Kandis mumbles under her breath as she hears a knock at the front door. She gets up from the kitchen table and walks through the house to the bay window in the living room. "What the fuck," she says, as her eyes take in the police SUV that is sitting in front of her house. *Why would they be here? Things are quiet now that Kyle is gone. No neighbours complaining. No wild parties in the garage. No drug dealers hanging around. What could they want?*

"Yes?" she says questioningly as she opens the front door. "Can I help you?" she adds.

"We were sorry to hear about the loss of your husband," Detective Helen Hodgins starts.

"Thank you, but Kyle has been dead for a while now. Why are you here?"

"The coroner has ruled his death a homicide and we have a warrant to search your house and the garage," Helen tells her.

"What? Why? When?" Kandis asks, stumbling away from the door as if she's been physically pushed, her daughter standing behind her watching the nightmare unfold. "You're kidding, right? In one breath you say how sorry you are and in the next you want to search the house?"

"I'm sorry that we are taking you by surprise. Didn't the coroner explain the results to you?"

"She did but she did not say that I was a suspect in killing Kyle."

"No, she wouldn't. Finding your husband's killer is police business," Alicia explains. "And once his death was ruled a homicide, we went to a judge and got a signed warrant for the search."

The four women stand for a moment; Kandis and Abbie in shock, Helen and Alicia waiting for the situation and their request to be understood before they add pressure.

Several moments later, Kandis says, "OK. Just give me a second. I'll get my purse, and my phone." She steps back from the door as Helen pushes it open wider and steps into the front hall.

"By all means, take your purse, but your phone and your daughter's are part of the search, and we will need to take them," Helen says.

"Mom. Do something. They can't take our phones. They can't just come into our house and root through our stuff looking for God knows what," the daughter cries, hugging her phone to her chest.

"The phones are included in the warrant that was signed by Judge Mitchell. You will have to leave the premises while our team searches," Helen advises the homeowner, her eyes moving towards the daughter.

Abbie steps back, still clutching her phone. "Mom?"

"There's nothing we can do about it right now. Get your purse and whatever you need for a couple of hours," Kandis advises her daughter. "They won't find anything. We'll be back before dinner," she declares looking at the detectives simply standing in the front hall.

"This is not right," Abbie declares. "Police harassment," she adds.

"And we will want to have a conversation in the next day or two about your husband's demise," Alicia advises. "It will need to be at the police precinct so we can also collect your fingerprints."

Kandis has a glazed look on her face, like she's just reached overload and is unable to handle this last piece of information.

"Mrs. Sheridan?" Alicia says, putting her hand out and touching the woman's arm to get her attention. "Did you hear me?"

Kandis shakes her head as if to clear it before turning to answer. "I did. I'll come to the precinct. Just give me a couple of days."

"Not a problem," Alicia replies, knowing that if she doesn't hear from the woman, they will be back to question her.

Helen and Alicia stand on the front porch and watch as the two Sheridans move to the old car in the driveway, the daughter cursing her father, the police, the situation. They watch Kandis start the car and pull away as the search team assembles on the front lawn, being given instructions from Connor, the forensics lead.

"Where do you think she's going?" Alicia asks.

"My bet is Maeve Preston's."

Chapter 89

Helen

The detectives lean against the fender of the police SUV, watching as the forensics team walk in and out of the Sheridan home, bags of evidence in brown paper bags piling up in the back of the police cube van parked in the driveway. The police presence in the neighbourhood has brought the looky-loos to their front doors, out onto the sidewalk, to the edge of the property, watching carefully and whispering among themselves.

"This will be interesting," Helen whispers, as they wait for the initial verdict from the forensic lead.

The slight, bespectacled middle-aged man steps carefully down the three steps from the front porch and walks directly to the detectives, pushing his large black frame glasses up on his nose, and gives them a big smile with his greeting, "Ladies."

"Connor," the pair reply in unison.

"Find anything interesting?" Alicia adds.

"We did," he confirms. "Found a bunch of stuff in the garage – car oil, gasoline, windshield washer fluid, antifreeze. There's also a shed out back with a bunch of gardening stuff in it. We removed a bunch of herbicides and insecticides. And under the kitchen sink, we found several different kinds of poison for mice. Looks like they might have had a problem, there was a lot of mouse poop behind the stove. It could be the culprit. There was old paint in the garage which could also be the problem, though drinking paint without knowing it, seems unlikely." He pauses, flipping to the second page in the notebook he's holding. "Also, under the kitchen sink – air fresheners, a bottle of ammonia, CLR, which could do a lot of damage if ingested, and a bunch of specialized cleaners including mildew, acid and oven cleaners. The team also found peroxide and drain cleaners in the bathroom. And from the laundry room, we took their chlorine bleach and washing detergent."

"Pick up anything else?"

"You said the deceased liked to party in the garage, so we went over it carefully. It looked like it had been cleaned up since the last party, but we did pick up a few things – a half-full bottle of coke sitting on a makeshift table, you know a piece of wood lying across two sawhorses. There were also a couple of shot glasses with some kind of residue in them and an almost empty rum bottle sitting on the floor beside a stool. We also picked up a funnel. It was sitting on the table beside an ice bucket. It has something on it. Might be oil or something for the car but it looked interesting, so we grabbed it."

"There's lots to test."

"Dr. Diamond has specifics for what killed Mr. Sheridan. Hopefully, we'll be able to match it to something that we've taken today."

"Great work, Connor. Thanks," Alicia tells her forensics lead before turning towards the street to take in the crowd of neighbours watching their work.

***

Helen holds the list of additional items seized from the Sheridan home – three cell phones, one belonging to Kandis Sheridan, the second belonging to the deceased Kyle Sheridan and the third to Abbie. *Wonder if they'll give us the passwords to get in. No bother if they don't. I'm sure Drew will be able to crack them.* Helen contemplates as her eyes continue down the list. A tablet was found in the mother's bedroom. *Probably used for email, googling stuff or watching YouTube. Yeah, how to kill your husband in one easy step,* she chuckles to herself. *Two laptops. Looks like one belongs to Kandis' company. Might have to step around the confidentiality of work materials but I'm sure there's also personal stuff on it. The second one looks like the family's. Now that might give us something. Oh, and an old desktop computer. Interesting. It was in the daughter's room. Probably being used for games, but you just never know in this day and age.*

What else? Banking info. Savings account, chequing account, a couple of registered education savings accounts, no stocks, no bonds, no RRSP contributions. Looks like they lived pay cheque to pay cheque.

And journals? That's interesting. It doesn't say who they belonged to or where they were found but aren't all personal journals filled with secrets?

Chapter 90

Alicia

"Hey Mom," Luke greets his mother, as she picks up her phone.

"Hi Luke, Hi Annie," Alicia says, knowing that her son has her on speaker phone. "What's going on?"

"Are you free?" Luke asks.

"Free?"

"We have some news, and we want to celebrate with you. And Jeff, if he's able to make it."

"What are we celebrating?"

"You'll see. How about meeting us halfway?"

"Jeff'll probably come with me, and we can just scoot down there. Not a problem," Alicia suggests, wanting to save her son some time and money.

"No, let's meet in the middle. Guelph is about halfway. Annie's just looking at restaurants in the area. See anything interesting, Annie?" he asks as she examines her phone.

"There's a couple. Take a look at this one, Luke," Annie says before Alicia can hear the two talking to each other away from the phone.

Several moments later, Luke is back on the phone, "How about the Shakespeare Arms in Guelph? Looks like they have everything on their menu – from appetizers to sandwiches and burgers to oriental bowls to pasta and even English stuff. Sounds interesting."

"Anywhere you want," his mother replies, not really caring about the food they will eat, much more excited with the thoughts of seeing her son and hearing his news.

"Perfect. I'll make a reservation for dinner. I'll send you the address, so you'll be able to find the place."

"Can't wait," Alicia replies, before her son disconnects the call.

***

"And you don't know what we're going to celebrate?" Jeff asks, as he manoeuvres his little convertible west on Highway 9.

"I'm hoping it's that they both passed their exams," Alicia says hopefully.

"That would definitely be good news," Jeff comments before they fall quiet for the remainder of the over two-hour drive, Alicia's mind wandering to other possible things that her son might want to celebrate.

***

The foursome are seated at their table in the traditionally styled English pub with their drinks in front of them. The restaurant has lots of dark wood, a huge bar with numerous beer signs and beer taps, a large stone fireplace and enough space to sit a crowd of people.

"What's the good news?" Alicia asks, looking across the table at her son and his fiancé, broad grins on both of their faces. Alicia's hands are in her lap, and she fidgets, preparing for her son's announcement, slightly nervous at the possibilities.

"You sure you don't want to wait until after dessert?" Luke asks.

Alicia laughs as she shakes her head. "This is not a birthday celebration. No presents to open," she says. "No reason to wait."

Annie lightly shoves Luke with her shoulder. "Don't be cruel. Tell her," she says.

"OK, my two favourite people have spoken," Luke replies smiling. "Drum roll, please," he adds, drumming his fingers on the table, raising the tension even more.

268

After several moments, he stops and holds Annie's hand before announcing, "Annie and I have both passed our exams," a brilliant smile on his face.

Alicia is instantly happy, stands up and moves around to the other side of the table as Luke and Annie stand up for their mom-hug, which they know is coming. The threesome stand embraced for several minutes as Jeff waits to shake each of their hands.

"That's fantastic news. No surprise to me though," Alicia comments, moving back to her side of the table, Jeff following her.

"We still have some on-the-job training in the next couple of weeks, but unless it goes terribly wrong, we will be certified to become police officers in Ontario."

"You both have already done some field work when you took the course at Georgian College, so that won't be a problem," she pauses as she lifts her glass. "This requires a toast. A toast to two new police officers."

The foursome touch glasses, smiles on all their faces and take a mouthful of their drinks.

As their glasses come down, Luke advises, "There is some other news we need to share." He lifts his glass again, the other three at the table following suit before he announces, "Annie has been offered a position at South Simcoe in Innisfil, and she will be starting there after graduation."

"Fantastic," Alicia says, putting her glass on the table and walking around the table to give her a big hug. "So proud of you," she tells her future daughter-in-law. "So proud," she murmurs again as she walks back to her seat and sits down, looking at her son expectantly. "And?" she asks.

"And what?" he replies, a huge smile on his face.

"And what will you be doing?" she clarifies.

Again, he drums his fingers on the edge of the table, going on longer than his mother can stand.

"Stop all the racket and just tell me,' she pleads.

"I have been offered a position with Barrie," he tells her. The words are barely out of his mouth when she jumps up and races around the other side of the table. She is silent as she hugs him, ecstatic that he will be close to her, but also deeply afraid of what it means to his safety to be on the streets.

After several moments, Alicia once again returns to her chair beside Jeff, who grabs her hand and smiles, knowing that this is her dream, working near her son.

Chapter 91

Alicia

Ten days after the search of the Sheridan home, the team have found the substance that killed Kyle Sheridan – antifreeze. Two sets of fingerprints were found on the jug – the dead man's and his wife's.

The almost empty bottle of rum has also been tested, and it included a substantial amount of the antifreeze.

The funnel that was picked up casually off the makeshift bar in the garage also reported a residue of the coolant on it.

Alicia and Helen have been given approval by the Chief to charge Kandis Sheridan with the murder of her husband, and the paperwork for the arrest warrant is ready for Judge Mitchell's signature.

Chapter 92

Kandis

Not again, Kandis thinks to herself as the police SUV pulls in front of her house and stops. *This is a fucking nightmare. They just keep coming back! Can't they leave us alone? Everyone is better off without that piece of shit. What could they possibly want now?* she thinks as she moves towards the front door.

"Yes?" she says questioningly, as she opens the door before the detectives have a chance to knock.

"Mrs. Kandis Sheridan?" Detective Helen Hodgins asks.

"You know who I am," she answers sarcastically.

"You're under arrest for the murder of Kyle Sheridan. Please step out onto the front porch and turn around."

Kandis steps back into the house, her hand still on the handle of the open front door. "What the fuck are you talking about? Murder? You think I killed Kyle?" she yells at the officers.

The three stand silent for a moment, the detectives watching the suspect closely, waiting for any sign that she's going to slam the door in their faces or try to run.

"It has been proven that your husband was poisoned with antifreeze that was stored in your garage," the detective continues, pulling handcuffs from a holster attached to her belt.

"And you think I did it? Why me? Anyone that had access to the garage could have done it," Kandis suggests.

"Please step out onto the front porch."

What am I supposed to do now? What about Abbie? She can't stay here by herself. She's only 16 years old – old enough for some to be alone but not Abbie. She's got too many addiction issues to be alone in this house. Especially with the bullshit that's going on with her dad's death. Now with me. I need to call Eric. He'll take her. It won't be for too

272

long, I hope, Kandis thinks as she pulls her newly purchased phone from her back pocket.

"Sorry, no calls," Helen advises, reaching for the phone as Kandis pulls back, cuddling the cell against her body like a child greedily keeping a toy from another. "Give it to me," Helen says, her hand out.

"Just let me call my brother-in-law. It will only take a sec. I can't leave Abbie alone. He's only ten minutes away. He can come over and get her," she explains, still gripping her phone.

Alicia, who is standing beside her partner, simply nods in the affirmative, knowing that if it were her, she would want to take care of her kid as well. Meanwhile, Abbie appears in the front hallway, surprise on her face. "What the hell is going on, Mom?"

The detectives watch and wait as Kandis has a quick stilted conversation on the phone, giving her brother-in-law only the barest of details before she disconnects the call. "He'll be here in 15 minutes. Can we wait?" she asks, tears sparkling in her eyes.

"We cannot wait," Helen says, forcefully pulling the accused out of the house and turning her around to place the cuffs on her wrists. As the ring-shaped metal devices click into place behind her back, a low moan escapes Kandis, and a feeling of helplessness and vulnerability envelope her being.

"There are a couple of patrol officers on the street," Alicia nods towards the road. "We'll ask them to stay until he arrives."

"Thank you," Kandis murmurs.

"Mom! What's going on?" Abbie demands, standing at attention in her crumpled flannel pants and baggy t-shirt.

"It's OK, Abbie. Uncle Eric will be here in 15 minutes. He's going to take you to his place until I can get this fixed," Kandis explains, as Helen offers the accused's phone to her daughter, who snatches it like a drowning person grabbing for a life jacket.

"They're taking you away? Why?"

Kandis looks directly at her daughter. "Call Maeve and tell her what's happened. Tell her to get that lawyer she was talking about. Simon something. Tell her to get him to the precinct ASAP," she says, just as Helen pulls her down the three stairs of the front porch before pushing her towards the police SUV, leaving Abbie alone, tears rolling down her face as she holds Kandis' phone in her hand, watching as her mother is led away.

This is unbelievable. What the fuck, Kyle. Even in death, you're haunting me, making my life hell. Now they think I killed you.

Alicia opens the rear door of the police cruiser as Helen directs the suspect to the side of the car. Alicia puts her hand on Kandis's head, pushing down as she manoeuvres awkwardly into the back of the car. Her hands are behind her, making her sit at the edge of the cushion; her knees are tight to the metal grill between the front and back seats of the vehicle. The car door slams and the prisoner jumps at the sudden noise.

"Where are you taking her?" Abbie yells, from the front porch, the phone to her ear.

"Police precinct on Fairview Road," Alicia answers before opening the passenger door and getting in. Helen moves in behind the steering wheel and starts the vehicle, pulling away from the curb slowly.

Oh my God. Couldn't they have just left it alone? The guy was a drunk. A fucking drunk. He partied endlessly and he would have killed himself with alcohol sooner or later.

Maeve's lawyer will help me get out of this ridiculousness, but it's going to cost a pretty penny. I'm going to have to ask Maeve to help me. I'll pay back every cent if that fucking lawyer can get this straightened out. He'll be on my side. He'll defend me.

Fuck. What if I have to sell the house to pay for my defense? What then? I'll have nothing. And my job? What about that? I'll end up losing everything and for what?

Son of a bitch. Even dead he's still making my life impossible.

Kandis sits alone in one of the interrogation rooms. She waits quietly hoping that Abbie was able to get through to Maeve and she in turn talked to the lawyer. Suddenly there is a commotion in the hallway, and voices are raised in argument, but she continues to sit, waiting for someone to help her make sense of this unbelievable situation.

The door opens abruptly, and Kandis can hear Maeve's voice. "Don't say anything. Simon is coming..." her friend yells before the detectives are able to enter the room and close the door, cutting Maeve's instructions off mid-sentence. *Maeve is here. Help is on the way,* Kandis thinks. She sits upright, knowing that she is not alone, that her lawyer and her friend are going to help her, and she just needs to wait for Simon to arrive.

"We would like to ask you a couple of questions," Helen starts, standing on the opposite side of the table.

"My lawyer is on his way," Kandis states matter-of-factly.

"We have a couple questions for you while we wait," Helen answers.

Kandis sits for a moment, remembering what she heard before the door was quickly slammed on her friend. *Don't say anything. Don't say anything*, she repeats to herself like a mantra.

She sits looking down at her hands in her lap for a moment, remembering the many crime-fighting television programs that she has watched through the years. *The detectives want me to say something to incriminate myself. They want me to tell them something that they can use against me. Nope, I'm not talking to them. They can't fool me.* She lifts her head and looks at the two standing across the table from her in their trim pantsuits, their guns visible in

275

their holsters under their arms and she smiles slightly. "I want my lawyer," she tells them.

"Why don't you just make this easier for yourself? For your daughter? Tell us what you did to your husband," Alicia solicits.

Kandis repeats, "I want my lawyer," watching as her words seem to knock the stuffing out of the detectives, deflating them and their aggressive presence before the pair move to the door, open it and slam it on their exit.

She pulls her feet up, hugs her knees and once again sighs deeply, waiting for help.

***

Kandis' head pops up as the door to the interrogation room opens and her friend Maeve rushes in, her arms wide open. Kandis stands up and falls into her friend's embrace. "Thanks for coming, Maeve," Kandis whispers in her friend's ear.

They embrace for a moment before the overly tall man with wisps of thinning blond hair, who followed Maeve into the room, clears his throat. The two break their embrace to look around at the interloper in his expensive navy-blue suit with red tie and matching pocket square.

"This is Simon Windsor. Scott recommended him. Simon is a criminal lawyer and will be able to help," Maeve says, stepping back and introducing the two.

"Mrs. Sheridan," the lawyer says, before he sets his briefcase on the table, sits down, and pulls out a pad of paper and pen. "Please sit down," he says, motioning to the chair that Kandis had recently inhabited. "The police have charged you with murder. There will be a bail hearing within the next 24 hours. Depending on what evidence they have, I may be able to get you out on bail." He stops and waits for his client's reply.

"I did not kill my husband," Kandis declares.

"Good. Good," the lawyer replies, absorbed in writing something on his pad of paper. "Tell me why they are charging you. Tell me why they think you did this."

Chapter 93

Maeve

"I told you no," Maeve says emphatically. "You need to delay it."

"Why? Why do you want me to delay reading the will?" Scott Wolfe asks. "We could do a preliminary and let everyone know what's coming. We could get it over with and put some people's minds at rest."

Maeve sighs deeply. "Scott, I know you're only doing your job. Doing what you think Lewis would have wanted. But Lewis is gone, and you now work for me. I do not want the will read yet."

"You know that Izzy is calling me almost daily trying to find out what her father left her."

"I do. And I know that you are doing me a favour by keeping the will private. I know that legally she could get her hands on a copy, but she doesn't know how to do that. It won't be of any help to her to know what's in the will in her present state anyway."

There's silence on the line for a moment before the lawyer asks, "What about Dominique Guillaume? Shouldn't she know what Lewis left her and her daughter?"

Maeve can feel her blood pressure rise instantly as her face flushes red. "Are you fucking kidding me? Do you think I care about that bitch? She can live in a ditch for all I care about her and her brat," she yells into the phone. Maeve breathes in and out several times, trying to calm herself before she continues. "She'll find out soon enough. It's not like she's starving or homeless or anything," she adds with contempt in her voice.

"Then when? When would you like the will read?"

"My understanding is that there's a lot of work that you could be doing before the will is read, like paying Lewis' debts and taxes, ensuring everything is legal and on the up-

and-up, checking all his assets, making sure that they are in order."

"Yes, those are all my responsibilities as his lawyer," Scott agrees.

"That should take you a while, don't you think?" Maeve asks to silence. "I would like you to hold the will until the cops find who poisoned Lewis," she finally confesses.

"That could be a while," Scott says tentatively.

"Could be," Maeve agrees before adding, "But I have faith in our legal system. I'm sure they will find the guilty party soon. And we've already installed you as Chairman as per Lewis' instructions. So everything is good," she finishes as she hangs up the phone, not giving her lawyer a chance to question her decision.

Chapter 94

Alicia

"We would like to talk to Abbie," Alicia advises Eric Sheridan as he opens the front door of his modest home.

"That's not legal, is it?" he asks, unsure of his niece's rights and his responsibilities as her temporary caregiver.

"It is legal, and it's done all the time as long as a guardian is present," Alicia advises. "I'm sure she must be upset with everything going on, losing her father so suddenly, then her mother being charged with his murder. We can talk here, or if that doesn't work, you can bring her down to the precinct."

Eric stands motionless for a moment thinking, looking closely at the pair.

He sure looks like his brother, just a slightly older version with laugh lines around his hazel eyes, unlike Kyle who had a red, flushed face, and dark circles under his blood-shot eyes. That's what years of drinking will do to you, Alicia thinks, waiting for an answer from this tall, trim, beginning-to-grey gentleman.

After a bit of introspection, he nods in the affirmative before holding the door open for the detectives. "Abbie is at the dining room table doing her homework."

"How is she doing?" Helen asks, as they step directly into the living room.

"Actually, better than I would have thought. I've had to change my life around a bit to accommodate her, drive her to school, make sure someone picks her up after school, and pick her up when she goes out with friends, but aside from that, she's doing well. Between you and me, I think she's relieved that it's quiet here. I live by myself. Kandis and my brother were both very loud, demanding people," he confides, walking across the living room to the dining area.

Abbie is seated at a round wooden table, with an open text and notebook in front of her as she tries to decipher an algebra equation. As the three approach, Abbie raises her head from her work and at once slams her notebook closed, followed by the textbook, a frown clouding her face.

"Why are they here?" Abbie asks, her uncle angrily as she piles her books together as if she is going to leave the table.

"They just want to talk to you," he advises. "And I thought it would be best to do it here instead of at the police station."

"They can do that? Don't we need a lawyer or something?" Abbie asks.

"No, you don't need a lawyer to answer a couple of questions, but if you've done something wrong, we can move this down to the police station and your uncle can call someone to represent you if that puts you at ease," Alicia replies, pulling out a chair and sitting across from the girl. *And she looks like her mom. Thin drawn face, brooding eyes. Though her attire is nothing like her mother's. Goth must still be in. The black hair, the black eyeliner, the baggy black t-shirt, and ripped jeans.* "You decide. What would you like to do?" Alicia asks, putting her open hands on the table.

There's silence for a moment as Abbie takes in the possibilities before turning to her uncle. "You're going to stay, right?"

"I am. And if it gets too intense, you just tell me and we'll stop," he agrees, moving behind Abbie, putting his hands on her shoulders.

"Go," she says simply, facing the detectives.

"Well, let me start by telling you how sorry we are about your dad," Alicia offers.

"And what about my mom? Are you sorry about that too?" Abbie asks, the fury in her voice evident as she stares the detective down, her uncle's hands still on her shoulders, like he's holding her back from jumping across the table.

"Well, that's why we're here," Helen offers. "We want to understand your family, your parents' relationship, what went on in the house, get your opinion of the situation, if possible."

"My mom did not kill my dad," Abbie yells, her eyes beginning to water.

"We hear you. If it wasn't your mom, we need to find out who did this to your dad," Helen rephrases, hoping to placate the adolescent.

There's silence for a moment before Abbie rubs her nose with the heel of her hand and asks, "What do you want to know?"

The detectives ask questions for the next hour. What kind of relationship did your parents have? Were they happy? Did they spend time together? Where did your mom work? Where did your dad work? Did your dad have friends over to the house? Who were they? How often? Did your mom complain about it? What did she say? Did your dad drink? Alcohol? Anything else? Did you hear your parents yell at each other? What did they fight about mostly? Did your father ever hit your mother?

Abbie's answers are what they had expected. The relationship between Kandis and Kyle Sheridan had been fractured for years. They didn't speak often and when they did it was typically a fight over him not working, or about the excessive noise from his band and his parties in the garage. Abbie told them about her mother going out on many occasions and asking, then demanding them to quiet down. She was typically ignored, and she usually came back into the house steaming mad.

The girl's demeanour changes drastically when the detectives begin to ask Abbie specifics about how her father treated her. Did your father hit you? Did he say anything inappropriate? Did he do anything that made you feel uncomfortable?"

Abbie's bravado continues until the last question is asked. She chokes up, coughs, and wipes her eyes and nose again with the heel of her hand, her lips curling in anger. "What the hell has that got to do with anything?" she finally blurts out.

"What did your dad do to you, Abbie?" Alicia asks quietly.

Abbie crosses her arms dramatically. She doesn't reply at once, but when she does her anger and resentment are clear as her voice escalates. "My father was a drunk and an asshole. He treated my mother like crap. He took, took, took from her, from everyone. Their money, their happiness, their life. He staggered around the house most of the time and yelled at us. Touch me? He probably couldn't even get it up," she finishes, her eyes glowing with fury.

There's silence in the room for a moment before Eric, who has been standing behind Abbie through the interrogation, moves to sit beside the girl, pulling his chair closer, and pulling her into his arms. But she fights him, pulls back, stands up pushing the chair forcefully against the wall, a loud bang reverberating through the house as it hits the drywall. Abbie looks at her uncle, her eyes flashing with rage. "And what? Do you want to make up for everything that he's done? Or are you just like him? Where were you when they were fighting? When he threw stuff around the house. When he took his fists to my mother. When I had to hide under my bed to stay out of his way. Where were you then, Unc?"

Eric shrinks back as bitter words are flung at him. "I'm sorry, Abbie. I swear I didn't know what was going on," he confesses, his face contorting in pain as he tries to justify his absence to his 16-year-old niece.

Abbie stares at her uncle for seconds before redirecting her anger back to the detectives sitting across the table. "And where the hell were you? How many times did the neighbours call about the noise? And not just the music kind. The fights were well known around the neighbourhood," she rants, her anger large on her face.

"The records show we did come out a couple of times," Alicia starts before being interrupted by the teenager.

"Yeah, sure you came out. Rapped him on the knuckles. Warned him to quiet down, which probably happened as long as it took for you fucking pigs to drive to Tim Hortons."

"Now, Abbie. Respect would be appreciated," her uncle admonishes.

"They don't deserve my respect," she replies, as her anger starts to wind down.

"Is that why you ran away from home?" Alicia asks, changing the subject, watching the girl as she picks up the chair, rights it and collapses into it.

The room is silent for a moment before Abbie finally confesses, "I couldn't stand it anymore. It was the same thing over and over. Nothing ever changed. And it's nice and quiet out on the street. No one yells at you. No one tells you you're a useless piece of crap taking up space."

"And that's when you started taking drugs?" Helen asks.

"Wow, you guys have done your homework," she says with mock surprise. "Yeah, I got mixed up with some bad stuff for a while, but I'm good now," the girl replies quickly as if trying to convince herself as well as the detectives.

"Good?" Alicia asks.

"Yeah, I've been clean for months now. My mom helped me. Said I could come home if I stopped."

"And how long have you been back home?"

"A couple of months."

"And were the arguments and the parties still happening at your house?"

"There would always be fights and craziness as long as my dad was there," she concludes.

"So why was this time different than before? Why were you able to quit?" Helen pushes to understand.

"My mom took my side. Told my dad that I was staying. Told my dad to leave me alone. Told him that if he didn't, we'd leave him," Abbie tells them.

"Told your dad to leave you alone? What was he doing to you?" Helen questions.

Abbie is quiet and doesn't answer. "Are we done here?" she finally asks.

The four sit for several moments listening to the silence of the house, only the ticking of the old grandfather clock cutting through the quiet.

Eric shakes his head, sorrow in his eyes. "I didn't know it was that bad," he professes, looking at his niece.

Abbie smiles, a strained grimace on her face, "It is what it is. It's over now. My father is gone. But my mom didn't do it. She had reason to, but she couldn't do it, wouldn't do it."

"What do you mean by that, Abbie? What couldn't your mother do?" Alicia asks.

"My mom was weak. No spine or she would have left him years ago," she pauses as if thinking before she continues. "It was probably one of those assholes that he owed money to," she says flippantly. "Are we done here? I've got to get back to my homework," she says, touching the books in front of her.

Helen and Alicia look at each other before Helen declares, "We are done. For now. If we have more questions, is it OK to come back and talk to you?"

"Sure, sure," the teenager says, dismissing them, opening her books, and picking up her pen.

The adults watch the adolescent for a moment as she pretends to be concentrating on her homework, before they get up from the table.

"Thanks for your time, Abbie," Alicia says, but there is no reply as the teenager stares at the open book in front of her.

Eric follows the pair to the front door, opens it for them, and follows them out onto the front porch before confessing, "I didn't know it was that bad. I swear. Kyle never let on and Kandis never said anything to me."

"What do you think their issues were?" Helen asks, after going down the three steps of the front porch and turning around.

Eric smiles weakly as he tries to explain the pairing of his brother Kyle and Kandis. "They had their problems. They were both running from their past – Kandis from a crappy childhood, Kyle from his time in prison." Helen and Alicia nod in understanding. "The first couple of months seemed OK from the outside, but then Abbie was born, and they realized that there was no more playing house. They had to buck up and become parents. Kandis did OK. She had a job at a call centre, took a few courses at night and got a few promotions. Worked her way up to manager of something or other."

"And Kyle?" Alicia asks.

"My brother struggled. Always has. Ever since he was injured playing hockey in high school. He always thought he was destined to play in the NHL but then he had all those concussions and buggered up his knee, and it was game over, literally. He started drinking, wrecked his car and killed his best friend. He never seemed to recover after that," Eric admits, as he rubs the 5 o'clock shadow on his chin.

Eric's analysis ends and the detectives stand for a moment, hoping that he will continue his ruminations on his brother and his wife, but there is only silence.

Chapter 95

Eric

"Hi, Maya. I won't be able to make it into the office today. Can you cancel my meetings for me? Rebook them for later in the week. Express my regrets," Eric says to his administrative assistant on his cell phone, as he locks the back door of his house.

"Not a problem, Eric. Everything OK?"

"Just tell them something has come up, something I can't get out of. Apologize for me. Make sure they know they are valued but something has come up that I have to deal with," Eric replies, as he gets into his car and pushes the key into the ignition.

"Is Abbie OK?"

"Don't tell them about my niece or anything else that's going on with my family," he directs, as he backs his car out of the driveway.

"Got it. I'll be very professional," his admin confirms.

There's silence on the phone for a moment, as Eric sits at the bottom of his driveway, waiting for a break in traffic.

"I'll call each of them personally. Are you OK? Is there anything I can do to help?" his admin asks sincerely.

"No, I'm not good right now. I'm on the way to the hospital. I'll be there for a while. Not sure if I have to turn my phone off, but if I do, I'll try and check for messages. I'll get back to you as soon as I can," he instructs, as he accelerates down his street.

"Hospital?"

"Abbie was rushed into Royal Vic."

"Oh my God, Eric. I'm so sorry. Was she involved in an accident?"

He noisily blows air out of his lungs trying to calm himself. "No, not an accident," he says. "She snuck out of the house last night after I went to bed, and I got a call from the

287

police early this morning. She was found unconscious at some meeting place downtown that's known for drug sales."

"Shit," his Admin says into the phone.

"Yeah, shit," he replies. There's silence for a moment, each in their own thoughts before he adds, "I'll call you later," and he disconnects the phone line.

Eric pushes on the gas pedal aggressively, forcing the car over the speed limit, as he races towards the hospital in the north end of the city, his eyes focused on the other cars, and the traffic. *Fucking kid. I can't believe she's using again. She told me she had stopped. Told me her mother had helped her get clean. Must be all the crap that's going on. Her father dying. Her mother being accused of killing him. And living with me. It can't be easy for a 16-year-old. She's seen way too much in her short life - my fucking brother's drinking, doing drugs, pushing his wife around. What the fuck was he thinking?*

What about the detectives? Should I call them? Tell them what their meeting did to her. Nah, they probably have contacts at the hospital that tell them everything. They'll find out that Abbie took a shitload of something. Took a fucking needle to herself. Cocaine. Heroin. Who the fuck knows? Hopefully, the cops got her to the hospital in time. The doctors pumped her stomach and gave her something to reverse whatever she took. But hell, was that enough to save her?

Chapter 96

Kandis

Maeve aggressively pushes the front doors of the Barrie Court House open, freeing Kandis after spending the last 36 hours in lockdown, waiting for her bail hearing. Kandis stands on the sidewalk for a moment, pulling in fresh air, before her friend turns around, a question on her face. "Coming?" Maeve asks, more like a demand, as she starts through the parking lot toward her white Lincoln Navigator.

Fucking assholes. Where the hell would I get $1 million from? Though I get that I only needed to put up 10% of it for bail, but still. Who has that kind of cash sitting around? Thank God for Maeve.

I should have been out of there in 24 hours, but with the exorbitant number of cases and the long weekend, it took a lot longer than expected. And I had to sit in that dirty, shitty dump with the scum of the earth, real goddamn criminals. Freaking bottom feeders. I feel unclean, and filthy and need a hot shower to get their germs off of me. Unfucking believable. They think I killed Kyle? Well, if they knew what I've been through the last 16 years with that piece of shit, it might be a logical conclusion. But they will have to prove it and Simon, Maeve says, is the best that money can buy.

Maeve had to sign a surety – put up her money for bail and promised to supervise me. Ha! She won't be far away, and she knows that she can trust me. I would never think of screwing her out of the money or hurting our friendship, especially when they have no evidence against me.

Thank God for Eric. He's has Abbie at his place. A confirmed bachelor with a teenager thrust on him with no notice. Hope she's OK. I couldn't even call. But Maeve checked in with him. I'm sure if there was anything wrong, or he was having any trouble, she would have helped him out.

The two jump into the big white Lincoln Navigator and Maeve touches the button to start its engine.

"We need to talk," Maeve announces to her friend, as she pulls out of the busy parking lot.

***

Maeve continues to drive, silence surrounding the pair for several minutes until Kandis asks, "I thought we were going to pick Abbie up from school." The silence continues for several moments, adding to Kandis frustration until she breaks. "What's going on, Maeve? You're driving in the wrong direction for Abbie's school," Kandis says, her volume beginning to increase. "What aren't you telling me Maeve?" Kandis asks, waiting for a moment before she demands, "Stop the fucking car. Stop it now or I swear I'll jump out," she threatens, putting her hand on the door.

Maeve quickly hits the button to lock all the car doors before offering, "Let's just get you home. Sit and have a coffee and I'll bring you up to date on what's going on with Abbie and Eric."

"Tell me now," Kandis demands, her lips tight, her jaw clenched. "What the fuck is going on? What's wrong?"

Maeve doesn't say anything for several blocks.

"Tell me now or I'm calling the cops," Kandis tells her friend, holding her phone in her hand.

"Are you kidding me? You just got out of jail, and you think calling them will help," Maeve says sarcastically. There's silence in the car for several minutes before she finally tells her friend, "There's been an incident."

"An incident? What fucking incident?"

Maeve pauses trying to find her words, her friend staring at her like she's never seen her before. "Abbie has had a relapse," Maeve finally tells her friend.

"A relapse?"

"Yes. It seems she snuck out of Eric's house. They found her at Memorial Square. Unconscious."

"And?" Kandis demands.

290

"She overdosed. Not sure what she took but the paramedics administered naloxone. They got her to the hospital where they pumped her stomach and gave her some other kind of antidote."

"And? She's OK, right?"

"It was touch and go for a bit. She stopped breathing," to which Kandis grasps and holds her chest before Maeve continues. "They did CPR and brought her back. Put her on a ventilator for a bit and she rallied."

"I want to see her," Kandis demands. Maeve hesitates for a moment before Kandis repeats, "I want to see her."

"You can't. She's been moved to a rehab centre and is currently undergoing detox. You'll be able to visit her in a couple of days, a week at the most."

Kandis sits in the passenger side of the luxury vehicle, a look of shock on her face, tears coursing down her cheeks. "Son of a bitch. The fucking guy is dead and it's like he's still here causing shit."

Chapter 97

Drew

Drew sits back from the computer screen, a look of awe on his face. *I can't believe that she would leave this on her tablet. She must have thought she was home free, that it would simply be ruled an accidental death. My God. This will put her away. I've got to tell Alicia and Helen*, he thinks as he stands up quickly, picking up the iPad from his desk before marching down the hallway to the Detectives' Den.

"Hey Alicia, Helen," Drew says as he arrives at the pair's workspace.

"Hey Drew," Alicia greets as she sits back in her chair, her hands leaving the keyboard. "What's going on?"

"I found something interesting."

"Don't keep us in suspense," Helen says, mirroring Alicia's actions, her attention moving from her computer to the visitor.

"There's a video on Mrs. Sheridan's tablet, one that was deleted but it was still on the hard drive. How to kill someone with antifreeze," Drew says, a big smile on his face.

"How to kill someone with antifreeze? You're kidding, right?"

"Nope. Not kidding," Drew says, pulling up a chair between the two as he continues to explain. "I checked the hard drive on the tablet, and found an old video from 20/20, you know the program that does investigative stuff?" he watches as the detectives nod. "They did a show which aired in 2022 entitled 'Home Sweet Murder' about a mother who used antifreeze to poison her husband, son, and daughter. Killed the husband and the son, but the daughter was lucky – hospitalized and survived," he pauses before adding, " She mixed the antifreeze with Coca-Cola. Sounds familiar doesn't it?" he grins.

"Unfreaking believable," Alicia says. "Have you watched it?"

"No, but I looked it up, got the description, and thought I would bring it to you. Want to watch it together?" he asks.

"Definitely," the pair say in unison.

Chapter 98

Maeve

"Why the hell would you call our lawyer and ask him such a question?" Maeve almost yells at her daughter.

The phone line is quiet as Izzy contemplates the question, knowing that whatever she answers will be wrong and won't be tolerated by her mother.

"Izzy answer me," her mother pushes. "What were you thinking?" She pauses a moment before adding, "Oh, yeah. You were only thinking of yourself again."

"I'm sorry Mom, but I was hoping that Daddy left me some money. I'm struggling with my influencer work. I need more followers and to get that, I need to go to better restaurants, wear designer clothes, go to exclusive parties, you know, have something interesting to write about so people will follow me."

Maeve sighs loudly at her daughter's explanation, appreciating that at least she was being honest about her need for the money and pleased that she is straight enough that she could form full sentences that make sense.

"I hear you, Izzy and I do understand. You chose a very difficult career," she puts her hand up to stop her daughter from butting in, even though they are on the phone and she cannot be seen. "I think it's time to rethink your choice of profession and to think about how you're going to support yourself without your father's help."

There's silence on the phone; Izzy sits on her bed, shaking from nervousness and jonesing for a fix, while Cody watches, and listens, hoping for a positive outcome.

"Izzy, do you hear me?" her mother asks. The girl nods her head in the affirmative, tears streaking down her cheeks as she cries silently. Maeve takes a breath waiting for her response but hears nothing from her daughter, "Scott will hold onto the will until probate is complete. It's going to be a

294

while until we know what your father put in it," she says ploughing ahead.

Izzy again nods her head and makes an 'ahh' sound in answer.

"You'll have to get a job. Work part-time or something until this is all sorted out. Why not get a job at one of those exclusive stores so you can get a discount on their clothes? That would be a good idea. They might even let you try the stuff on and video it, so you can put it online. You wouldn't have to use your money to buy anything. Give them some free publicity," Maeve suggests.

Izzy is silent for a moment, knowing that isn't really an option as she would need to be straight, need to have poise, grace and style to wait on customers, need to be able to blend in with the upper class, something that she hasn't ever been able to do.

"Or maybe that boyfriend of yours could get a job. I'm sure there's something legal that he could do," Maeve suggests to the silence on the phone line. She waits for several moments before adding, "Once the police figure out what happened, I'm sure Scott will book a reading of the will. I'll make sure that he calls you when that happens," she finishes before disconnecting the line.

Where the hell did we go wrong with her, Lewis? Maeve thinks, looking around her luxurious home. *We gave her everything. We tried to raise her right, but somehow she just didn't seem to get it.*

Shit, I better phone Scott and tell him to look after the condo in Texas. Rand's going to be calling soon enough about it. Scott can look after moving him, paying the condo fees, giving him an allowance and selling Toronto. That's what I pay him for. To look after things so I don't have to!

Chapter 99

Kandis

Kandis paces back and forth from one side of the expansive reception area to the other of the rehab centre, as her brother-in-law Eric watches. They are waiting to see Abbie and have been waiting for over 40 minutes. *What the hell! I don't understand why we have to wait. I'm her fucking mother,* she thinks, as she approaches the sizeable windows on the south side of the building. She stops for a moment, looking out at the green grass, the trees, the park-like area that none of the residents are allowed to use as it is outside of the residents' fenced-in area. *What a waste. They could have made better use of that space,* she thinks, as she turns to continue pacing.

Before she can take a step, a woman dressed in scrubs opens the locked door between the foyer and the facility and smiles. "Mrs. Sheridan? Mr. Sheridan?" she asks, stepping into the waiting area and closing the door.

"Yes. I'm Kandis Sheridan, and this is my brother-in-law, Eric Sheridan," Kandis answers, as she quickly moves towards the nurse.

"You're here to see Abbie?" the nurse asks, looking from the mother to uncle.

"We are," Kandis agrees. "She's OK, right?"

"Abbie has had a bit of a rough morning but she's in her room now," the nurse explains.

"Rough morning? What happened?"

"She was involved in an argument with another patient. It started during group therapy and then escalated over lunch. The two came to blows. We had to sedate her, and she is now resting in her room," the nurse explains.

"Can we see her?" Eric asks.

The woman hesitates for a moment before clarifying, "I'm sorry, not today. As I mentioned, we had to sedate her and she's sleeping. She'll probably sleep for the rest of the afternoon."

"How about tomorrow? Can we see her tomorrow?" he pushes.

"If everything is calm this evening and tomorrow morning, then yes, you will be able to see her tomorrow afternoon," the nurse concedes.

Eric stands for a moment, looking at his sister-in-law.

"Thank you for looking after Abbie," Kandis finally tells the nurse before turning around and walking across the lobby to the front door, silent tears streaming down her face.

Chapter 100

Alicia

"Are we almost done?" Alicia asks, as Luke hands her a box out of the back of the rented U-Haul parked in front of the house where he and his fiancé will be living.

"Just a couple more, but I'll get them if you're sore."

"You take the big one," Alicia points to a box in the back of the truck. "I think it's full of books. I'll take this one," she nods.

Luke jumps into the truck and grabs the large box, pushes it to the edge of the truck bed before stepping down. "What are you up to later? Annie and I are going out for dinner. We're just going to walk away from all the boxes for a while," he smiles. "Have some good food and enjoy being back in the city. You and Jeff are more than welcome," Luke says, as he grabs the big box and Alicia holds the smaller one.

"Hmm, that sounds nice, thanks, but you guys go and enjoy yourself," she tells him, as they walk towards the door, their arms full.

"Are you sure?"

Alicia smiles, happy to have her son closer to home but knowing that he and Annie will have a much better time without her hanging around. "I'm sure. Thanks. We're going back to Jeff's, order some food, fall asleep in front of the TV, maybe even stagger to bed and go to the spa tomorrow," she says putting the box down in the living room.

"If you're sure," her son smiles.

"I am, but thanks for the invite."

Chapter 101

Alicia

Alicia and Jeff sit in the hot tub at the Scandinavian spa, a look of contentment on their faces, as they relax in the swirling, bubbling water. "Hmm," she murmurs, her body relaxing in the heat, soothing her muscles, and putting her in a pleasant, tranquil state. *Wow. The cold plunge was intense. Only 30 seconds, but my God it was invigorating. I'm just going to relax here for a little bit, warm up and then we're off to our massages,* she thinks. Her eyes are closed in the quiet sanctuary of the resort, until a boisterous laugh erupts from another pool area across the courtyard. She immediately sits up and opens her eyes to take in the situation.

She stares for another few seconds before nudging Jeff, who is sitting beside her. He opens his eyes slowly as if awaken from a tranquil sleep.

"Do you have your phone with you?" she asks quietly.

"I do," he replies, his eyes shifting to the pair that Alicia is eyeing.

"Can you get it for me, please?"

"You're not supposed to take pictures in here," he tells her, as he stands to get out of the hot tub. He moves to the chair where he left his robe, pulls it out of the pocket, signs on and hands the phone to Alicia.

She clicks on the camera app and holds it up to her eye, zooming in on the couple in the pool, snapping five or six pictures before reviewing them.

Unfreaking believable, she thinks as she sends all the pictures to Helen with a short note, 'Look who else is enjoying the spa.'

After hitting send, she looks up at the couple again, shakes her head, before she stands up and hands the phone back to Jeff.

"Everything OK?" he asks, as he puts his hand out to help her out of the tub, pocketing the phone with his other hand.

"Great. Everything is great," she says quietly, not wanting the couple to notice her.

Quite a day. A very enlightening day, she smiles to herself as they move into the resort for their couples massage.

Chapter 102

Alicia

"Good weekend?" Helen asks, as Alicia walks up to her desk and slumps into the chair.

"Fantastic. Luke and Annie are back in the city. We helped them on Saturday and then spent yesterday at the spa. Did you see the pictures I sent?"

"Interesting, don't you think? Guillaume and Rizzo. She moved on pretty quick," Helen replies almost laughing.

"Definitely. And it didn't look like they were just getting to know each other, if you know what I mean," Alicia adds.

"I agree. Those pictures were pretty intimate. Guess they thought that no one would recognize them at the spa," Helen agrees. "I called Fallon Shipley after I got your text and asked her to send me Dominique's resume. I got it this morning, and she did work for Rizzo Enterprises before she went to Preston Construction."

"Well, we knew that. Antony Rizzo admitted it to us when we went to see him," Alicia counters.

"He did but he didn't elaborate on what she did or why she left. He just kind of sloughed it off if I recall correctly, like he didn't really know her."

"So why did she leave? Or should I ask what did she tell Preston Construction was her reason for leaving Rizzo?"

"She was an admin in the executive offices at Rizzo's. Her resume doesn't specifically say who she worked for. She said she was looking for a new challenge, felt underappreciated."

"Interesting. Was she simply looking for something new or did she get a job at Preston's so she could spy on the competition for Rizzo? Was she involved with Antony Rizzo before she came up here? Or maybe even when she was with Lewis? Her moving up here, working for Preston could have been a setup," Alicia says.

"Yup, lots of questions. I'm not sure either Dominique or Rizzo will give us the answers, probably sic their lawyers on us. I think we need to go back to the orders for the sodium nitrite, the customer and the email lists from the Suicide King, to find something that points to their involvement in Lewis' death. There are a lot of unique acronyms or maybe they combined their names or initials or something."

Chapter 103

Maeve

"Fucking bitch," Maeve mumbles as she leaves the gym after only finishing half of the pilates class. She walks quickly to her car and gets in, slams the door, before starting the engine and roaring out of the parking lot.

That goddamn Julie gossiping about Dominique. She was whispering to that bitch Val about Dominique's new boyfriend. Does she think I'm hard of hearing? And her bloody smile while she was doing it. Smirking in my direction while she spewed about the whore, who's forgotten my husband already, and taken up with another asshole.

Fucking Lewis. I told you. I told you she was using you. And she's already whoring around, forgotten you already.

Chapter 104

Helen sits back from her laptop, her eyes blurring from exhaustion, almost unable to see the screen. *It's like looking for a needle in a haystack. We've been at this for a while and have found nothing. Not an email, not an order, not an inquiry that we can trace back to one of the suspects. We've sent a bunch of possible email addresses to the telecommunications company and hopefully they can supply IP addresses with specific account information or something, anything to help find who did this.*

It amazes me. All the creative email addresses people create – dienow, letmego, hadenough. I guess Kenneth Lawlor's customers didn't want to use their regular email addresses – needed something that was untraceable. I did find a conversation with user LPD, which if you use your imagination could stand for 'Lewis Preston dies'. Hopefully that IP address will help us locate the user and it's one of our suspects.

Helen opens her eyes again and continues to review the contact list, searching for something to tie Guillaume and Rizzo to the purchase of sodium nitrite and the murder of Lewis Preston. *What about this one? ARDG. Their initials? DG could be Dominique Guillaume. Shit, AR is Antony Rizzo. Damnit. That's it. Those two were in on it. That's the proof. They bought the sodium nitrite and killed Lewis Preston. Shit. And look, they bought a 50-gram package of 99.999% pure sodium nitrite. All for the low cost of $59.00. My God. They killed someone and it only cost them $59.00!*

And how did they pay for it? Let me get into this asshole's financials and look for ARDG. Hmm, come on. A cheque would be perfect. Or a credit card. Something that we can trace. Shit, here it is. Cryptocurrency. Fuck there's no way to trace that.

OK, let's see where it was sent. Wouldn't it be great if they had it delivered to the house that Lewis bought for Dominique? The irony of that would be too sweet. Nope, looks like a post office box in downtown Toronto. Hmm, wonder how close that is to Rizzo Enterprises? Maybe he picked up the package during his lunch break.

No sense in calling the post office. They won't give us anything without a warrant, not like Nico who lucked out with the London Construction stuff. Wonder if Judge Mitchell is in his office today.

Chapter 105

Simon

Simon Windsor sits behind his substantial desk watching the women sitting across from him.

I don't think either of them have a clue that this case is open-and-shut. And not for us! The crown has the antifreeze, which was found in the defendant's garage; they have her fingerprints on the jug; they have a funnel coated with the toxic substance and they have a bottle of Captain Morgan's Black Label rum mixed liberally with the antifreeze, also with her prints on the bottle.

The consensus from everyone that my private investigator has talked to is that Kyle Sheridan never ever shared his bottle with anyone. It was always by his side. He guarded it like it was something precious.

And the garage was cleaned up. Supposedly her kid always tidied up after the parties, that her dad gave her $10 to do it, and that all may be true, but it looks like Kandis tried to hide the evidence. It's possible, it's even probable that it's the kid's job to clean up after her old man, but it sure as hell doesn't look good.

And don't forget the degenerates that hung out in the garage and their testimonies that the wife would come out, yell at her husband to turn the music down and on several occasions threatened his life. What was she thinking?

Oh yeah, she wasn't. Just like she wasn't thinking when she kept those frigging journals. And not just one journal but a bunch of them. Christ! I haven't got them from the crown yet but I'm sure there are lots of threats, promises, rants about the husband, stuff that won't look good in court. The guy was a drunk, a violent out-of-control drunk. I get it and if writing down your thoughts helps you make it through, go for it. But at the end of your kumbaya moment, get rid of them. Burn them. Shred them. Destroy them so no one can examine your inner thoughts.

And they just found that fucking video on her iPad. Killing someone isn't hard to do, it's covering up the evidence that you leave behind that will put you behind bars, and the video, her fingerprints, her journals are going to do just that.

Everything is circumstantial, but the court will be directed to treat both circumstantial and direct evidence equally and she's got the deck stacked against her.

And so far, she's the only one with means, motive and opportunity to kill Kyle Sheridan.

The lawyer sits for a couple more moments, before announcing, "We have an uphill battle. I have a private detective digging around trying to find other suspects, someone else that could have done this. We need to put some doubt in the jurors' minds so they will have to acquit you. Right now, we need to talk about how you're going to plead," Simon says looking at his client.

"Plead?" Kandis repeats, question in her voice.

"Yes, plead," Simon reiterates again, taking control of the conversation. "When you go to court, the judge will ask you how you plead. You have a couple of options. Guilty which means you are admitting to the crime, that you are taking responsibility for Kyle's death and the court will sentence you accordingly. You can also plead not guilty, at which time the court will set a trial date to hear the evidence in the case."

Kandis looks to Maeve for help, tears flowing down her cheeks, unable to make a coherent sound.

"Is that it? Are those her only options?" Maeve asks on behalf of her friend.

The room is silent for a moment before the lawyer offers, "Basically, though she could plead guilty with an explanation."

"An explanation?" Maeve questions.

"She was mentally incapacitated due to his constant abuse. She didn't know that what she was doing was wrong, didn't know what the consequences would be, only that she had to do something to get out of the situation," Simon stops, looking at the accused. "It would be tough. We would need some psychiatrists to weigh in, say you were in a fugue state, and didn't know what you were doing, but it is a possibility."

"She would have to confess to killing Kyle?"

"Yes," Simon answers.

The pair look at Kandis, who has horror plastered on her face as she shakes her head adamantly before yelling, "No, I will not confess. I won't. I'm pleading not guilty. Period."

Simon nods his head, not in agreement with her, but to acknowledge her decision for a difficult and almost impossible trial.

"I will argue on your behalf against everything that the crown brings to court. I will suggest the evidence is tainted and offer alternate persons that would have wanted your husband dead, anything to draw attention away from you, but it's going to be a battle. One you need to prepare yourself for."

Chapter 106

Abbie

"Take care, Abbie," the nurse says, as Eric and Abbie walk through the locked door from the rehab centre proper into the spacious lobby. Eric smiles at his niece as she races through the space. She hits the double doors leading out of the facility and bursts through them, shoving with such force that they both smack into the outer wall.

"Whoa, slow down. It's not a race," Eric says, as he catches up to his niece.

"Free. I'm free," Abbie replies, slowing down slightly. "Where's your car?" she asks, looking around the parking lot before spotting his old black classic Mustang sitting alone in the corner farthest from everything. She smiles before turning to her uncle. "Think someone is going to hit you?" she laughs. "Is that why you park as far away as possible? So, no one will open their door and dent your precious antique?"

Her uncle's huff in frustration is his only reply.

Eric throws his niece's bag into the back seat of the car before getting into the driver's seat. "Your mom should be home by the time we get there," he tells her.

Abbie sits for a moment, her once stolid face breaking as tears creep to the edges of her eyes, her breathing fast as the stress of freedom hits her.

Eric turns to his niece and puts his hand on her shoulder, knowing that she doesn't appreciate human contact. "It's OK, Abbie. It's OK," he says, not knowing what else to say.

The two sit for several minutes as Abbie's emotions bubble up and escape her carefully created frosty exterior. "It's OK, Abbie," he repeats.

They continue to sit for another couple of minutes before he says, "Your mom couldn't come this morning. She had an appointment with her lawyer that she couldn't get out of, but she's anxious to see you."

Abbie sits for another minute, and Eric watches as she puts on a brave face for the world.

Chapter 107

Kandis

A noise comes from down the hall, and Kandis looks up at the clock on the stove. *Abbie's getting up. She's been through hell too. As soon as I shake these fucking charges, we're going to have to do something special. Maybe go somewhere together.*

Kandis wipes the tears from her face as her daughter steps into the kitchen. "Morning Abbie," Kandis greets.

"Morning," Abbie mumbles as a reply, looking at the sadness etched on her mother's face, her tearful eyes, and her unsteady hands. She walks to the fridge, opens it, and pulls out a Diet Coke, popping the tab and taking a drink.

"You know that's not good for you," her mother tells her, a shallow smile on her face.

"I would say it has the same health rating as the many, many cups of coffee that you consume every day," her daughter replies, as she sits down. "Why are you so sad? I thought you would be happy to be rid of him."

Kandis tries to smile through her tears. "Happy to be rid of him?" she asks, her voice raising in question before continuing. "I'm not sure happy is the right word. Am I relieved that his chaos is gone? The answer would be yes. Will we be more comfortable, less on edge, always waiting for the other shoe to drop? The answer is yes. Will we be in a better economic place? Definitely." Kandis stops for a moment and wipes the tears from her face before continuing. "But I also miss your father. When he was sober, when he was straight, when he tried, he was an incredible individual."

Abbie listens closely to her mother's voice, shaking her head. "You still love him," she states, wonder in her voice.

Kandis sits silent for a moment before admitting, "I love the past shadow of your father. I love who he was when we first got married. I love who he was when he stopped

311

drinking, stopped doing drugs, when he actually remembered that he had a wife and a daughter."

"Unbelievable. I don't get it," Abbie replies taking another swig from her can of Diet Coke. "After all the shit he did to you, to me, to us. He destroyed our lives, Mom. I don't know how you can feel anything good about that piece of shit," she finishes, abruptly slamming the can on the table, pop exploding out of the top from the force.

They sit for a moment, both thinking of Kyle Sheridan, Kandis thinking of their good days, while her daughter squeezes her hands into fists, her anger close to the surface. Kandis' phone shrills in the silence between them, and she picks it up and looks at the call display. "Shit," she mumbles as she clicks the button to answer warily with, "Hello Yara." She listens for a moment, nodding her head occasionally. After several moments, Kandis tells the caller, "Not a problem. I understand. I'll be there in an hour." She listens again, nodding her head before she says, "Goodbye" and ends the call looking at her daughter.

"I was going to take the day off, but some emergency with one of our vendors has come up. Apparently, they think I'm the only one that can fix the issue," she explains, dropping her shoulders in submission.

Abbie says nothing, giving her mother a shrug in reply, as she gets up and walks down the hall into her bedroom and slams the door.

Chapter 108

Alicia

The detectives are at the post office looking at a registration form for the rental of a mailbox filled out by Dominique Guillaume.

"Timing is right," Helen comments.

"Would she use her real name as contact information though? I mean she goes to the trouble of renting a post office box in another city, pays for it with cryptocurrency, and then is stupid and puts her real name and address on the form?"

"Maybe it was automatic. She just filled it in and didn't think about it," Helen suggests. "Not sure this is enough to charge her," she continues. "Anyone could have filled this in."

Alicia looks away from the computer terminal and looks around the room. She spots a camera over the doorway with a direct view to the bank of mailboxes which holds the one rented by Dominique. She turns to the postal employee who is standing behind them and asks, "How long do you keep your surveillance videos?"

He smiles before replying. "The cloud is a beautiful thing. Unlimited space to store hours and hours of videos. Do you have a specific date you're looking for?" He moves between the detectives who are using his laptop. "Here let me show you," he says, minimizing the registration form and moving to another platform.

"We're not sure," Helen offers. "How about the full three months that this post office box was rented?"

He chuckles again. "It's going to take a while for you to go through that much video. I can download it onto a couple of flash drives, and you can take it with you," he tells them as the detectives look at each other. "No flash drives?" he continues. "There's a Best Buy just down the block. Why don't you walk down and grab some of the big ones, the two

313

terabyte ones? I'd say about a dozen of them and I'll download it all for you."

Chapter 109

Abbie

Abbie lies on her bed, the conversation with her mother flooding through her thoughts. *I can't believe her. Maybe he was a sweetheart when they met, maybe he was her soul mate, whatever the fuck that is. But the abuse, the beatings, the rapes, the disrespect for as long as I can remember sure as hell trumps what she seems to want to remember of that asshole.*

She closes her eyes, relaxes, empties her mind of all thoughts, letting sleep take her. She dreams that she's sitting at the kitchen table, writing something in one of her books from school when her father walks into the room, a big grin on his face. He takes the chair beside her and grabs her, pulling her onto his lap. "Awe baby," he says, his lips close to her ear, his smelly booze breath reaching her nose.

"Dad," she yells, squirming to get out of his grasp. "Let me go," she demands, twisting and turning, trying to stand up as he grips her tighter.

His lips, still by her ear, whisper, "Come on sweetheart. You know you love Daddy."

Abbie begins to chant the words, "Let me go," as she struggles to get away from him, but her father is strong. He stands up and picks her up in one fluid motion.

"You're mine, little girl," he says, as he carries her down the hallway, pushes through her bedroom door and throws her on the bed.

Abbie screams as she wakes from her nightmare, jumping up from the bed as if it's on fire, looking around frantically for her father.

"Where the fuck are you?" she cries. "You want me? Come and get me!" she shrieks, but she is alone.

She slowly backs away from the bed and backs into the corner of the room, her knees collapsing as she slowly crumbles onto the floor.

He's never going to leave me alone. He's stone-cold dead, but he's never going to leave me alone. He'll always be here, taunting me, torturing me, treating me like a piece of shit, doing whatever the fuck he wants to me.

I thought once he was gone that I could have a life, she cries, big fat tears rolling down her face as she groans in anguish. *I thought that I could be normal. But he's not going to let me. He's going to haunt me forever. I couldn't live with him, and he won't let me live without him.*

Too many secrets, Daddy. Too many secrets.

Chapter 110

Kandis

Kandis is deep in thought as she pulls her car into the empty driveway, turns it off and sits for a moment in silence. Fucking idiots. *Not a freaking brain among them. They could have looked after all that without me. Just a power trip. Knowing that my life is fucked right now, knowing that I've been charged with Kyle's murder, knowing that I need the job, the money. But hell, they need to get their shit together. Or maybe it's me. I need to be stronger. I need to stand up to them. I'm not a fucking doormat.*

She slams the car door as she gets out and stops for a moment listening. *Quiet. No guitars. No drums. No music. No Kyle.*

"Abbie," she yells as she walks in the front door. "Abbie are you here?" she repeats as she kicks off her shoes and notices her daughter's shoes, bag, and jacket in the front hall.

"Abbie," she shouts again as she moves into the house, throwing her purse and briefcase on the kitchen table before walking down the hallway to the bedrooms. "Abbie? Are you in there?" she asks, as she knocks on her daughter's door and it creeps open slightly. "Abbie?" she repeats as she pushes the door fully open.

"Abbie!" she shrieks seeing her daughter's placid body sprawled across her unmade bed. "Abbie," she yells again, as she grabs her shoulders and shakes her daughter like a rag doll, but there is no response.

Kandis lets Abbie fall back onto the bed. She runs into the bathroom, throws open the cabinet under the sink, tossing things around the room as she searches for the black zippered kit with the red cross on it. *Where the fuck is it? There it is,* she thinks, as she grabs the edge of the kit and pulls it from its hiding place.

She stands up, ripping the package open as she runs back to her daughter's bedroom. *Fuck, we only have the nasal spray. Shit. Shit. Shit,* she thinks as she approaches her daughter. Kandis arranges her daughter on the bed, supports her neck, tilts her head back, pushes the tip of the nozzle of naloxone in one nostril and presses the plunger firmly, watching as the mist goes into her daughter's nose. She watches and waits for several moments. *What the fuck! She's still not breathing.*

She pulls her daughter onto the floor and starts CPR, counting as she performs 30 chest compressions and two rescue breaths.

She stops again, watches, and waits but nothing. Tears are coursing down her face as she opens the second nasal spray and puts it up her daughter's nose, pushing the plunger. "Fuck," she yells before she tries compressions again. "Come on, Abbie. Come on," she cries, before standing up and running to the kitchen to grab her phone.

***

Kandis sits in her dark living room; her legs folded under her on the couch. She is awake, her eyes are open, but they are unseeing as she stares straight ahead. Her mind's eye is far away, reliving the last couple of hours as if on a loop that repeats over and over.

She sees herself coming into the house, calling for her daughter, and finding her lying still on top of her rumpled bed. Instantly, she thinks that her daughter has taken some drugs, that she's overdosed, and she sees herself rushing to the bathroom to get the naloxone, running back and administering it, doing CPR, waiting but Abbie doesn't breathe, Abbie doesn't come to, so she does it again and again, frantic until the EMTs arrive and push her out of the way.

They inject Abbie with something and perform CPR, accompanied with a couple of loud cracking sounds as Abbie's ribs break with their force. Kandis continues to

318

huddle at the end of the bed on the floor watching the ghastly scene play out. Then they lift her daughter onto a stretcher and rush her out of the house. Kandis runs after them, is helped into the ambulance by one of the EMTs and she watches as they continue to work on her little girl, as the ambulance races through the last of rush hour traffic to the hospital.

Kandis can see the EMTs push the stretcher into Emerg and then push it down the hall into a room as nurses run around, all with some task to perform, while she is left to stand in the hall for what seemed to be hours before Dr. Lee finally came out. He holds her hand, guides her into another room, and tells her to sit down but she doesn't. She paces, keeps asking about her daughter, asks what was going on, asks when she could see her, until he says the most horrible, unbelievable words that she will ever hear – your daughter is dead, we couldn't save her.

Kandis is numb as she sits in her dark living room, the movie reel starting again. It runs again and again until she hears a crumpling sound through her darkness. She looks down at her hands, where the noise is coming from, and sees her fingers gripping the letter that she found on the floor of her daughter's room. Her fingers are tightly wound into a ball, crushing her daughter's last words. Tears stream down her face as she recalls her daughter's almost-illegible scrawl telling her that she had mixed her father's rum with antifreeze, that he deserved to die for the things he had done to her, how he had raped her time and time again and how she thought killing him would stop her pain. But it didn't. He was still here. He was still haunting her. He still wanted her. He wouldn't let her live a normal life. She was just plain tired of the pain, so she did the only thing she could. She made a mixture of antifreeze, with just a touch of Diet Coke, kinda like she'd made for her dad, and drank it.

Tears choke Kandis, and she is unable to breathe as the reality of her daughter's life of hell unfolds. *That fucking piece of shit. Touching his own daughter. Telling her that he would kill me, that he would kill her if she told anyone. It had been going on for years under my nose, and I didn't know. I should have looked harder. I should have known something was very, very wrong. I should have known when she started to do drugs. I should have figured out what the asshole was doing, what hell he was inflicting on our child.*

What a fucking useless mother I was. I didn't protect her. I swear I didn't know what her asshole father was doing. He took us all for a ride. Used his own daughter for sex. Raped me time and time again. Used his fists on me. And I let him. I let him destroy me. Destroy Abbie.

He deserved to die. You did good, Abbie. And if I have to rot in jail to keep your secret, the secret of your abuse at the wicked hands of your father, the secret of why you left your home so young, and what you finally were forced to do to stop the monster, I will. I will take it to the grave if I have to. He deserved to die. It should have been me that killed him, not you, my angel. Not you, she thinks as big fat tears drip down her face, and the reel starts to play again in the mirror of her mind. *I will keep your secret. I will keep our secret.*

Chapter 111

Helen

The detectives spend days reviewing the videos meticulously looking for anyone using the post office box rented by Dominique Guillaume. Finally, on the third day of watching the videos, Helen stops the feed and stands up. "Got it," she says, smiling at Alicia.

"Is it her?" Alicia asks, abandoning her laptop and moving to stand beside Helen. "Are you sure?"

"Definitely," Helen says, a genuine grin of pleasure on her face.

Alicia sits down in front of Helen's laptop and eyes the screen, a shot of a woman, wearing a dark tracksuit, a hoodie pulled up over her head covering her face, though the woman's long dark slightly curly hair has escaped its cover.

"She definitely knows where the cameras are. She's got the hoodie covering her face, hanging so low that it's even covering her eyes. And she's got a scarf around her neck, covering her chin, so we can't see her face. Even zooming in isn't helping," Alicia says, as she expands the picture trying to get a better view of the woman about to open box number 790.

"It is hard to tell with that hoodie on but look at her hair. It's Dominique's long hair," Helen offers, as Alicia fiddles with the picture.

The detectives continue to look at the screen, until Alicia looks up and confirms, "Yup, that's her."

"What are you seeing? Why so definite now?"

"Check out the nails," Alicia says sitting back in her chair as Helen moves closer to the screen again.

Both detectives sit looking at the enlarged picture, zeroing in on the offender's long, sharp stiletto nails painted a bright blue with little red hearts on each of them.

Chapter 112

Kandis

"The crown has released copies of your journals that will be brought up in court. Talk to me about them, Kandis," Simon Windsor asks his client. "Explain to me why you would write such things down."

Kandis sits across from her lawyer, his substantial desk between them, ringing her hands in her lap. She looks up. "Those journals were supposed to be private. No one was ever supposed to see them," she starts.

The lawyer sits watching his client, waiting for her explanation.

Kandis thinks for a moment before continuing. "I was told in Al-Anon that journaling was a good way to face the issues, my concerns. We were told to think about what was going on, what bothered us, and try to figure out what we could do to make the situation better, how we could live through the tough times," she tries to explain.

The lawyer nods his head in understanding. "There are some very incriminating pieces in your journals," he replies. "I've reviewed them, and we need a solid defence of what you wrote, why you wrote it and how we can reposition it as therapy and not a to-do list."

He makes a note on his pad of paper before continuing. "I'll call someone from Al-Anon to the stand, get them to talk about the program, the suggestion about working with journals, try and downplay everything that you've written, but it will be difficult for the jury to ignore the blatant threats you made against your husband."

Kandis simply nods her head, knowing that what she had written, if taken out of context, would be difficult to refute.

"OK, I mentioned the last time that we met that I hired a private detective who is trying to dig up other suspects, find some way to introduce someone else that could have done this. It's important, even with all of the evidence against us, that we offer them other explanations for who could have done this and why."

"Yes, you mentioned that. Have you found anyone? Kyle had a lot of friends that used to come to play music in the garage. I'm sure half of them probably have criminal records of some kind."

The lawyer is silent for a moment, looks at his computer screen before looking back at his client. "I was so sorry to hear of your daughter's passing," he starts as his client nods her head, saying nothing. "I know this is going to sound drastic, but would it be an option to include Abbie as a possible suspect?"

"A suspect?"

Simon nods his head. "We need to take the spotlight off of you. We need to make the jury see that other people may have committed this crime," he pauses watching as his client's face crumbles. "You've admitted that your living arrangements were difficult, that your husband was very demanding, and that Abbie struggled with drugs," he peters off.

Kandis is shaking her head before he even finishes, tears pooling in her eyes. "No fucking way. She is off-limits. Off limits," she repeats.

Simon is quiet, watching Kandis'fierce reaction to the suggestion and they sit in silence for a moment before he continues, "I understand how it sounds. It's nasty. It's despicable to even bring poor Abbie's name into this but think about it for a minute. Sadly, she's gone. Sadly, she can't talk for herself, but she must have loved you very much and I'm sure would have done anything to protect you."

Kandis continually shakes her head, tears falling down her face as the lawyer continues to push her.

"I understand that you want to honour your daughter, that you do not want to have her name mixed up with the death of her father, but this might help you Kandis." Simon pauses for a moment before continuing. "I would be diplomatic, compassionate when I suggest Abbie's possible involvement in her father's death," he pauses before continuing. "Just think how much it would help your case."

Kandis abruptly stands up. "No. No mention of Abbie."

The lawyer opens his mouth to speak, but Kandis puts her hand up in a stop motion. "I said no. No mention of Abbie. None."

Chapter 113

18 months later

Alicia

Alicia stands back and admires the décor – potted plants and groups of pink and white helium ballons placed strategically placed about the rooftop and the fairy lights twinkling in the waning sunlight. A full bar is set up at one end of the patio with a bartender. Patio chairs and couches are sprawled about in small groups. There's an enormous empty table ready for the food that she has ordered too. *Have I forgotten anything?* she asks herself as she looks around again at the soft whimsical surroundings set up to celebrate Luke and Annie's elopement.

She hears the door to the roof open as she surveys the wonderland and turns just as arms wrap around her waist. "Looks fantastic," Jeff breathes into her ear. "They will love it," he says, kissing her cheek.

"I hope so. I know they didn't want anything big, but I didn't want this momentous occasion to go by without at least a small celebration."

Jeff laughs as he lets her go and moves to stand in front of her. "Small celebration? You've invited half the force. Or should I say the two forces – Barrie and South Simcoe."

"You're right. There will be lots of cops here tonight."

"Safest place to be in the city tonight," he smiles.

"Thanks for helping put this together. Getting the use of the rooftop patio from the condo, getting the bar, stocking it, and arranging for a bartender," she nods at the solitary man standing behind the refreshment counter, waiting patiently for guests to arrive.

"For you, almost anything," Jeff comments as he steps towards the bar. "Would you like anything? A glass of wine to calm your nerves?" he asks.

Alicia nods her head. "Yes, please," she replies just as she hears the door to the rooftop open again. She turns to see Helen and Wyatt coming onto the patio, both smiling, holding hands, as they look around at the fanciful surroundings.

"Thanks for coming," Alicia greets them both, nodding at Helen's date.

"It's beautiful, Alicia. Absolutely gorgeous," Helen gushes. "Are the bride and groom here yet?"

"Not yet. Any minute, I'm hoping," Alicia answers as the door opens again and more guests arrive. "The bar is open," Alicia motions to the far end of the deck. "Help yourself. Dinner will be served once Luke and Annie arrive," she finishes before moving to greet the newcomers.

***

The party is well underway - a lavish smorgasbord of food available for the guests, plentiful drinks from the bar and a DJ playing soft background music. Alicia smiles looking out at the crowd, content that the evening is going well as Helen approaches and takes her arm, leading her away from the centre of the party.

"Great party," she comments to her friend.

"Thanks. It looks to be going OK," Alicia answers before changing the subject, "Great to see Wyatt. Things still going well?"

"They are. We're having some fun. Nothing too serious," Helen pauses before adding, "But that's not what I wanted to talk to you about. Did you hear about Greco and Beckham?" Helen asks but continues without giving Alicia a chance to answer. "The trial was quick. Took less than a week. They were both found guilty of fraud over $5,000 and theft over $5,000, and the judge sentenced them immediately. Both received 10 years in jail."

"No, I hadn't heard. Good for our judicial system, getting it right."

"You knew that Greco and his wife, what was her name?"

"London, like the city," Alicia fills in.

"Yeah, London. Well, they split up when the hubby and her dad were first charged. She moved into her parents' condo in St. Maarten."

"Tough life," Alicia replies.

"And the verdict for Dominique was delivered this week too. She was given life for the first degree murder of Lewis Preston."

"I heard she was found guilty, but I'm not so sure it was that cut and dry. I still can't wrap my head around why she would kill Preston. She was sitting pretty. He was going to leave his wife for her. Bought her a house. Took responsibility for the kid. Doesn't make sense to me."

"$22 million. That's why she did it. And don't forget the $2 million for her daughter," Helen pauses before adding, "She thought she could have it all. The money. And the good-looking rich Antony Rizzo."

"Yeah, maybe," Alicia replies, watching over Helen's shoulder as Wyatt winds his way across the floor, two drinks in hand, a smile on his face. "We'll talk later," she says as Wyatt reaches Helen and passes her one of the glasses.

"I didn't mean to interrupt," he says stepping back.

"No, no stay," Alicia urges. "I've got to go and check out the buffet table. Make sure there's enough of everything. We'll talk later," she says, leaving Helen and Wyatt together.

Chapter 114

Kandis

Kandis lies on the lower bunk in block B, cell number 13 in the Grand Valley Institute for Women. The door has been secured for the night, and she is locked in the small claustrophobic room until morning. Her roommate Maria, is in the bunk above her, already snoring loudly even though the lights will be on for another half hour.

Kandis holds a photo album, the only personal item that she was allowed to bring with her. She looks through the worn pages at the smiling faces and remembers the love, the hope that she had back in the early days of her marriage.

What the fuck ever happened to this picture-perfect family, she wonders to herself as she slowly turns the page to a picture of her holding Abbie in the car on their way home from the hospital. *Happy, we were happy. But it dissipated quickly. Kyle seemed to resent me, to resent Abbie and he pulled away from us, turned to his friends, turned to drugs, turned to alcohol. I should have left him then. Should have stood on my own two feet, been an adult and looked after my little girl.*

I almost did a couple of times, but he would woo me back. He always seemed to know when I was at my wit's end and he'd pull out all the stops, sweet talk me, treat me like a queen until I forgot about leaving him. And then it would happen all over again.

I so wanted to kill him at times, but I was just a scaredy cat, too chicken to do the right thing, so my little girl, my Abbie, had to do it. And he deserved it. He deserved to die for what he did to her, what he did to me, for being the useless human being that he really was.

The best thing I ever did was create my Abbie, but I didn't keep her safe. I didn't look out for her. I let her beast of a father mistreat her, take advantage of her, and hurt her to the core.

If I have to stay in this hell hole, then that will be my penance for being a horrible, self-centred, stupid mother, she thinks as the lights suddenly blink out in the cell.

She carefully closes her photo album and stuffs it under her pillow, keeping it close, keeping it away from her roommate and the guards. She rolls over on her side, her back to the room, looking at the grey block wall as tears leak from her eyes, the sadness of her situation enveloping her. *I will live with your secret, Abbie. I will take what you did to your father to the grave.*

Chapter 115

Maeve

"It's such a beautiful day," Maeve comments out loud, though she is alone as she carries a large tray loaded with a single glass, a jug of freshly made margaritas with crushed ice, a couple of limes, a bowl of the salted mixture for the rim of the glass, plus a plate of fancy biscuits, her cell phone and a small speaker. "The pool's a perfect 28 degrees. Great day for a dip. Too bad there's no one to share it with," she tells herself, as she lowers the platter onto the glass table in front of the elegant sectional couch on the back patio.

She sits down in the centre of the thickly padded wicker settee, picks up the lone highball glass from the tray, rubs the already-cut lime around its rim before dipping it into the salt mixture and pours herself a cocktail from the large pitcher. She pushes her butt back on the couch, lifts the concoction to her lips and takes a long pull of the cool, refreshing drink.

Kandis should be here. Simon has appealed the verdict, but it's taking longer than expected. I can't believe she's in that rotten place. I guess I should go see her, give her some hope or something, but it's so far, and the fucking security. You have to book a visit. Have to leave your purse and belt and anything dangerous in a locker. Have to be scanned before you can actually get to see her. She's so sad, and she looks miserable in that ugly grey uniform that she has to wear. And she's probably lost more weight.

What the fuck did Abbie say in that god-forsaken suicide note? It was like a switch was flipped. The change in Kandis was unbelievable. It must be devastating to lose your daughter, but something else happened to her. Something that she couldn't seem to come back from. Something she won't tell me about.

Either way, I will always be grateful to her. She did great when she picked up the sodium nitrite in Toronto for me. I had a hell of a time getting fake ID in Dominique's name so

330

Kandis could rent the post office box, but it all went off without a hitch. Maeve smiles to herself, remembering the wig and fake nails she put on Kandis twice – when she went into the postal station to rent the box and then to pick up the package of sodium nitrite. *It was so easy to mix the white powder in with the sugar, knowing that he would put three heaping spoonfuls of it in his morning coffee. He must have felt like shit for a couple of days, but he deserved to suffer for what he was going to do to me.*

And then I simply threw the sugar and the sodium nitrite out when I got home, when I couldn't find him. Flushed it down the toilet so there was no trace. So easy, so simple.

It took the cops a while to figure out ARDG, but they finally did and now I'm free of that bitch running around town with her bastard child.

What a shame. Kandis and I started this journey together. But she fucked up on the timing. She was supposed to wait. Wait until the dust settled from Lewis. I don't know what the fuck she was thinking. Something must have happened. He must have done something that pushed her right over the edge. What else was going on in that house? Something toxic. Something very, very bad.

We just had Lewis' will read this week. Poor Izzy. She was in tears, and her boyfriend was livid. Sorry baby girl, but you need to get straight before I share any of that money with you. Thank God Lewis listened to me about that. He was just going to give her the money, no strings attached. She needs to learn, and this will certainly give her some incentive.

Rand wasn't too happy either. Probably thought he was going to get more. Well, he'll just have to be content with what Lewis left him and either make big bucks as a football player or get a real job. The buck really does stop here.

Note to self - follow-up with Scott to see what's going on with Dominique's inheritance. Thank God for the Criminal Code that freezes all assets when you are convicted of a crime if it is believed that you benefited from the crime financially. And that bitch sure did, Maeve smiles to herself.

That money should be mine. Scott says that won't happen, but I would rather see anyone, even the government have it before Lewis' whore.

"Hmm," she sighs, looking up at the back of her massive two-storey home, clad in field stone, windows across the rear of the house looking out at the pool, and beyond to the lake. *I've spent a lot of years making this the place what it is today, transforming it into the perfect home, everything that Lewis and the kids could want, a place where the family could gather, where we could be a family. But the kids are grown up, or almost grown up, and only come around when they want something. And Lewis is gone now. It's his own fault that he's not here. I didn't like his dalliances over the years, but I could have put up with them. But buying that bitch a house. Having a baby. Thinking he was going to leave me. No fucking way!*

Her head turns to the Olympic-size pool, taking in the burst of water shooting up in the shallow end, the tinkling noise of the fountain cascading into the pool. She looks at the slide in the deep end, which was used constantly through the years by her children. Her lips move into a smile as the memories come faster – the kids yelling and screaming as they climbed the ten-foot ladder to the top and slid down, hands in the air, shouts of glee until the moment before they hit the water.

She shakes her head before taking another pull from the glass. *This is my house. My castle. My family. My life. I couldn't let him and that bitch take it all from me,* she thinks as she holds the glass up to her lips, downing the last drops.

She reaches for the jug sitting on the coffee table, grabs its handle and proceeds to refill her tumbler before leaning back on the sofa. A sigh escapes her lips as she sits for a moment, taking in the resort-like backyard – the crystal-clear swimming pool, the lounge-like furniture around its perimeter, the burst of colourful flowers that surround the deck, the brilliant blooms that intersect with the rocky staircase which leads down the slope to the large double docks and Lewis' boats – one a centre-console fishing boat and the other a large cabin cruiser.

The bastard had it coming. And that conniving bitch deserves to go to jail. Lewis was stupid, he let his pecker do his thinking for him. He didn't believe me when I warned him about the bitch. Said I was wrong. Well, I wasn't. After it all went down, the whore actually took up with Antony Rizzo again. Not sure who's stupider, Lewis, Dominique, or Antony. Maeve smirks to herself as she sips on her ice-cold drink.

She moves to the edge of her seat, picking up her cell phone from the table and taps the music app, searching her playlists for something soothing, settling on Burton Cummings' mellow voice singing the Guess Who's hit song 'These Eyes.' Her anger falls away slowly as she listens to the song about lost love. It gives her strength, knowing that she loved her husband absolutely and that she will never have another love like his. And that it was Lewis that brought their world to an end. She only did what was necessary for her survival.

We had a great life, but it wasn't enough for him. Always out wheeling and dealing. Always looking for the next woman to bed. I should have left him years ago, but I loved him. He made me do this. He forced me to protect myself and I sure as hell was not going to live with his secrets.

Acknowledgements

First, I want to confirm that no husbands were killed during the writing of this book!

Second, I want to remind you of the legal stuff at the beginning of the book – 'this book is a work of fiction. Names, characters, businesses, organizations, places, events, and incidents either are the product of the author's imagination or are used fictitiously. Any resemblance to actual persons, living or dead, events or locales is entirely coincidental'.

Though I will admit that Chapter 2 includes a lot of what I did with my best friend Wendy throughout the years, including going to Playa del Carmen for a special birthday celebration and drinking through the bar menu (we did not drink through the alphabet), but that's where the similarities end – except maybe the description of Maeve as the two stand at the airport on their way home. Everything else, I swear, is my imagination gone wild.

The more I write, the more I realize how much I rely on the guidance, advice, and wisdom of other people. Their ideas, suggestions, support and encouragement help me create exciting and distinct adventures for my characters. My warmest and heartfelt thanks to **Lori Bentley, Kathleen Chalmers, Felice Cohen, Mary Crouteau, Heather Neilson, Anne Page, Lisa Prentice** and **Cheryl Zavot** for their unfailing support, their insightful ideas, suggestions and their generosity with their time. This book is as much yours as it is mine. Thank you!

And to you the reader – thank you for picking up this story and getting to the very last page. I hope you enjoyed it.

www.ingramcontent.com/pod-product-compliance
Lightning Source LLC
Chambersburg PA
CBHW021530250626
47154CB00006BA/2053